PATHS IN DREAMS

Asian and Pacific Writing 7

General Editors:
Michael Wilding
&
Harry Aveling

In This Series

Atheis
by Achdiat K. Mihardja
translated by R. J. Maguire

Tropical Gothic
by Nick Joaquin

Black Writing from New Guinea
edited by Ulli Beier

Padma River Boatman
by Manik Bandopadhyaya
translated by Barbara Painter
and Yann Lovelock

Contemporary Indonesian Poetry
edited and translated by Harry Aveling

A Heap of Ashes
by Pramoedya Ananta Toer
translated by Harry Aveling

Paths in Dreams
by Ho Ch'i-fang
edited and translated by Bonnie S. McDougall

PATHS IN DREAMS)

Selected Prose and Poetry of Ho Ch'i-fang

translated and edited
by
Bonnie S. McDougall

University of Queensland Press

Published by University of Queensland Press,
St. Lucia, Queensland 1976

Printed and bound by Silex Enterprise & Printing Co.,
Hong Kong

Distributed in the United Kingdom, the Middle East, Africa, and the
Caribbean by Prentice-Hall International, International Book Dis-
tributors Ltd., 66 Wood Lane End, Hemel Hempstead, Herts., England

National Library of Australia
Cataloguing-in-publication data

Ho, Ch'i-fang, 1911–.
    Paths in dreams.

    (Asian and Pacific writing; 7).
    Index.
    Bibliography.
    ISBN 0 7022 1260 1.
    ISBN 0 7022 1261 x Paperback.

    I. McDougall, Bonnie S., 1941–, trans.
    II. Title (Series).

895.115

To Agnes & Mabel
in love and gratitude

Acknowledgments

When several years ago I began to study the writings of Ho Ch'i-fang, I was trying to find a link between the different stages in his life: in the nineteen-thirties, a romantic poet and essayist; in the forties a communist poet and propagandist; in the fifties and sixties a leading figure in the academic establishment of the People's Republic of China. Looking back it seems to me now that in a way Ho was typical of many Chinese intellectuals of his generation, the offspring of landowners or the city bourgeoisie, who came to reject their past and accept communism during the Sino-Japanese War of 1937–45. In selecting his work for translation in this series, I have concentrated on pieces which seem to illustrate this progress, rather than provide a fully representative range, and the introduction is primarily concerned with providing the necessary background to these translations. Unless otherwise indicated all notes are my own.

I should like to express my very deep thanks to the staff and students in the Department of Oriental Studies at the University of Sydney for their help and encouragement on this project over many years. In particular I should like to thank Professor A. R. Davis who suggested this topic to me and who has guided my work ever since, and Professor W. P. Liu, Dr. Mabel Lee, Dr. Agnieszka, D. Syrokomla-Stefanowska, Dr. H. F. Yang, and Mr. K. H. Louie for their assistance and advice. I should like to thank Michael Wilding for his encouragement and suggestions, and Harry Aveling for his careful revision of the manuscript. I am also very much indebted to J. Szabo, A. G. Frankovits, D. Morrissey, A. Hansson, and to my parents.

Contents

Acknowledgments   vii
Introduction by the General Editors   xi

INTRODUCTION by Bonnie S. McDougall

The early life and times of Ho Ch'i-fang   3
Ho Ch'i-fang and the New Literary Movement   11
Literature into politics: the War of Resistance to Japan   15

POEMS AND PROSE

Poems and essays from *The Han Garden* and *Painstaking Work*   31
    The prophecy   32
    Footsteps   34
    Lament   35
    Love   36
    Do not wash away the red   37
    Summer night   38
    Night of the full moon   39
    The cypress grove   40
    The ancient city   41
    Early summer   43
    The wall   45
    Step insects   46
    The fan   47
    The pillow and its key   48
    Day of the duststorm II   49
    Afterword to *The Swallow's Nest*   51
    Paths in dreams   54

Prose poems and essays from *A Record of Painted Dreams*   61
    Mists and clouds on a fan   62
    Dusk   65
    A record of painted dreams   66
    Lament   72
    Magic plants   76
    Lute-strings   79

Essays from *Diary of a Visit Home*   81
    The essay and I   82

The sobbing Yangtze   89
Streets   97
The scenery of the district town   104
In the countryside   111
Our fortress   119

The Laiyang poems   121

Funerals   122
Mr Yü Yu-lieh   123
Sound   124
Let's get drunk   125
Clouds   126

Prose from *Sparks*   127

On work   128
On basic culture   134
On saving the children   137
Notes on the Szechwan-Shensi road   142
I sing of Yenan   147
A Taiyuan primary school boy   153
The common people and the army   159
An ordinary story   163

Poems from *Night Songs*   173

Chengtu, let me shake you awake!   174
Night song I   177
Night song II   179
Night song III   182
Night song IV   185
Our history is racing forward   188
I see a little donkey   193
I should like to talk of pure things   194
Here is a short fairy tale   195
How many times have I left my daily life   196
North China is aflame! (Part I)   198
North China is aflame! (Part II)   207

CONCLUSION by Bonnie S. McDougall

Ho Ch'i-fang's literary achievement   223
"Love, thoughtfulness and self-sacrifice"   231

Bibliography   233
Index   239

Introduction by the General Editors

Asian and Pacific Writing is a series making accessible to English readers some of the world's most exciting and dynamic new literatures. The primary concern is with modern and contemporary work. The series contains both translations and work written originally in English, both volumes by single writers and anthologies. The format is flexible so that it can respond to the variety of an area that spans the world's oldest and youngest literary traditions. A forum for contemporary writers and translators in Asia and the Pacific, the series gives expression to an expanding literature outside of the European, Soviet, and American cultural blocs. Edited and published from Australia, Asian and Pacific Writing marks Australia's developing awareness of her place in Asia. And it marks, too, an international mood of literary exploration, an interest in new forms and new stimuli, a spreading interest in getting to know other cultures, a determination to break down language and other barriers that have prevented literary interchange.

Michael Wilding
Harry Aveling

INTRODUCTION

The early life and times of Ho Ch'i-fang

Ho Ch'i-fang was born in 1911, the year of revolution which brought to an end twenty centuries of dynastic rule in China. Subsequent waves of disorder and rebellion swept through his childhood, causing his wealthy family to seek refuge in one place after another to protect their lives and property. Peasants in secret society uprisings, bandits and local warlords (the one barely distinguishable from the other), fought over territory amongst themselves and against the troops of the central government—that is, the government of whichever warlord was currently acceded Western recognition as the ruler of China. His early experience of bandits, warlords and the aggression of foreign powers taught Ho Ch'i-fang at a very young age to distrust political and military leaders and to hate war. As he grew up, he made himself ignore the periodic calls to armed resistance and war which inflamed students and intellectuals during the turmoil of China's emergence into the modern world.

He was too young to remember the Northern Expedition of 1926-27 which ended the period of warlord hegemony in China and established Chiang Kai-shek as the ruler of a unified country. In fact, this "national government" had complete control only over the central provinces around the new capital, Nanking. Outlying provinces, like Ho Ch'i-fang's native Szechwan in the west, continued under warlord rule, which, depending on the individual warlord, could be more or less humane and efficient than the Nanking government. Ho's family lived in the mountainous countryside around Wanhsien, the first commercial port on the Szechwan side of the Yangtze River gorges. One of his most distressing childhood memories was of a local warlord by the name of Yang Sen, who in 1926 was bold enough to engage British warships in a gun battle only a short distance from the centre of the town itself. Not long afterwards, Yang Sen was persuaded to support the Northern Expedition, and was temporarily permitted to retain control over his east Szechwan domain.

Throughout the early part of his life, Ho Ch'i-fang tried to remain remote from politics and war. But as he pursued his studies in the great coastal and northern cities like Shanghai, Peking and Tientsin, he became, regardless, involved in the violent struggles of the age.

In the decade 1927-37, China was shaken by two major power struggles: Nationalist-Communist civil war, and Japanese economic and military encroachment. When the Communist Party of China was founded in 1921, there was already in existence a revolutionary party of many years' standing, the Nationalist Party or Kuomintang, led by Sun Yat-sen. The Nationalist Party (under its earlier name of the Alliance Party) had helped bring about the republican revolution of 1911, but was very nearly destroyed itself shortly after. Following a long period of exile, Sun Yat-sen accepted Soviet Russian advice on revolutionary tactics and began the reorganization of his Party along Leninist lines. Communists were admitted to the Nationalist Party, and the Northern Expedition was undertaken as a joint Nationalist-Communist effort. To Chiang Kai-shek, leading the right-wing faction of the Nationalists, the Communists were uncertain allies, threatening his proposed alliance with the wealth and power of native and Western capitalism. Early in 1927, he expelled the Communists from the government, banned the party and its cultural front organizations, and set in progress a ruthless extermination of Communist and left-wing influence in China. Ten years later, he had not yet managed to achieve his aim, but had in the process deeply weakened the country with dissension and bloodshed.

The civil war was waged most fiercely in the central provinces of China; in Peking, Ho Ch'i-fang was largely able to ignore it. Though large numbers of young writers and students were jailed and executed there for showing left-wing tendencies, Ho's literary friends avoided political comment and pursued literary beauty in the secluded atmosphere of the universities.

If the internal conflict could be avoided in the north, the external aggressor, on the other hand, was most apparent there. The ever-growing military and economic power of Japan had been a constant factor in Chinese political life since her military victory over China in 1894-95. The initial economic exploitation of China in the nineteenth century was mainly carried out by Western powers such as England, France, Germany and Russia. The diversion of these countries' interests during World War I had allowed Japan to build up her position in China, and as an ally of the Western powers she was awarded at the Versailles Conference the former German possessions in Shantung, in north-east China. It suited Japanese interests to maintain warlord regimes in China, and the nationalist and socialist policies of the Northern Expedition came as a considerable threat to her position. After the Nationalist government had been established in Nanking, Nationalist forces continued their march north towards

Peking. On route, they found Japanese troops lined up to protect Japanese investments in Shantung. An armed clash took place in May 1928, when the Japanese occupied the provincial capital, Tsinan, and blocked the Nationalist advance. This provoked a mass student demonstration in Shanghai, in the most effective display of student power since the May Fourth Movement of 1919. (Students were regarded as leaders of the new nationalism of resistance to Japanese and Western imperialism. In 1919, students staged a series of demonstrations during May and June against the provisions of the Versailles Peace Treaty and the complicity of the Chinese government in this betrayal of Chinese territory. Their success in mobilizing all sections of the people behind them to force a change in government policies won them considerable public esteem.) Ho Ch'i-fang was attending senior middle school in Shanghai when the "Tsinan Incident" demonstrations were taking place. But just as in the Wanhsien Incident of 1926 (the confrontation between Yang Sen and British gunboats), Ho only shrank further into himself, desperately choosing insignificance and non-involvement. While the students were demanding from a reluctant government the right to military training and the inclusion of anti-Japanese studies in their curricula, Ho Ch'i-fang buried himself in poetry. Among his most treasured discoveries of that period was Paul Valéry, who had spent World War I in a minor bureaucratic post writing his long poem, *La Jeune Parque* (The Young Fate).

In September 1931, Ho Ch'i-fang enrolled at Peking University, the oldest and most famous university in China. Ho has written at great length about the loneliness he suffered in this great northern city, first in the bleak university dormitory and later in the slightly warmer atmosphere of Szechwan student lodgings. But only rarely does he even mention the violent background to his solitary life. On 18 September 1931 Japanese troops seized control of the main railway centre in the north-east provinces of Manchuria; the "Mukden Incident", or "Manchurian Incident", as this became known, provoked a special League of Nations investigation of Japanese activities in China, but in the end, nothing was done to prevent the Japanese from spreading more and more deeply into Chinese territory. After consolidating their position around Mukden, the Japanese occupied the neighbouring province of Jehol in January 1933 and then forced their way into Hopei, the ancient province which contained Peking itself. On the twentieth of May, Japanese troops were only thirteen miles outside Peking, and the Chinese army which had failed to stop their advance was preparing for a desperate struggle to defend the city. The Tangku Agreement negotiated by the Nanking government temporarily deferred this crisis, though in doing so it created further problems.

As enemy planes flew low over Peking, university authorities advised students to leave the city, beginning the summer vacation a few weeks earlier than usual. Their exodus aroused some condemnation, but the students may have acted more in despair than cowardice; judging from the Nationalist government's record in these matters, students must have had little hope that their resistance would have gained any official support. Ho Ch'i-fang joined the flight from the city, but characteristically refused to turn aside from his "gentle essays" to witness and record those terrible days. Gentle beauty and romantic love were all that could engage him.

He returned to Wanhsien for a few weeks' vacation at home. Recollections of his childhood days stirred a new vein in his imagination, and he began to write simply and tenderly about figures he remembered from the past, lonely men and women whose lives were circumscribed by old customs. On his return to Peking, he began to take part in the active literary life of Peking, and his writing became affected by more advanced and self-conscious literary fashions. The confusion between illusion and reality became one of his favourite themes, and the failure of a tempestuous love affair increased his desire to retreat from the world and let his imagination drift into twilight dreams of romance and illusion.

After his graduation from university the pressure of the real world, that is, the need for him to earn a living, forced him to awaken from his daydreams. His first job was as a teacher of Chinese in a well-known school in a prosperous commercial city, Nankai Middle School in Tientsin. But Tientsin, particularly in contrast with the mellow beauty of Peking, was ugly, dirty and foul. Agnes Smedley, who visited Tientsin in 1929, was horrified by the feudal decay on the outskirts of this modern industrial city:

> In Tientsin I visited the outposts of death. A taxi took me to Nankai University to meet a group of professors. Leaving the well-paved streets of the foreign concessions, our car bounded along the rutted dirt road which the rains had turned into a quagmire. On the drab mud flats crouched many small mud-and-thatch villages. Here men made their last stand against death. Ragged, dirty children with small baskets picked at garbage heaps. In the fields and along the road were many grave-mounds from which the earth had fallen away, exposing the decaying coffins level

with the earth. Frightened by the roar of our engine, curs leaped from the crumbling bones which they had been gnawing, and fled snarling into the fields. (*Battle Hymn of China*, 1944, p. 40)

Several years later, the dogs, the coffins and the swamps around the Nankai buildings were still there to greet the new teacher.

Too miserable and overworked to find the heart for poetry, Ho Ch'i-fang spent part of his precious spare time arranging for the publication of his early poetry and essays. Some of his poetry appeared in a joint anthology with other poems by two of his friends from Peking University, Pien Chih-lin and Li Kuang-t'ien. The anthology was called *The Han Garden*, after the location of the university, and Pien Chih-lin was its editor. Ho's essays from the period 1933-34 were collected in a separate volume, *A Record of Painted Dreams*, which appeared in July 1936, a few months after *Han Garden*. *Painted Dreams* was the more popular work; it won the *L'Impartial* (*Ta kung pao*, a prominent Tientsin newspaper) Literary Award for 1936, and was reprinted many times during the thirties.

Early in 1936, Ho Ch'i-fang regained enough energy and self-confidence to attempt his most ambitious project yet, a full-length novel "in defence of individualism". By the end of May, four short chapters or "sketches" had been completed, under the general title of *Sketches of the Passing Scene*. But on the very same day that he finished the last fragment, his life was once more shattered by a sudden and deeply disturbing intrusion of the outside world.

During 1934 and early 1935, there was a lull in Japanese activities in north China, as the Japanese began to use more subtle tactics to secure their interests in China. In the spring and summer of 1935, they forced the central government to suppress more firmly all signs of anti-Japanese feeling, and to remove from positions of power in north China all military and political figures hostile to them. The Japanese then proposed to establish an "autonomous region" in north China to fill the vacuum thus created: this was to include the provinces of Hopei, Shantung and Shansi, as well as Chahar and Suiyuan in the north-west. To the alarmed residents and students in cities like Peking and Tientsin, this was tantamount to placing the Japanese in direct control over all north China. Although the student movement had lost most of its leaders during the White Terror of the early thirties, students in Peking made one last desperate attempt to protest against the submission of the central government to Japanese demands, braving the bitter cold and police brutality in their mass demonstrations of December 9 and December 16. Despite Nationalist countermeasures, the protest movement grew stronger over the next few months, and similar demonstrations were held throughout China. By April and May in the following year, leadership of the movement passed to Tientsin, as the original Peking students were arrested or otherwise intimidated. A huge demonstration of students and workers in Tientsin was planned:

> On May 28 several thousand Tientsin students had paraded the streets, overcome police resistance, presented demands at the Mayor's office, distributed handbills, addressed crowds of people, and held a mass meeting in protest against the increase of Japanese troops in North China, on the Nankai University campus. Spurred by strong Japanese representations, the local Chinese authorities had clamped down martial law and occupied school and university campuses. The Tientsin students then declared a five-day strike, which spread to Peiping (Peking) . . . (T.A. Bisson, *Japan in China*, 1938, p.137).

The students burst into the school yard outside Ho Ch'i-fang's rooms, and despite his later professions of admiration and support, he made no move to join them. Instead, he and his colleagues filed into their classrooms and talked to the empty walls.

The end of the school year could not come too soon. Early in June, Ho Ch'i-fang thankfully took his final leave of Tientsin and went for a short holiday in Wanhsien. At the request of a friend, he wrote up his experiences of homecoming in a series of travel essays later that autumn. Although the subject-matter is the same as the essays written two years earlier after another visit home, the emphasis and the tone are totally different. Instead of lonely figures like pedlars, fortune-tellers, maiden aunts and others living outside society, he now became conscious of the harshness of peasant life, the meanness of the petty traders in town and the backwardness of the local educational bureaucracy; instead of gentle nostalgia and a sense of individual destiny, an angry awareness of social injustice was coupled with a growing suspicion that individualism was no more than a cowardly retreat from social responsibility.

After his month's vacation, Ho Ch'i-fang went to a new teaching post at Laiyang, a small district town in the Shantung peninsula. Putting off the continuation of his novel, he worked steadily on his travel essays during the autumn of 1936. Then early in November, something happened. In one week, and breaking more than a year's silence, he suddenly wrote three violent, bitter poems, unlike anything he had ever written before. The same intensity was carried over in another travel essay completed two weeks later, and into several more poems over the next few weeks. Ho Ch'i-fang has never publicly admitted to any specific reason for this extraordinary outburst, which considering the extent of his later self-explanation is surprising. Perhaps it was a purely private affair. One possible cause could have been the riot which took place in Tsingtao in late October following a lock-out in a Japanese-owned mill, and its forcible suppression by Japanese marines. It might also have been caused by the martyrdom of a twelve-year-old girl in Peking on November 3 who was reported to have shouted "Down with Japanese imperialism!" as she flung herself under an enemy tank. Perhaps it was her death which led Ho Ch'i-fang to write, "This is the age of funerals..."

In May 1937 Ho Ch'i-fang looked back on the changes which had taken place in his outlook on life since he quit Peking in the summer of 1935:

> I almost forgot poetry completely. But after I had lost my passion for it, I reached in my new clarity a conclusion, one which I had not reached (then); poetry, just like all other branches of literature, must have its roots deeply planted in the world of men, in this great land full of misery and dark oppression. If you pluck it from this fertile land, it will surely wither and die, because it is not at all, as some illusionists and escapists have supposed, a tree which can be uprooted to grow and even flourish in emptiness.
>
> But even now there are still people who hold on to this vain hope.
>
> Into every corner floats a lightly drifting song.
>
> The whip of reality will eventually strike, and a man's most important need is sincerity, so that when the unfeeling whip lashes his back, he should awake from dreaming, distinguish whence it came, and angrily and courageously begin to fight back.
>
> As for me, though I don't deceive myself as to my ability to play the clamorous trumpet, I want my songs to become whips to flog the back of this unjust society.

The Laiyang poems are more like self-flagellation.

While Ho was writing the last of his Laiyang poems, he may have gained some slight feeling of relief from the unexpected alliance being formed by the Communists and Nationalists to resist further Japanese demands. On 12 December 1936 the Manchurian general

Chang Hsüeh-liang arrested Chiang Kai-shek, President of China and his own Commander-in-Chief, on a charge of having failed to check the Japanese invasion of his homeland by tying up Manchurian troops around the Communist base in northern Shensi. In the strangest irony in modern Chinese history, Chou En-lai stepped in to mediate between the two parties. He persuaded Chiang Kai-shek to abandon the civil war between the Communists and Nationalists and to resist Japan in a nation-wide united front, and at the same time, persuaded Chang Hsüeh-liang not to eliminate the only man in China who could command general national support. On Christmas Day, Chiang Kai-shek was restored to freedom amid the rejoicings of all classes of Chinese.

No official announcement was made on the reversal of the Nationalists' domestic and foreign policies, but the direction soon became clear both to the Chinese people and to the Japanese. When a brief exchange of fire between Chinese and Japanese troops at the Marco Polo Bridge outside Peking early in July was followed by further Chinese military action instead of the expected negotiation and submission to Japanese demands, large numbers of Japanese troops poured in from Manchuria to surround Peking and Tientsin. Then on July 17 Chiang Kai-shek made an official announcement of the Chinese intention to resist Japanese aggression: the "special un-declared war", according to the Japanese, or the "War of Resistance," according to the Chinese, had begun.

The outbreak of war had a profound impact on Ho Ch'i-fang, radically affecting his outlook on literature and life. Before describing the new direction of his literary activities, we should backtrack a little into the history of modern Chinese literature to examine the rise of the New Literary Movement in the early twentieth century.

Ho Ch'i-fang and the New Literary Movement (1917-37)

Ho Ch'i-fang's losing battle to defend literature from the demands of politics and revolution echoed the same struggle, on a much wider scale, throughout the development of modern Chinese literature. When the literary reformers of the early twentieth century repudiated China's classical literary heritage, one of their main charges was its traditional scholarly remoteness from the dust and strife of the real world. Although some of old China's most outstanding poets, such as Tu Fu and Po Chü-i, concerned themselves with the hardships of the common people, this "rebellious" tradition seemed in the recent past to have fallen away.

Despite the violent language used by the literary reformers to characterize traditional literature, not even the most radical among them were totally opposed to the past. They distinguished between two different streams in literature, the classical literature of the scholars and the colloquial or vernacular literature of the common people. The former was written in a highly allusive, gnomic style, bound by prosodic and genre regulations; it consisted essentially of poetry and essays, but in a wider sense also included historical and philosophical writing, and all official documentation. The common people, whose education rarely extended beyond a few basic characters, relied on folk song, story-telling and the theatre for their literary entertainment. The lively expressiveness of many of these forms attracted the attention of the educated classes, who would record or obtain written versions of performances for their private amusement. Some of the more unconventional scholars would even write original scripts for private circulation. Despite official disapproval of the vulgarity or subversiveness of vernacular literature, novel-reading became as popular a pastime in Chinese homes in the last three or four hundred years as in Europe over roughly the same period.

When it came to creating a fresh, new literature, however, the old vernacular literary forms seemed to be just as stilted and threadbare as the classical literature itself. In contrast, the newly-discovered literature of Western realism and romanticism offered a wide variety of forms, which themselves had been evolved in the creation of national vernacular literatures in post-Renaissance Europe. The young writers of the May Fourth generation fell onto Western literature with a voracious hunger, translating, describing and analysing in passionate excitement great quantities of literature from all countries and periods. By the early twenties, the acceptance of the vernacular as a serious literary medium was virtually complete, and a wide range of Western literary forms was available for literary experimentation. The New Literary Movement moved into its first creative phase.

To aid in the encouragement and dissemination of the new literature, a large number of literary societies sprang up in the twenties, some leaning towards the realistic fiction of France and Russia, others emphasizing English and German romanticism. Common to almost every literary group was, however, the insistence that literature must be involved with life, that is, with the problems of contemporary Chinese society. The Northern Expedition of 1926-27 drew into its ranks some of the most valuable literary talent of the period, such as the realistic novelist, Shen Yen-ping (who had yet to write his first novel, under the pseudonym of Mao Tun), and the romantic or expressionist poet, Kuo Mo-jo. During the intense political activity of these few years, writers were assured of a keen (if comparatively minute) audience of radical and liberal young intellectuals, some already in positions of power. This led inevitably to the dominance of political themes and directions in literary works, while the introduction of Marxist criticism and Soviet literature provided concrete examples as well as a theoretical framework for this tendency.

The sudden and complete collapse of Nationalist-Communist cooperation in 1927 and the subsequent White Terror of the late twenties and early thirties brought chaos into the literary world. Among the left-wing writers, the shock of failure and the disillusionment of powerlessness at first provoked only mutual hostility and suspicion between different literary cliques. Increasing government oppression eventually brought some measure of unity, and the League of Left-wing Writers was founded in 1930 in Shanghai. Its aims were perhaps more political than literary, but it survived as a highly influential body up to the eve of the Sino-Japanese War.

On the other side, many writers gave active or passive support to the new national government. Some, like Hu Shih and Lin Yü-t'ang, grew alarmed at the excessive authoritarianism of the Nationalist regime and criticized the government for betraying the ideals of the cultural renaissance. While more conservative writers welcomed the official revival of classicism, the moderates or liberals sought refuge in the northern universities, avoiding as far as possible open political commitment. The group with the longest record of devotion to art for art's sake was the Crescent Society, led by the poets Wen I-to and Hsü Chih-mo. Friends since 1924, they shared a passion for English romantic poetry, and experimented with adaptations of English verse forms for Chinese vernacular poetry. Towards the end of the twenties, political differences between the two began to emerge. Hsü Chih-mo, at the time of his premature death in 1931, had become an outspoken anti-Communist. Wen I-to never at any stage became a Communist, but his awareness of the sufferings of the people would not allow acceptance of the status quo. During the thirties he wrote no poetry at all, and after a period of academic seclusion, he began to support any political or literary movement which urged social reform. His criticism of the Nationalist government for failing to carry out its responsibilities to the common people led to his assassination in 1946 by the secret police.

As a young student, Ho Ch'i-fang's sympathies were with the Crescent group, and during his university years he developed friendships with some of its writers. In his earliest prose writings, his protagonists are the retired scholar of classical Chinese tradition, and a more modern hero who broods over the passion which has wasted his life; both live apart from the world, and scorn the common man's pursuit of happiness and comfort.

When forced into the world of the common man to earn his living, Ho Ch'i-fang passed to the more realistic position of defending the rights of the individual in contemporary life. He acknowledged "the more urgent call of life; the shared anger of accumulated misery; or the shout on the brink of danger"; but he could not see himself as a trumpeter of the revolution. He could only offer a pathetic plea for the loyalty the artist has to his own lyre. By the autumn of 1936, even this loyalty was beginning to fade. His Laiyang poems and essays lay bare his lack of faith in the individual, the society around him, and even the value of art itself. It was a period of extreme mental anguish, judging from the violence of his writing, as feelings of inadequacy and guilt in the face of his country's suffering threatened to overwhelm him.

While Ho Ch'i-fang had been vainly trying to uphold the independence of literature, the Left-wing League of Writers was examining the problem of aligning it with politics. One of their major debates was on the question of literature for the masses. The left-wing writers conscientiously attempted to write about the masses, rather than about their own petit-bourgeois circles, but even that required a more intimate acquaintance with the masses than most of them possessed. As for the masses producing their own literature (of a kind acceptable to the left, that is), this was apparently an even more remote possibility. Two methods of overcoming this problem were "popularization", or simplifying the language and forms favoured by educated writers, and "elevation", or educating the masses towards greater literacy and literary appreciation.

The New Literary Movement was from its inception deeply influenced by Western literature, and many of the left-wing writers had learned their profession by translating Western books. With the general spread of Western learning among literate Chinese, a new literary idiom was being created, so that the "vernacular writing" of the new intellectuals became virtually a new language, almost as unintelligible to the vast majority of the peasant masses as the former classical language had been. With the outbreak of the war, the problem of mobilizing the people to resist Japan became acute, and the campaigns for popularization and elevation were stepped up. "Elevation" now involved intellectuals going to the countryside to teach and carry out propaganda. Their actual dispersal throughout the country was in many cases a direct result of the war itself: some, like Ho Ch'i-fang, fled from the cities to their own native villages; others were driven into remote areas where northern university graduates and teachers had never before ventured. "Popularization" meant the development of literary forms suitable for propaganda. Chief among these were the *tsa-wen* (miscellaneous essay), reports, declamatory poetry and street theatre, all of which were short, simple and openly didactic.

The *tsa-wen* was a short satirical essay which had already achieved great popularity among the writers of the left; Lu Hsün had defined its essential characteristics in the late twenties, and it was used extensively in the literary debates in the thirties. A basically provocative or aggressive form, it commonly dealt with an abstract political principle currently under debate, while some recent experience of the author provided its starting-point. It could be personal and humorous in tone, but its brevity and didactic purpose allowed no genuine self-revelation. When Ho Ch'i-fang first turned to writing propaganda in 1938, it was the relatively sophisticated *tsa-wen* that became his favourite form.

Literature into politics: the War of Resistance to Japan

The War of Resistance was the major event in Ho Ch'i-fang's lifetime, transforming him from an individualist into a socialist and nationalist: it is doubtful that he would otherwise have found his way to communism. In this he probably resembled many of his countrymen, although the Japanese intervention in China was designed to prevent the east from turning red.

During the autumn of 1937, the Chinese people in the cities and villages along the coast and in the north-east welcomed the prospect of ridding the country of the Japanese, who had long since replaced the British as the most hated foreign power in China. But from the very beginning, the war went badly for the Chinese. Despite a spirited defence by local troops, the East Hopei area, including Peking and Tientsin, fell to the Japanese by the end of July. The Japanese then moved west towards Shansi, and south to Shanghai. Fighting raged in Shanghai for three months, but not even the best of the well-equipped government divisions could withstand the heavy enemy bombardment. Chinese withdrawal was sounded on October 31 and the flight of refugees from the coastal areas inland began. In December, the Japanese pressed the attack up the Yangtze to Nanking, the national capital. The government abandoned the city, moving executive headquaters further upstream to Hankow while gradually shifting the apparatus of bureaucracy to the far west provincial city of Chungking, in Szechwan. The Japanese entered Nanking on December 14 in horrifying scenes of bloodshed, brutality and rape; on the same day, a Japanese puppet government was established in Peking. Meanwhile, in the north-west, the Japanese took the Shansi capital of Taiyuan in November, thus gaining control over all railway communication in the north.

The Shantung cities of Tsinan and Tsingtao, in which Japanese investments in China were most heavily concentrated, were discreetly left outside the war zone by the Japanese until local Chinese sabotage forced their military occupation in late December and early January. Long before this, however, Ho Ch'i-fang had quit Laiyang to return to his native district in Szechwan.

When the Japanese occupied the northern cities of Peking and Tientsin, one of their first acts was to close down the schools and universities—only foreign-owned institutions were allowed to carry on. Teachers and students, as well as writers and artists of all kinds, joined the flight of the refugees to the south-west. After a brief pause in the temporary capital of Hankow, they were forced even deeper into the recesses of the Chinese interior, virtually a foreign land for the educated Chinese of the north. They finally came to a halt in the remote mountainous province of Yunnan, south of Szechwan, where the "United University" continued to function for the duration of the war.

The writers in Shanghai were on the whole not attached to academic institutions, many of them being in hiding from the police in the International Settlement and existing as best they could on various kinds of literary hackwork, journalism, translation, proof-reading, and so on. After the retreat from Shanghai, some continued to enjoy the sanctuary of the Settlement, while others fled further south to the temporary safety of Canton and even Hong Kong. Many left-wing writers, however, took advantage of the Nationalist-Communist truce to emerge from hiding and offer their services to the government. Kuo Mo-jo, for instance, returned from exile in Japan to write official propaganda, accompanying the government first to Hankow and then to Chungking. Others who had been under arrest in Nanking, now found the way open to the Communist head-quarters in Yenan, in the north-west province of Shensi. Despite their precipitate flight from the north-east, Chinese intellectuals on the whole enthusiastically supported the national resistance movement, rejoicing in the new spirit of national unity and for the first time in perhaps a decade, full of hope for the future.

In September 1937 Ho was back in Wanhsien, teaching in the small district normal school. It was no time now for tender reminiscence or compassionate observation of rural hardship, only immediate disil-lusionment. With bitter shock Ho Ch'i-fang surveyed the backwardness and corruption of the local gentry, still seemingly un-touched by the state of national emergency.

A few months of this reactionary atmosphere made Ho Ch'i-fang unbearably depressed, and he decided early in 1938 to go to Chengtu, the capital of Szechwan, in search of more congenial surroundings. Together with a friend, he began to write, edit and distribute a small magazine, *Work* (*Kung-tso*). His first contribution was an article on the proper meaning of work in the present situation: his material, the backwardness of those provincial schoolteachers and the shortsightedness of intellectuals who believed that literature could stand outside of life.

During that Chengtu spring, as Ho Ch'i-fang began to use literature consciously as a weapon in the political struggle, his former diffuse style became clearer and more concise. His social attitudes also became firmer, and the objects of his attacks more precisely defined. His reports on provincial backwardness, for instance, are distinctly harsher than the Wanhsien tales of 1934 or the travel essays of 1936: he shows less tolerance towards the complacence or outright corruption of the middle classes, and more anger as he describes the neglect of children and the sufferings of the poor. Above all, the note of personal doubt begins to fade.

Traces of self-pity still linger in the first of these Chengtu *tsa-wen*, but by March he had produced the first of his writings not concerned with his merely personal situation, "On Basic Culture". The problem of how China should react to Western culture had been cropping up in one form or another since the 1870s. The original formula devised by Western-inclined reformers was "Chinese learning for essentials, Western learning for practical use", and referred to the determination of the reformers to retain Chinese culture and society intact alongside new industrial and commercial techniques. By the time of the May Fourth Movement of 1919, this half-hearted approach had been discredited, and the more progressive intellectuals made serious efforts on a personal level to absorb all aspects of Western culture, literary and social as well as political and economic. Because of the confused political situation, even the most enthusiastic of the Westernizers had little chance to put their ideas into practice, and even with the establishment of a national government in 1927, a basic division soon emerged among the "new conservatives". Some still thought that China needed a programme of "wholesale Westernization" to develop into a modern state along the lines of the Western democracies, while others wanted to hang on to traditional social and cultural patterns while carrying out "partial Westernization" only in so far as it was necessary to secure state power. Hu Shih, for instance, defended "wholesale Westernization", but the majority of Nationalist thinkers, including Chiang Kai-shek himself, supported traditional Confucian beliefs and the re-introduction of classical education in schools. At the same time, the left-wing movement also began to move away from its former internationalism. Some of the proponents of "national forms" were still adamant on combining these with "international content", but the outbreak of war interrupted the working-out of this theoretical compromise. The

Nationalists, of course, were greatly strengthened morally by the declaration of resistance to Japan, and talk of "national essence" and "basic culture" became widespread in Nationalist centres in the early war years.

In his essay on "basic culture", Ho Ch'i-fang avoided both the left-wing and right-wing approaches. Still preoccupied with the relationship between the individual and society, he pointed out that in some cases, at least, their interests were identical. Here and in other *tsa-wen* written between March and June, 1938, Ho adopted an impersonal tone. It is not neutral, for on the contrary, his attitudes show through very clearly; it is simply that his own feelings are no longer the subject under discussion. He had found a social and political position he could set forth without guilt, conscious of his identity with enlightened and progressive elements in China and the world. The key to this new faith was Romain Rolland, who had replaced Paul Valéry or T.S. Eliot as his literary idol. Rolland seemed to have found a balance between social responsibility and individual freedom, particularly in regard to the problems of a writer in contemporary life. Unfortunately, it is difficult to be sure of which aspects of Rolland's teaching were adopted by Ho Ch'i-fang.

Romain Rolland, like Ho Ch'i-fang himself, was a writer who changed his beliefs several times during his lifetime. Born in 1866, he formed part of the reaction to the *fin-de-siècle* withdrawal from life by symbolist and other neo-romantic movements, and reached maturity as a writer under the slogan of "serve the people". It was not until the outbreak of World War I, on the threshhold of his fifties, that he established the position for which he achieved an international following: the responsibility of the intellectual to maintain his independence of mind. During the first years of the war, the destructive patriotism of the press and public aroused him to the defence of internationalism, or the universality of human culture; subsequently, the vicious personal abuse which his pacifist stand was met with convinced him of the moral necessity of individual freedom of thought. It was during this period that he wrote *Au-dessus de la mêlée* (Above the Battle, 1915). Towards the end of the war, the Russian Revolution reawakened his old socialist beliefs, but with his stronger faith in the "independence of the mind", he gave it only limited support. His ambivalence in this matter is hinted at in *Les Précurseurs* (The Forerunners, 1919). On the day the armistice was declared, he published in *L'Humanité* his famous "Declaration of the Independence of the Mind", in which he called for freedom of thought beyond the "selfish interests of a political or social clique, of a state, a country, or a class". This declaration, which was signed by some of the most notable writers in Europe and America, was warmly received by the May Fourth generation in China. Rolland justified his refusal to support the "class interests" of the Russian Revolution on the grounds that "in the common work of struggle and reconstruction, each contingent of workers had its own peculiar task, and that of the intellectuals was to maintain the independence of the mind as a televising instrument, from the vantage point of which, beyond the clashes of the day, it would be possible to guide the armies." (Romain Rolland, *I Will Not Rest*, London, 1936, p. 17.) In the following years, however, as he watched the increasing alienation from the struggle of the "free minds" and "independent spirits" around him, he began to doubt the correctness of his own individualism and pacifism. The rise of fascism in Italy forced his hand, and in 1927 he openly enrolled in "the army of proletarian progress". Against imperialism abroad and fascism at home, Rolland turned to the Soviet Union as the sole defender of social justice. In 1935, he claimed to have been in the front line for the last fifteen years, "where it was not a question of some infamous war between nations that are kin, but of a sacred war on behalf of those very nations and against a cursed and murderous society composed of exploiters and enslavers." (*I Will Not Rest*, p. 50) He began to quote Stalin on "the true nature of freedom," and to state with Marx that "the free development of each is the condition of the free development of all." (p. 64).

In his *tsa-wen*, "On Work," Ho Ch'i-fang referred to his admiration for Rolland's *Au-dessus de la mêlée*, while three years later he quoted from the 1931 "Greetings to Gorki" which was published in *I Will Not Rest*; when Ho identified himself with Rolland as the defender of individualism, to which Rolland was he referring? Perhaps he wasn't too sure himself. Within one month, Ho Ch'i-fang was able to write in his new style, "if we cut ourselves off from life, from the age, from the struggle for national freedom and the suffering masses, no work we produce could possibly be a masterpiece;" and then, reverting to his former humanism, "No matter whether in the east or in the west, man everywhere is man, and there should be a culture of mankind." Admitting the shortcomings of individualism, Ho Ch'i-fang nevertheless upheld the rights of man without reference to his class origin or political allegiance.

In the middle of this high-minded humanitarianism, Ho Ch'i-fang launched an attack on a former literary hero, Chou Tso-jen. Chou Tso-jen had a long and honourable history in the New Literary

Movement. Together with his elder brother, Lu Hsün (Chou Shu-jen), he was the first to introduce into China the realistic and humanist literature of Eastern and Northern Europe. Later, in 1917 and 1918, both brothers were among the first to support the call for vernacular literature, and while Lu Hsün became the best-known writer of short stories and *tsa-wen* in the new literature, Chou Tso-jen went from "new poetry" to essays and literary criticism. Chou Tso-jen also played an important role in founding the Literary Association in 1920-21, and the Thread of Talk Society in 1924: these two societies were notable for maintaining high literary standards throughout the twenties. Lu Hsün was also associated with them, but by the end of the twenties, he had become a leader of the left-wing literary movement. Chou Tso-jen, meanwhile, had been moving steadily towards the right, restricting his literary output to anti-quarian essays and personal musings. Lu Hsün died just before the beginning of war with Japan, but there is not the slightest doubt that he would have offered total resistance; Chou Tso-jen, on the other hand, was one of the small minority of writers who came to terms with the enemy. He stayed in Peking, pleading ill-health and his attachment to his surroundings, and even collaborated with the Japanese in the reorganization of education in north China.

The reaction of other writers to this betrayal was naturally hostile, but Ho Ch'i-fang felt a personal sense of shock: one of his closest friends at Peking University, Li Kuang-t'ien, had been a protege of Chou Tso-jen's in the early thirties. The news of Chou's treachery made headlines in Chengtu on May 8, and three days later, further evidence of his collaboration appeared in the newspapers. That night, Ho sat down and wrote a furious denunciation, not only of Chou's present behaviour, but also of his past:

> To people who are rather more fully acquainted with the situation in cultural circles over the last few years, it is no great surprise that Chou has descended to such a level. It was not some accidental slip, nor even an unforeseeable apostasy, but the result of his way of thinking and the circumstances of his life. He is following his own path to the grave... Although he taught at the university where I was, I did not really know very much about him. I did not study Japanese, nor did I take after a classmate of mine whose subject was also philosophy but who spent most of his time attending lectures of "famous men" in other departments. It wasn't till I became intimate with a student who said he was going to write an article on Chou Tso-jen but who finally did not, that I learnt from him just what a ridiculous person Chou was. According to him, Chou always came to his classes late and left early, and after his classes he left the school in a great hurry because he was afraid that the "com-

mon" students would bother him. On the streets he made a special practice of not greeting people. Besides, he was secretly jealous of Mr Lu Hsün. He once said to my friend, "Everyone says that Lu Hsün is good to the young people...", implying that it wasn't really true...

At this time countless young people had with great hardship and courage devoted themselves to the struggle to save the nation. At this time the insane and yet cunning enemy had already stepped up its invasion. And at this time, Chou wrote some "Glimpses of Japan". What were these glimpses? The glasses he looked through were probably made in Japan, so that all he saw was the "beauty of human nature" in the Japanese. Although he did not see any beauty in the Japanese fascist militarism, neither did he forcefully indicate its ugliness. In his peacetime writing, he condemned both fascism and socialism; he regarded the German Nazi Party which advised starving people to "tighten your belts", and the Soviet Communist Party which had completed two Five-Year Plans and wiped out unemployment and illiteracy, as foxes sharing a common lair...

Ho Ch'i-fang's bitter condemnation of a former hero turned traitor was shared by many. There were others, out of a sense of loyalty perhaps, who tried to defend Chou Tso-jen at least from the attacks on his personal life. One of these was Chu Kuang-ch'ien, a literary critic influenced by Croce and I.A. Richards. At the beginning of 1937, Chu was the editor of a Peking literary journal and an associate of prominent Peking writers such as Chou Tso-jen and Shen Ts'ung-wen. Chu Kuang-ch'ien was not a traitor—he had fled with the others into the interior—but he opposed the general criticism of Chou Tso-jen on two grounds: firstly, that Chou's collaboration had not been proven; and secondly, that attacks on a person's private life and weaknesses are out of place in a serious discussion.

Chu Kuang-ch'ien's critical remarks were obviously pointed at Ho Ch'i-fang, among others, and Ho rose to defend himself. His reply began politely enough, to the effect that Chu and he were both agreed that in no way could Chou Tso-jen be regarded as an evil person who had deliberately sold out to the enemy. The question of proof of Chou's betrayal remained open, though events were to prove Ho correct: Chou Tso-jen was eventually appointed minister of education in the puppet government, and was convicted of treason after the war. But on the question of Chou's private life, Ho Ch'i-fang remained unforgiving:

> ...I believe that Chou's confused thinking and attitude towards life in recent years should be attacked. His pessimism and lack of faith in the future of mankind and our own people, his indifference to and secret

ridicule of the struggle of countless young people on the eve of this great epoch, and even his whole attitude, described by Mr Chu as that of "an aesthete who burns with a white hot flame" or "a sophisticate who fears involvement in controversy," all these are totally incorrect and harmful, they should be vigorously exposed and attacked. It is precisely beeause he thinks in this confused way, precisely because he has led this confused kind of life, that he has become cut off from the age and from the people, that he chose to stay in Peking after it had fallen as a "modern-day" Su Wu, that he sank into this wretched mire...

... Why do I want to bring up his "private life"? Because to understand a person we must understand his life, otherwise we may be deceived by the fact that while what he writes and says may sound very pleasant, his personal behaviour may be another matter altogether. Which parts are "private" in a person's life, and which are "public", or which parts we may speak of and which we must ignore, is something which never occurred to me when I wrote my previous article, and I have no intention of letting it worry me now.

It is true that few people in this world are perfect, but to consider therefore that all men are equally good or bad, or to know the difference between good and bad and the difference between various degrees of good and bad and yet still feel neither hate nor love, or different degrees of hate or love, is in my opinion incorrect. It may well be that everyone has his bright side and his dark side. But we must find which side is the dominant one. If the brighter elements predominate, then we should love him. Otherwise, we should hate him... The superficial expedient of putting the blame on his age and infirmity won't do, for what about Romain Rolland, who is over seventy, and Bernard Shaw, who is in his eighties? Chou is only in his fifties...

And as for the principle of "live and let live" in Mr Chu's final remark, "Towards ourselves the utmost severity, towards others ungrudging generosity", I have something to add to that: I believe that "generosity" should be shown to some people, but I cannot be "generous" to people I hate...

This controversy shows a significant change emerging in Ho's way of thinking. It is not just his use of phrases like "cut off from the masses" (these had been creeping into his prose as early as 1936), but his unrelenting attitude towards someone who had always tried to be an individual and lead his own life outside normal convention. There are perhaps two reasons for the vehemence of Ho's attack. In the first place, it was people like Chou who had encouraged his own early tendency to regard all political and military activity as senseless and wicked. Chou's quietism in the face of Japanese occupation was foreshadowed in Ho's own writing in the years 1934 and 1935, and Chou's submission in 1937 and 1938 might nearly have been made by Ho himself. Secondly, perhaps under the influence of Romain Rolland, Ho Ch'i-fang was moving closer to a Leninist outlook, in which no distinction is made between a person's public and private life, and no sentimental allowance is made for renegades, no matter what their former achievements may have been. "I cannot be generous to those I hate"—this kind of moral righteousness can only be the result of a drastic change in Ho's way of thinking. It is a clear echo of a talk given by Mao Tse-tung in September the previous year, "Combat Liberalism":

> To let things slide for the sake of peace and friendship when a person has clearly gone wrong, and refrain from principled argument because he is an old acquaintance, a fellow townsman, a schoolmate, a close friend, a loved one, an old colleague or old subordinate. Or to touch on a matter lightly instead of going into it thoroughly, so as to keep on good terms. The result is that both the organization and the individual are harmed. This is one type of liberalism.

And liberalism to Mao at this time,

> is a manifestation of opportunism and conflicts fundamentally with Marxism. It is negative and objectively has the effect of helping the enemy; that is why the enemy welcomes its preservation in our midst. Such being its nature, there should be no place for it in the ranks of the revolution. (*Selected Works of Mao Tse-tung*, Vol. II, 1965, pp. 31 & 33.)

The confident idealism of that Chengtu spring proved to be no more than a brief interlude between the loss of one faith and the adoption of a new one. In his disillusionment with liberalism, Ho Ch'i-fang was not alone. The mutual bond of support between the Nationalist government and the intellectuals was foundering, as the Nationalists failed to prosecute the war as vigorously as they might. Not only were they losing steadily to the Japanese on the war front (it could not then have been foreseen that the loss of Hankow in October would be the last major battle for several years), but the government was also losing the propaganda war to the communists.

The former Red Army was now operating as the Eighth Route Army in the north-west provinces of Shensi and Shansi, in cooperation with central and local Nationalist troops. While the Nationalists were losing the positional battles for the larger towns, the Eighth Route Army was waging a limited but effective guerrilla war on enemy outposts and communication lines in the countryside. News of the high troop morale, the mobilization of the peasants and the new democracy of the base areas filtered into occupied and Nationalist China. Universities and academies were established in the Red capital, Yenan, and intellectuals and students were encouraged to see for themselves the new China which was being created in the ancient birthplace of Chinese civilization. While the government urged students to remain in schools and educate themselves for the post-war future, and foreigners commented unfavourably on the frivolity of the wealthy and educated young in Hankow, thousands of other students were setting off by bus, truck or on foot for the north-west, the real centre of anti-Japanese resistance.

In the summer of 1938, Ho Ch'i-fang made up his mind to investigate this new "Mecca" of the young. Up until then, Ho had first tried to avoid or ignore the forces which had changed his life, and then more recently had accepted their direction with some relief. Now, he was striding out to meet the new era, voluntarily and deliberately. Perhaps he was still not fully conscious of the import of his journey, for after all, his stated purpose was only to visit the front. But it was not the Nationalist front to which he was heading, but Yenan, home base of the Eighth Route Army and headquarters of the Chinese Communist Party.

The journey from Chengtu to Yenan was long and hazardous. The railway connecting the neighbouring provinces of Szechwan and Shensi had been left uncompleted by the war, and even the motor road was in poor condition. Edgar Snow, making the same journey a year later, speaks with disgust of the "miserable road" and "foul inns" of Szechwan, particularly in contrast with Shensi. All around him, Ho Ch'i-fang saw evidence of personal corruption and official incompetence. At night, under the lamplight in wayside inns, he jotted down his experiences and impressions to be written up later as "reports". The report (*pao-kao*) was another literary form which became popular as an instrument of wartime propaganda; it was factual and positive rather than satirical. Ho Ch'i-fang's use of this form suggest that he regarded himself as a reporter and not as a critic on this visit to Yenan.

From Sian, capital of Shensi province, to Yenan in the north, was a further three-day journey, this time along a road in worse condition even than the Szechwan roads. Communications between the two cities had been restored since the formation of the National Front, and Ho's party was joined by a group of Eighth Route soldiers returning to Yenan from Sian. It was the first time that Ho had come face-to-face with Communist soldiers, and as they jolted along together in the uncovered truck, he realized that they were not the same kind of men as the soldiers who had terrorized his childhood. As he wrote a year later, "Not only did I neither hate nor fear them, I even felt I could be friends with them." They told him stories of guerrilla warfare in Shansi, of the Long March, of their families and their childhood. By the time they reached their journey's end, when they said goodbye and shook hands, "I did not think of these hands at all as killing people. On the contrary, I thought that from these coarse, peasant hands, a free, new China would be established and a rich human life achieved."

They arrived in Yenan in September 1938. Despite his original intention to remain an objective observer, Ho Ch'i-fang burst into immediate admiration. On the day following his arrival, he addressed a gathering of the Lu Hsün Academy of Art, concluding with these words, "Breathing in the atmosphere here, I feel only happiness. I seem to have always been dreaming of a just society, a just land, and now it's as if my dream has come true." During the next few weeks, besides writing up his travel notes, Ho Ch'i-fang went about collecting material for an article on Yenan itself. The eventual result was more a paean of praise than a report, as may be guessed from its title, "I Sing of Yenan". In it he mentions by name for the first time the Chinese Communist Party, and "the great leader of our people, Comrade Mao Tse-tung".

It was now November, and Ho Ch'i-fang was anxious to be on his way to the front. The Eighth Route Army made a practice of encouraging groups of writers and artists to visit guerrilla bases to witness the effectiveness of their operations and also their close relations with the common people. These were known as "comfort corps", and were ostensibly to raise the morale of the troops; as Ho himself remarked, the "comfort" they were able to bring was negligible. The real gain to the Eighth Route Army was in the glowing reports generally brought back by these visitors to the rest of China and the world. One "comfort corps", for instance, organized in the winter of 1937-38, included the Chinese writers Chou Li-po and Hsiao Chün, and also the American journalist, Agnes Smedley. Perhaps the most remarkable visitor to the front in those early years was Evans F. Carlson, an officer in the U.S. Marines. Carlson had been sent to China to protect American interests against Chiang Kai-shek's Northern Expedition of 1926-27, but he gradually came to sympathize with Chinese nationalist aims. The Chinese resistance of 1937-38 convinced him that the "twin stars" of China were Chiang Kai-shek and Mao Tse-tung, as he visited many centres of Red and Nationalist resistance in north China; on the whole he found the

Eighth Route Army to have the highest levels of morale and efficiency. (Details of these and other eyewitness accounts are given in the Bibliography.)

On the north-west front, the first major Japanese target was Taiyuan, capital of the strategically important and coal-rich province of Shansi. Despite a valiant defence by provincial troops, who were supported by central government troops, other local units and guerrilla detachments of the Eighth Route Army, the Japanese entered Taiyuan in November 1937. This gave them control over all big towns and railways north of the Yellow River. By the end of 1938, however, the Japanese had not made much further progress. Their rapid advance over north China had left behind large areas of the countryside which were impossible to patrol. The Eighth Route Army and remnants of the provincial troops formed bases behind the Japanese lines: their constant guerrilla raids on the enemy's communications and surprise attacks on isolated units were damaging to enemy morale, and tended to keep the Japanese confined to the major cities under almost siege-like conditions. But due to the scarcity of supplies, and also, perhaps, the need to avoid large-scale retaliation, guerrilla operations during the first half of the war did not lead to substantial victories.

In 1938-39, the period in which Ho Ch'i-fang visited the front, the Eighth Route Army controlled three separate areas in the north-west. The best-organized was the base area in the Wutai Mountains in north-east Shansi: it was here that the Shansi-Hopei-Chahar Border Government was established in February 1938, the second Border Area Government after Yenan itself. To the south, along the border with Honan and Hopei, was a combination of Manchurian, Shensi and Communist forces, the latter under the command of Chu Teh and P'eng Teh-huai. To the north-west of Shansi was Ho Lung's 120th division, with headquarters at Lanhsien. Ho Ch'i-fang arrived here at the end of 1938.

Lanhsien was a small town some fifty miles north-west of Taiyuan, and the centre of guerilla operations along the important Tat'ung-P'uchou Railway. There was an intelligence group there, and even a few Japanese prisoners, who were rare at that stage of the war. When Ho Ch'i-fang arrived in Lanhsien, Taiyuan had been in enemy hands for more than a year, and many stories were circulating about the atrocities committed by the Japanese. For his first report from the front, Ho wrote a long article, "The Tragedy of the Japanese". Compiled mainly from captured diaries of Japanese soldiers and Chinese traitors, it recounts these terrible stories in a remarkably restrained way; it even includes the story of how a Japanese officer at Nanking refused to rape a helpless young girl, and mentions the small group of Japanese fighting on the Chinese side. Ho Ch'i-fang tries to find a reason for the "inhuman behaviour" of the Japanese: as in his analysis of the backwardness of his own countrymen, in "On Basic Culture", he blames the authoritarian nature of Japanese family and social life. It is the same system of submission and obedience which creates unresisting apathy among the Chinese and unrestrained cruelty from the invading Japanese—though Ho Ch'i-fang does not make the analogy explicit. Even the title of this piece indicates a sort of ironic sympathy for the Japanese: their tactics presumably designed to create terrified sub-mission among the Chinese people only provoked stubborn resistance from a hitherto fatalistic peasantry.

Apart from examining captured documents and interviewing new recruits, Ho Ch'i-fang had little to do in Lanhsien. A week after he arrived, the town was bombed, but this was an infrequent excitement. He was therefore willing to go along when Ho Lung led one of the division's two brigades, with one guerrilla detachment in support, across Shansi into central Hopei early in 1939. The crossing was dif-ficult and dangerous: in Shansi the mountainous terrain made the going perilous enough, but when the loess mountains gave way to the vast alluvial plains of Hopei, they were exposed to the continual danger of enemy attack.

Ho Ch'i-fang was careful to bring his fountain pen and notebook along, but there was no leisure for writing. Even when they reached their new base, Hochien, they were not on safe ground. Hochien lay only one hundred miles south of Peking, deep in occupied territory. Carlson, who visited this area in mid-1938, was offered the chance of secretly entering Peking with the guerrillas, who could apparently go in and out at will. But there were still frequent encounters with the enemy, and Ho personally witnessed at least one serious clash, in which they were saved only by the timely return of the division's other brigade from an expedition in Suiyuan. This dramatic rescue made a strong impact on Ho, and he later wrote a long report on the exploits of this brigade, the 715th. He concluded "how insipid history is, compared to real action. I now know how clumsy legend is, com-pared to living events, and how colourless imagination and reasoning are, compared to life itself. I now know that I would rather be a failure in life than a successful teller of tales."

In fact, Ho Ch'i-fang wrote only some notes in his diary and a few letters after he left Lanhsien. Although he had stayed with Ho Lung's division for more than six months, he had never become a part of the army itself. He had first travelled to the divisional headquarters in a "comfort corps", that is, as a reporter from outside. Then, finding this too restrictive, he moved over to the political group, and in this way followed the division into enemy territory. Still, as he later admitted, he played the part of a guest. In his notebook he recorded conversations he had with peasants in the villages through which they passed, but these only reveal the unconsciously superior attitude he held towards the common people. He boasted that he wore the padded cotton uniform and cap of the Eighth Route Army, but he did not take part in any action. Much to his later shame, he did not even share the life of the common soldier, but kept to a small circle of educated men like himself in the political group. Under these circumstances, it was inevitable that he took down only a few superficial anecdotes and descriptions to illustrate conditions among the peasants and soldiers. There would have been several reasons for his self-imposed isolation: firstly the conflict between his sense of duty to the common people and the war effort on the one hand and to the abstract virtues of independent objectivity as a reporter on the other; in addition, his former pacifism, nurtured on Rolland and Einstein, would have reinforced the natural fastidiousness of the educated middle-class Chinese brought up to despise soldiers and manual workers. But as he became preoccupied with the problems he encountered in his new life, he came close once again to being overwhelmed by his own feelings of inadequacy and guilt.

The Ho Ch'i-fang who returned to Yenan in the autumn of 1939 was after all not so very different to the man who had returned to Szechwan two years before. Finding in himself only "a barren wasteland", he resolved his lack of faith by becoming part of a mass movement with unarguable aims, so that from 1937 to 1939 he devoted himself to propaganda for the war effort. The final stage in his rejection of the past came in the period 1940-42, when he learnt to rid himself of his former introspection and passivity through the acceptance of the resolute discipline of a revolutionary party. The Yenan Forum on literature and art conducted by Mao Tse-tung in 1942 became the final turning-point.

The story of Ho Ch'i-fang's gradual acceptance of communist direction and his emergence as a party and academic bureaucrat is so foreign to his earlier life that it is difficult to reconcile the two in the one context. This volume therefore contains only a selection from his early writing and his own account of his life up to 1942. Further material dealing with his later career is listed in the Bibliography.

POEMS AND PROSE

Poems and essays from *The Han Garden* and *Painstaking Work*

This section consists of poems from *The Han Garden* (1936) and *Painstaking Work* (1937), plus two essays on poetry from the latter.

The poems are divided into three groups: (i) mainly love poems, from autumn 1931 to spring 1933; (ii) nostalgic and dramatic poems, from autumn 1933 to early summer 1934; (iii) poems on the themes of illusion and fantasy, from summer 1934 to early 1935. Poems from the first two groups formed Ho's contribution to *The Han Garden*, under the subtitle *The Swallow's Nest* (*Yen ni chi*); the remainder were published in *Painstaking Work*. Many of these poems were later republished in *The Prophecy* (*Yü-yen*) in 1945, but since Ho did not have the originals with him at the time, he could only include those he could remember; there are some minor differences in punctuation, use of particles etc., and in some cases a few lines are missing in the *Prophecy* versions. The two essays were first written for magazine publication in 1936, and were included in the first two editions only of *Painstaking Work* as a kind of appendix.

The Prophecy *(Yü-yen)*

This heart-stirring day has finally drawn near,
Like a sigh of night, the sound of your footsteps approaching
I can clearly hear — not the whispering of forest leaves and night wind,
                          nor
The faint patter of flitting deer along mossy paths.
Tell me, with your song like a peal of silver bells, tell me
Are you the Young God in the prophecy?

You must have come from the warm and easeful south,
Tell me of its moonlight, its sunshine,
Tell me how the spring breeze unfolds the hundred flowers,
How the swallows dote on the green willows,
While I close my eyes to sleep in your dream-like singing,
That warm fragrance I seem to remember yet seem to forget.

Please stop, stop your long journey's ceaseless flight,
Come in, and sit on this tiger-skin cushion,
Let me burn the fallen leaves I gather every autumn,
Listen while I softly chant my own song,
That song like the firelight, now low, now leaping high,
Like the firelight, telling the story of the fallen leaves.

Do not go on, ahead is the boundless forest,
Where ancient trees take on the spots and stripes of savage beasts,
Half-alive half-dead the creepers python-like intertwine,
Through the dense leaves not a star can gleam,
In fear you will not dare to make the second step,
When you hear the empty echo of the first.

Must you go? Wait for me to go along with you,
My feet know each safe path,
My unceasing song will dispel your weariness,
I'll give you again and again the warm comfort of a hand,
When the heavy darkness of the night separates us,
Your eyes can gaze unwavering into mine.

But after all you do not listen to my passionate song,
Your feet do not pause despite my trembling,
Like the silent, mild breeze floating through this dusk,
Your proud footsteps fade, fade away . . .
Ah, at last you came, without a word, as in the prophecy,
And do you leave without a word, Young God?

Autumn 1931 *(Han Garden*, pp. 4–7.)

Footsteps *(Chiao-pu)*

Often your footsteps sound low in my memory,
On my pensive heart they tread a sweet sad movement,
Like a lute in an empty pavilion, the touch of dear fingers long absent,
When the twilight wind passes, the strings tremble with tidings of
          yesterday,
And like the fallen leaves of aspens, drifting through a wordless
          wasteland,
They sigh, as they pass and touch, like trees rustling.
Ah! It was an autumn night south of the Yangtze!
          The deep autumn was heavy with dreaming,
And yet clear and fragile, as if unequal to your low, faltering steps.
So furtively you leant across the curved railing,
So lightly you came running — above, one lamp guarding the night chill,
With such childlike delight you gave me a page of manuscript,
Asking me to read your new poems,
          That first night you knew I wrote poetry.

          1 May 1932 *(Painstaking Work*, pp. 85–86.)

Lament *(K'ai-t'an)*

How much have I lost of the freshness of clear morning dew?
How much of the quiet of starry night skies, filtered down through
            green shady trees?
The jests of spring and summer? The joy of flowers and leaves?
The songs of spring that I withheld for twenty years?

Drinking the bitter tears that unhappy love has given me,
Day and night I await the coming of familiar dreams restoring me to
            sleep,
Not caring about the calls from outside, like weeds greenly spreading,
Like hands knocking on my tightly closed door.

Now I regret the years that I have wasted,
As I regret the unopened flowers lying dead on the green bough.
Love though in pain bears red fruit,
I know they fall off easily, and gathering them is hard.

25 June [1932]
(Painstaking Work, pp. 87–88.)

Love *(Ai-ch'ing p'ien)*

The dawn light opens on the dew-laden pomegranate flowers;
The shadows of the noon sun are laggard footsteps
Playing among the weeping willows and bôdhi trees;
And when the south wind blows in the night across the lake of sleeping
                lotus,
The moors still overflow
With the scent of star-anise and night-borne tuberose:
It is the evergreen ivy spreading everywhere
And the dodder twining up around the trees.
Love in the south sleeps deeply,
Even the flutter of its awakening draws us into sleep.

The gleaming hawk drifts through the cloudless autumn sky,
Hunters gallop over the distant heath;
The evening sun sinks down below the ancient citadel,
Wind and moonlight caress the leafless trees;
Or the sound of camel bells, instinct with patience,
Lingers on the withered grass of the long, long road,
A white falling star like a sigh,
Or like a cold teardrop, streams through the vastness of the night.
Love in the north is awake, alert,
And has a quick and cruel step.

Love is old, very old, but not weary,
It can be the dimpling smile of a baby,
It is the golden crown of a storybook prince,
It is the blue cotton smock of the peasant girl.
You, you have love,
Yet you too weep because of its coldness!
Let us burn the fallen leaves and broken branches,
And sit in the glow and crackle of the fire.
Let the trees awake and trembling
Eavesdrop as we softly talk of love.

23 September [1932]
(Painstaking Work, pp. 100–102.)

Do not wash away the red   *(Hsiu hsi hung)*

The lonely sound of the pounding stone scatters over the cold pond,
Transparent ancient waves quiver lightly as if beaten.
My idle arms want to reach down,
What can I pick among this gold and green?

Traces of spring, shades of joyous laughter,
As the silk clothes lose their colour, fade silently away.
Frequently washed in sunshine and in storms,
Do not rosy dreams dissolve in just the same way?

I beat my stone, the cold autumn light approaches,
Bathing its feet in the icy water,
Treading the hoar-frost on the wooden bridge:
My gleaming shadow shivers.

26 October [1932] (*Han Garden*, pp. 18–19.)

Summer night   *(Hsia yeh)*

Newly washed in the June locust-flower breeze,
Your hair exudes a subtle perfume, cool and smooth,
A round green shade is our sky,
In your eyes is a starry smile.

Lotus flowers sleep silently among the dreams of green leaves,
Their faint fragrant breath like the gliding firefly's golden wings
Flies to the lakeside, flies to the dim grassy bank,
And brushes against your uncovered knees.

Your soft arms like grape-laden vines,
Encircle my neck, blending with your whispers, ripe and sweet.
Tell me, do you hear the throbbing in my breast,
Like tree-roots on hot summer nights stirring in the mud?

Yes, a strange new tree has grown in my heart,
And soon on my lips a red flower will bloom.

1 November [1932] (*Han Garden,* pp. 20–21.)

Night of the full moon *(Yüan yüeh yeh)*

The full moon scatters a silvery calm,
Soaking the green grass like chill water.
The sleeping lotus in a dream opens up its virgin heart,
Bashful petal tips redden as if kissed.
The summer night's painted gnats are not asleep,
Their wings, like pollen-laden wasp's feet,
Steal away our whispers and tell them to the reeds.
Tell me, what grief, what chill shakes
Your heart, like forest leaves trembling in the moonlight's caress,
Shakes from your eyes unsullied pearls, unhappy dew?
"Yes, I am crying, because the night is so beautiful!"
Your voice, soft as an angel's snow-white arm,
Turns each second of time to gold.
Do you think I am a cruel lover?

If my breast were as seductively soft as the blue ocean waves,
I would pillow your head with its seaweed breath on my heart's pulse.
Its beating is like pearl bubbles spat out by fish,
A circlet of silver to rock you in a lullabye.
A dim, faint dream rests on your eyebrows,
Your eyes are like the twin-stemmed early orchid still unopened,
Hoarding the mysterious musk of night.

Do you hear the golden stars falling among the forest trees?
They are the ripe yellow locust-flowers leaving broken-off branches,
Do you hear a green shadow pressing against your hair?
It is the breeze gliding down the dense leaves.
The latticed shadow has moved up to our feet.
What answer does your hushed red mouth await?
The silent fall of flower-like lips?

> Spring 1933 (*Painstaking Work*, pp.107—9.)
> also called "Summer night"

The cypress grove *(Pai lin)*

_____

The sun shines on the broad leaves of the *pi-ma** tree,
Seven-*li*** bees hive in the Earth God shrine,
Here with my shadow as a racing partner,
Completing a great circle I return,
Suddenly conscious that time has come to a stop.

But on the green grass, where
Are the little hands that chased the crickets' cries?
Where are the joyful shouts of my childhood friends,
Which rose straight up to the tree-topped sky?
This vast kingdom of my youth
Under my feet, soiled with foreign mud,
Is pitifully small.

Travellers in the desert treasure water,
Boatmen fear white waves beyond their oars.
For a long time I thought I had paradise,
And hid it in the darkest corner of my memory.
Now I begin to feel the loneliness of adults,
Only to love still more the wilderness of paths in dreams.

[1933] (*Han Garden*, pp. 24–25.)

* *pi-ma*: Castor-oil tree (Ricinus communis)
** *li*: approximately one-third of a mile

The ancient city   *(Ku ch'eng)*

There was a traveller back from beyond the passes
Who said the Great Wall is like a long column of galloping horses,
Which just when rearing their necks and snorting were turned to stone,
(By whose black art, by whose curse?)
The grass, withered under horses' hooves, every year puts forth new
            shoots,
The ghosts of Khans of ancient times sleep silently in
Mongolian sands, the white bones too, on distant guard no more
            complain.

But the Wall cannot keep back the Mongolian sand
And the Gobi wind from beyond the passes
Blows through this ancient city,
Blows lake-water into ice, uproots trees,
Uproots the heart of the wanderer.

Late at night I trod the marble bridge,
Fondling the marble tablets by the Great Lake,
(While the moonlight fondles the tablets' vermilion characters,)
Later I asked everyone I met
Where is the Jen-tzu Willow? — no-one understood.
Grieving that this is an ancient kingdom, I wish to flee,
And yet I linger; I imagine a lofty tower thrusting up before my eyes,
As I lean against the high railing . . .

            Falling to the ground
Yellow locust-flowers, heart-wounding tears.
On the pillow at the Hantan inn
A dark brief dream
Has taken me through a lifetime's grief and joy,
I hear the startled door close,
Leaving the long cold night to freeze
On the earth's crust; the earth's crust is stiff in death,
With only a faintly trembling vein,
Perhaps the shaking of distant iron rails.

Run, ah, run to an even more desolate city
In the twilight mount the ruined battlements and look afar,
Even more cramped by this northern world.
They say it is a clap of thunder on a level plain,
Mount T'ai: the Eighteen Paths winding up amid the clouds and mist,
Seem also to have a hopeless bearing, a hopeless cry,
(By whose curse, by whose black art?)
In the setting sun I cannot see the boatsails on the Yellow River,
I cannot see the Three Blessed Isles in the sea . . .

Grieving that the world is so narrow, I run back again
To this ancient city: the wind still blows lake ice into water,
In the long summers under ancient cypress trees
People are still sitting around tables drinking tea.

                    24 April [1934] (*Han Garden*, pp. 40–44.)

Early summer *(Ch'u hsia)*

The green leaves mass and spread under your eaves,
The long-legged bee seeks out its old hive,
Is this the first month of summer? On my way back from the
                  borderland
I mistake a stretch of calm water for a river.
Under the few, tall trees I linger,
Thinking of my native district, our native fishing-boats . . . .

It's true I saw you off, letting the steam-train carry you,
Thin and weak, over the Yellow River's Iron Bridge.

Already several Mays have passed. I sort out my clothes,
Last year soaked in the rain in my native district,
And grieve that I did not visit you then in your illness,
To see the pool by your home, to see your fishing-rod.
At home I acted like a guest from a distant land,
A hurried guest from afar; not once, under the window,
Did I think of those bygone childhood times,
Nor did I in the dust of the attic cobwebs
Bring to light the small armchair with missing legs.
Not once did I go to visit my childhood friend
(Five years already sleeping in the graveyard),
I always liked the man of old who hung his sword before the grave,
But never did I go with traveller's tales
To tell him, but left and came back here.

At twilight I sit in the dark in the high-backed chair
And think of the man who sells straw shoes from his bench
(Dawn to him is the same as dusk),
Looking at the long cobbled street outside the door:
So many people come and go,
So many people, wearing the straw shoes he has made,
Going to buy cloth in town, or peddle medicines in the mountain wilds.
He remembers the White Lotus uprisings,
He remembers the old strings of cash with copper coins,
He keeps his white and wispy queue
And laughs at the passage of time, at changes in the world,
Passers-by say he gets stronger as he gets older,
Like a tree, he himself knows he will soon fall . . . .

From *The Han Garden* and *Painstaking Work*   43

I think I am this old man in the story,
Not caring whether it is dusk or dawn,
As I sit in the dark in the high-backed chair before the window . . . .

You would come and invite me for a stroll,
If we were now still together in the boarding-house,
And I invite myself into the deep forest,
To wash clean my dust-covered body.
But in the northern parks there are no forests,
Or else, "Excuse me, where are the cherry blossoms?"
"They've already faded, sir, you came too late."

7 May [1934] (*Han Garden*, pp. 45–49.)

The wall *(Ch'iang)*

Creaking, the song of the water-cart
Opens the dawn's long road.

Grey walls make the long lane longer,
I will pause with a gentle sigh.
See the wistaria, hanging half-way down the wall
Green, like a belt someone has left behind

To summon my mind to the lawn within the wall
Where tall tree shadows at noon ascend . . .

In drowsy numbness I feel I am a snail
Crawling around chinks, losing my way
A leaf's green shadow, blending with dewy chill
Sends me to sleep, in a long, morning dream.

Awakening, I lightly fall,
Plop, outside the wall again.

15 August 1934 (*Painstaking Work*, pp. 125–26.)

I hear the grass quivering between the cold steps,
I hear the white dew roll along the moss and lightly shatter,
The great hero growing old remains sleepless throughout the night,
In vain he recalls the sound of dice within the bowl,
Or the jade spittoon he beat time on when the singing started.

Oh yes, I am a captive from Ch'u* in my southern hat,
I can compose Ch'u songs: when one leaf falls autumn is here.
I unfurl my sails, my wings,
Going through sunlight, through mist and rain
To a place of clouds and waves, to be as carefree as the water birds.

But where can I find my vast and mighty river,
As vast as the Silver River fallen from the sky?
I dare not open the door to look at the frosty moon which fills the
                    courtyard,
I am even more afraid of the cock crow at daybreak:
One night of insect noises turns my hair white.

(Painstaking Work, pp. 127–28.)

---

* Ch'u: an ancient state in the south of China.

The fan *(Shan)*

If there were no mirror in a young girl's dressing-case,
She might gaze all day at the palace fan hanging on the wall,
At the towers and pavilions, like reflections in water,
Blurred with spilt powder and tear stains, like mists and clouds,
Lamenting the years drifting quickly over its silken surface,
The lost Fairy Spring can never be found again.
Yet mortals on the cold, chilly moon,
Gazing each night on this apple-shaped globe,
Might think that under the dappled shadows of its hills and valleys,
Its inhabitants were very fortunate . . .

11 October [1934]
(*Painstaking Work*, pp. 129–30.)

The pillow and its key *(Chen yü ch'i yao-shih)*

"When the waters of the Ts'anglang are clear," someone sang,
"Roll up a *wu-t'ung** leaf to make a cup,
One drink will banish memory."

I do not ask whose dream like dew on grass
Has made me a nightlong tomb:
I'm just afraid that when the moon is clear and the wind is fresh and
                    falling,
I'll have lost the key to the tomb door.

Someone made his pillow an immortal's sleeve:
On the wall inside the sleeve is written "grief at parting".
I do not ask from whose dream I am awakening,
But silently regret that my sorrow is bright and pure
Like a frail boat, which cannot bear a single teardrop.

12 February 1935
(*Painstaking Work*, pp. 131–32.)

---

* *wu-t'ung:* the Chinese plane-tree, *Sterculia platanifolia.*

Noon: when the river-boats unfurl their white sails
I lower the rush screens outside my window.
Le soleil detéste la pensée.

With my rush screens lowered,
I am in a rocky cave on some deserted island.
But am I the Duke of Milan, who was cast into the sea,
Or his orphaned daughter, Miranda?
Miranda! I call my name but there is no response.
In the distance the tempest gathers like an angry billow,
And suddenly gathers up the whole expanse of sun and sky,
Surely this isn't my magic?
Surely the flying, crying locusts which fill the air
Can't be the grains of yellow sand I scattered from the gourd?

Or am I thinking of an October yellow London fog.
"Wife, are you tired of sunlight and flowers?
Are you tired of sunlight and leaves?
Let me drive the carriage like a boat
Through the foggy streets as on a river.
A reef? A reef looms before us,
We are changed into foam, and never heard of again."

A great wind, such as has not been seen for many years,
Blows through the old trees by the water's edge, transforming them
                                    into dragons,
And sends flying an archway, a piece of wall,
Then reaching the ass's head is never heard of again.
I should really like to take a long siesta,
I should really like to paint on a wall
And then step into it
And wake to find myself falling near the Immortal's Isle,
To hear someone clapping and laughing at "the scholar in the water".
But let's listen to your fantasies.
(Why are you always lost in fantasies now?)
Thirsty? Perhaps you want some water? An orange?
... An orange grown beyond the Huai becomes a bitter fruit,
Maidens call it love-in-idleness,

Do not sprinkle that flower juice on my eyelids
The first thing I see when I awake might be
A bear, a wolf, a monkey . . .

. . . What's up, you plants, always so straggly at my bedside?
Asking, asking, I turn over and knock
The basin and tray to the floor. The dream is broken.
I was dreaming of a woman in a novel
(Natasha, are you happy?
Does the sound of tearing silk or breaking fans make you laugh?)
I dreamt I was a white-headed madman,
My hair dishevelled, the jug upraised, running towards the white waves.

I roll up the screens on my window to see if it is really night
Or whether half a day of yellow sand has buried this Babylon.

[1935] (*Painstaking Work*, pp. 133–38.)

Author's Notes

Title: For "Day of the Duststorm I", see *The Han Garden*
l.3: A saying by Oscar Wilde, quoted in Gide's *Oscar Wilde*.
ll. 6–7: See Shakespeare's *The Tempest*.
ll. 28–29: See "The Immortal's Isle" in *Strange Tales from a Chinese Studio*
                (Liao chai chih i).
l. 34: The original line from Shakespeare's *A Midsummer's-Night Dream*.
l. 42: Natasha is the heroine in Dostoevsky's novel *The Idiot*.
ll. 44–45: See the entry under "The K'ung-hou tune" in *Notes Ancient and
                Modern (Ku chin chu)*.

Translator's Note

This is the first and only time that Ho annotated his poetry. It may be pointed out
that *Ku chin chu* is a 4th century Chinese commentary on poetry and other
matters, and that *Liao chai chih i* is a seventeenth century collection of stories.

Afterword to *The Swallow's Nest* (*Yen ni chi hou hua*)

Last year when the Literary Supplement of *L'Impartial* asked me to write on new poetry and to discuss some of my own experiences in that area, I felt it would be a very difficult topic to handle. Even if I were to attempt it, I still wouldn't be able to manage more than a glancing blow or sideswipe at the issues. Then I began to write "The Stringless Lute". I began by describing the man of ancient times who refused to bow his head for his five pecks of rice; I described how he had hanging on his wall a stringless lute, and every fine day in spring or autumn, when the mood took him, he brought it down and played it. What I was trying to say was that from time to time it was my wish too to play the lute. But in the end I never finished this piece, showing clearly enough that my wish eventually faded away.

Now a small book lies before me: *The Han Garden*. Opening it up: *The Swallow's Nest*.

The Swallow's Nest? Can this really be the tombstone of the ashes of my emotions, with so delicate and yet so strange a name? In spring this year, Chih-lin sent me a letter to say that each of our sections should have its own title. There was one name which I had for some time intended to use, but for a certain reason I was unable to do so. Chih-lin then passed the words "swallow's nest" on to me. I immediately wrote back to say that I liked this title very much, because it reminded me of a childhood joy, and I now seemed like a swallow myself; I could not say in which direction I was flying, but I had already forgotten the mud nest left in fragments on the empty beams where with an aching heart I passed my former days. Yes, I had long forgotten it, until now, when this volume was placed before me to let me sadly mourn my former self, to let me once again savour those former emotions, those melancholy dusks and those evenings, when I lingered alone under the deep blue sky, when I picked a few small soft white flower-buds; and brought them home, to make a poem. But evenings like these are only related to the first part of my collection. I am slightly biased in favour of the short poems from this first part,—I say biased, because now I am a stranger, and I do not trust my own judgement. However, from the criticisms of other people I found a word, or a reason: joy. Reading these poems, I felt a lonely joy; in my memory I opened up a tropical land in the arctic, a northern summer night, so that without the slightest hesitation I recognised my own self, as described in another poem, "Summer night" (not included in this collection):

> Tell me, what grief, what chill shakes
> Your heart, like forest leaves trembling in the moonlight's caress,
> Shakes from your eyes unsullied pearls, unhappy dew?
> —Yes, I am crying because the night is so beautiful.
> Your voice, soft as an angel's snow-white arm,
> Turns each second of time to gold...

I am a man who lingers in time: so I like to explain in my own words the famous line from the eighteenth-century mystical poet, "to hold eternity in an hour". In the second part of the collection, there are deep sighs and the relentless tossings of sleepless nights. The trembling of a distant railway, the cruel sound of an engine whistle, or the braying of a donkey in the grey dawn. Shadows so heavy. Not even the silence of despair. This *pien-cheng* note could not go on indefinitely, but I was seeking the golden key I had lost, which could open the doors to illusion and allow me to return to that green shady garden, though laden with years, trouble, dust. But still I found a wasteland. I discovered that I did not even have a stringless lute, and gradually the urge to play it faded away.

And now when I examine that mud nest where I patiently passed my former days, I feel a stranger's surprise.

I am a reed; I don't know how strange a wind it was that passed through me, drawing forth sound. When the wind passed, I fell silent. I was not willing to become a flute or trumpet.

But then I realised that writing lyrics in metrical form was a mistake. A perfect poem is a miracle. We want to use rough, fumbling, cold words to build up a graceful and balanced form, which is as difficult as a sculptor striving to express his thoughts and feelings from a slab of Tali marble which stubbornly resists his chisel. When we are young, our spiritual eyes gaze towards the sky, towards love and beauty (either in the world of men or in dreams), and we seem to pluck a few small soft white flower-buds, a few pearls, and a few uncut precious stones. But what does this amount to? A true artist must be conscious in his creative activity. How much bad poetry has been written, not only by our contemporaries but even by the ancients whose fame remains undimmed despite the ravages of time! Art is impersonal, it requires more than just the sincerity of the artist. Tragedies will inevitably occur, and there are many people like that hero who was filled with a fierce ambition to conquer the world, but who failed in the end and died alone on St Helena.

I am not trying to suggest here that the future looks bleak. I am in fact far from despairing about the future. However, I do grieve over my own poetic poverty, and yet (let me be perfectly frank), the other voices that I hear are also very faint and weary.

8 June 1936, for the first issue of *New Poetry* (*Hsin shih*)
(*Painstaking Work*, pp. 63-67.)

Paths in dreams (*Meng chung tao-lu*)

Now I begin to feel the loneliness of adults,
Only to love still more the wilderness of paths in dreams.

This couplet, which concludes one of the short poems in *The Swallow's Nest*, seems to mark a boundary stone in my emotions: since then, filled with dying midsummer memories, I have entered a season of desolation. The images in the poem are derived from an unhappy experience. That year I returned to the place where I grew up, and as though visiting an old friend, I entered alone the kingdom of my childhood, a cypress grove. Under the shade of its dense foliage were still the green grass, the solemn gravestones, the white mountain goats, the sounds and wings of insects in the grass; and there were still the footprints, the laughter and fears of my childhood. In those days when I ventured forth into the depths of the cypress grove, I experienced fear, a mysterious sensation of vastness; but now, those gigantic ancient trees humbly bowed their heads, and the shadows which had oppressed my childish spirits dispersed like the mist, while "under my feet, soiled with foreign mud", the kingdom of those former days was "pitifully small". I stood there stupidly for a few moments. I sighed over losing so many precious things. When I returned to this desert land again, I felt like the Indian prince who set out on a journey and achieved enlightenment under the bodhi tree; like Adam, who was banished for eating the fruit of knowledge, I had lost my Eden and yet felt no remorse. Since then I have formed views on all aspects of life in the real world, and my thoughts are like a river which has dried up and in which not a single fish, a single waterweed can remain hidden. I am no longer a star-gazing dreamer.

But why did I say I preferred that wilderness?

I remember there was a time when I was very melancholy, "I was always hesitating between yesterday and tomorrow". I would often think of a man of ancient times, who was walking along a road when suddenly the pot he carried on his shoulder fell to the ground and broke into many pieces; without looking back, he simply kept on walking. Sometimes I feel that this is the attitude of a wise man. At other times I feel it becomes a kind of affectation.

Once I used to look back on the past, again and again, to such an extent that I was unable to realise that I still lingered there. But now my intelligence has been set free, and when I look back and caress my broken dreams with a gentle glance, I don't feel any grief at all, although I speak so tenderly, so nostalgically.

The way in which I came to write poetry is a path in a dream.

I once experienced a burst of great enthusiasm for writing poetry, although it was very brief. I listened to the words of my drifting soul. I grasped at images which gleamed for a second with a golden light. My greatest joy or distress was in the success or failure of a new piece of writing. In the end I became addicted to this kind of solitary work; I did not ask what kind of wind it was that inspired me, seeming to draw forth harmonious sounds from my emptiness, and neither did I wonder within myself what chance event prompted me to pour out my feelings.

When we are young we like to collect tiny playthings, an ancient copper coin, a cowrie shell, or a string of pearls from an old palace lamp; even when we are adults, we still want to grow with our own hands and in our own gardens a few rare and fragrant flowers.

Books, my intimate friends, first made their appearance among my playthings in the form of stories. Gradually I was able to appreciate the beauty of writing itself, apart from the plot and characters. I became able to read all kinds of books. I wondered at, tasted and finally lost myself in the colours and patterns of writing, the interweaving of allusions and the subtlety and richness of meaning. In a small attic room amid the soughing of the dense pine trees, during those long, quiet days or under the lamplight, I leafed through the books in the old and battered wooden chest, as if looking for something delicious to eat.

A change of scene made me forget these companions of my lonely home. First I had one and a half free and easy years at school. It was only when a wave swept me to a desolate city in a strange district that I regained my peace and quiet, and with excessive precosity I allowed myself to be shut up in solitude. I did not open to my fourteen and fifteen year old contemporaries my friendship, joys and sorrows, but redoubled my reading until my face grew pale and wan. Then finally I discovered the new literature. I often went to the ruined city walls to listen to the melancholy waves flowing towards the dawn; or sat late at night in my tiny room listening to the rain dripping from the eaves, writing my immature emotions and disjointed thoughts in a small, secret notebook in the forms which were popular then.

After this I spent a year by the desolate seaside. The vast sky and the fresh air were of no benefit to me at all. I was like a tree with roots in stony and barren ground, without sunshine, without rain or dew, and my tiny but proud young shoots only hindered my growth.

The old, decaying capital in the north became my second homeland; in that arctic climate and desert aridity I developed a new hardiness, putting forth flowers of grief. Had those few years been spent elsewhere, I do not know what kind of fruit they would have borne. But the cloudless blue sky, the pigeon whistles, the palace gates with their faded splendour, gleaming in the evening sun, inspired many dreams in me.

> Oh dream how sweet, too sweet, too bittersweet,
> Whose wakening should have been in Paradise...

At that time I cherished the poems of Christina Georgina Rossetti and Alfred, Lord Tennyson, reading them often and with deep feeling. A faint, rustic melody stirred in my heart. In the space of one day and night I wrote a fluent, commonplace story of over one hundred lines, in a metre which had gained some praise from one friend and over-generous appreciation from another friend in the distant south. This imperfect tune continued for half a year. These brittle, long-fallen yellow leaves could only produce a single blaze of light in the fireplace. Until summer, when a humid rainy season brought a strange wind to caress me, disturb me and destroy me, and finally left me with a clear and glorious autumn; and just as a piece of polished jade shines with its own lustre, I heard a pure music welling up of its own accord in my soul. Those exaggerated emotions of the nineteenth century which weighed on me like a shadow changed into tranquillity and clarity; I seemed to be breathing a fresh current of air. A new gentleness, a new beauty. In the clear dawn or in the starry night, when I leaned alone against the long white stone bridge, lingered alone under the shade of the locust-tree*, or sat with closed eyes in the dark before the small window, from time to time those delicate sensations would suddenly rise up and then disappear again. Once again I began to contrive a few lines of poetry. But I do not have any natural creativity or patience; and from this beginning I came to understand that my small constructions were awkward, broken-down, worthless. I realised that I was a stream whose source had run dry, incapable of producing any healthy-looking waves and in constant danger of disappearing altogether. My only wish was to make a few toys for my own amusement. At the time I was reading the delicate, bewitching poetry of the T'ang and Five Dynasties period. I was seduced by the charm of those beauties in distress and

---

* locust-tree: the *huai (Sophora japonica).*

sought also a similar intoxication in the works of the post-Parnassian French poets.

The first section of *The Swallow's Nest* consists of the remains of my work during this period. Originally there was more than three times as much. I cherish those few, brief days, because I had many pleasant dreams.

Afterwards I crossed over a boundary line: since then, filled with dying midsummer memories, I have entered a season of desolation.

When I returned to this great city in the north after my first journey home, the sky seemed to have changed colour and could no longer lead my imagination towards far-off, gentle things. I lowered my wings. I adopted "a hopeless bearing, hopeless cry". I was reading T.S. Eliot. Even this ancient city had become "a wasteland". I listened to the sound of the woodpecker and the nightwatchman's rattle, and when I wandered outside the ruined palace, with its double gates closed and bolted, I even seemed to hear a low, choked sobbing; I could not tell whether it came from imprisoned spirits or from my own heart.

In that dark year I also carved out some short essays; I felt that this kind of prose composition was more suited to the expression of my melancholy and despair. However, I still did not forget that goddess I had worshipped for so long. I still wanted to find a road back to my former peace and clarity.

> I do not ask whose dream like dew on grass
> Has made me a nightlong tomb:
> I'm just afraid that when the moon is clear and the wind is fresh and falling,
> I'll have lost the key to the tomb door.

I really seemed to have lost my key, but with stubborn patience, I continued to write a little, only to feel the more destitute. I have passed one full year in deep silence. If I begin again, perhaps it will be with a song which will startle even myself.

I used to say something very brave: the only thing which moves me in life is its appearance. I do not have a sense of right and wrong. In passing judgement on anything, I only say I like it or I don't. A role in a play which is commonly found distasteful can be performed so skilfully by some actors that involuntarily I pause and become lost in admiration. Flowers with beautiful colouring require all the more a beautiful form.

It's also the same with writing. Sometimes a metaphor or an allusion can suddenly catch my attention, but whatever meaning it has is absolutely unrelated to my enjoyment.

Once I showed a friend a four-line poem by Wen T'ing-yün:

The waters of Ch'u course like steeds into the distance,
The moors are covered with bitter purple and grieving red.
The savage earth for thousands of years has resented the injustice
That to the present day it is fired for mandarin duck tiles.

I said I liked it, he said it wasn't particularly good. At that I felt very lonely. Later I came to understand that my friend and I were quite different in a number of ways. He was a deep thinker, he wanted to find some meaning in the illusory passage of time; I had lived under the spell of literature since I had first read the books I found in a wooden chest in the attic as a child. I loved the ways in which literature is wrought, the blending of colours, the mirrored flowers and river moons. I loved T'ang "cut-short" poetry, and the way in which its form was more important than its meaning, like a smile or a handshake.

This tendency appears in my own work too. I am not inspired by an idea first for which I then seek a form; what float into my mind are actually colours and patterns.

To express these colours and patterns in our spoken language really cost me much bitter effort. I selected from time-worn poetry and prose words which could burn with a new flame. I used allusions which could evoke new associations. My only pleasure was the completion of some small, painstaking task. But this pleasure was no more than a sigh of relief, because the piece of work which had just left my weary hands to stand alone was no longer fresh or new to me. I was familiar with each rafter and cranny, I could not find the intoxication of a foreign clime in it as in the works of others.

Sometimes I loathe my own refinement.

At present some people condemn the obscurity of new poetry; I do not know whether I am included in this condemnation or not. The real difficulty lies not in the style, unless the poem is confused or too hastily written, but in our inability to follow the writer's imagination. Great writers are always sparing in indicating the connexions between one image and another, it is as though they leap over rivers without pointing out where the bridges are; if we do not have wings on our spirits we cannot follow.

There are also those who enjoy criticising a flower which blooms out of season. Someone who keeps up with the latest trends may of course dress in accord with the current fashion, but he need not hold a grudge against the world for being so vast and having so many people who do not share his tastes.

However, nothing these people say affects me. I have my own loathing for my refinement. Why have I been reduced to such a state? Why, when I look back, has my stumbling, unaided progress proved no more than a path in the wilderness?

19 June 1936, for the first issue of *L'Impartial* Poetry Supplement.
(*Painstaking Work*, pp. 69-79)

Prose, poems and essays from *A Record of Painted Dreams*

The essays from *Painted Dreams* fall into three groups: (i) prose-poems, of which "Dusk" is the only example translated here; these were written during the first half of 1933; (ii) two prose narratives written around the end of 1933 and an undated composite of three stories concerning illusion and reality under the general title of "A Record of Painted Dreams"; (iii) essays inspired by Ho's visit home in 1933, dating from January to July, 1934.

In place of a preface to the collection, Ho has included a "dialogue" written in a fit of depression one night in Tientsin; *Painted Dreams* was published a few months later, in July 1936, in the "Literary Collecteana" series edited by Pa Chin. These essays are probably Ho's most admired work; the book won the *L'Impartial* literary award for 1936 and had gone through eight editions by 1943, while the individual essays have been reprinted in several collections.

Mists and clouds on a fan (a preface) (*Shan shang te yen yün—tai hsü*)

> If there were no mirror in a young girl's dressing-case,
> She might gaze all day at the palace fan hanging on the wall,
> At the towers and pavilions on the fan, like reflections in water,
> Blurred with spilt powder and tear stains, like mists and clouds ...

"Are you trying to say that our senses of hearing and seeing are pitifully limited?"

"Yes. One summer day, I was strolling in the country with a friend who is colour-blind; I picked a red flower and he said it was blue."

"Then you felt sorry for him?"

"Actually I felt sorry for myself."

"Then you believe in mysterious things?"

"Actually I enjoy imagining far-off things. Non-existent people. And countries whose names cannot be found on any human map. I don't know how many days and nights it must have been, as the story goes, that I sat facing the picture on the wall, lost in thought, before I walked into the picture. Only my wall had no picture on it. Still, the golden door, the door which leads to heaven or to hell, has opened for me."

"Then your attitude to life—?"

"The only thing that moves me in life is its appearance. Ever since I sailed down to the sea, and a storm cast me upon this desert island a long, long time ago, I haven't spoken to anybody. But today, I find I have something to say."

"Then speak."

"I want to say that in the last few days I've taken great pleasure in an ancient saying: 'To me, all is but a drifting cloud.' It pleases me as a good footnote to the line: 'I have of late,—but wherefore I know not,—lost all my mirth ...' At that time, I had been listening to the soliloquy of a Danish prince; true madness or feigned insanity? This sterile promontory appears no other thing to me but a foul and pestilent congregation of vapours; one drop of wine loosens my tongue, I shock people without meaning to. But what I want to praise now is the beautiful expression of this image, without reference to its meaning. Sometimes I sigh over the difficulty of finding images. I've been unable for a long time now to forget two beautiful images used by a Hungarian writer in one of his works: he describes a group of labourers with bowed heads, at twilight, beneath the window of a wineshop, as ships with lowered sails and masts moored in a quiet harbour; later on, he describes a young girl in one delicate phrase, saying that her eyes shone like golden keys."

"Did he say they would open the gates of heaven or hell?"

"And once I was sitting with my head bowed, beside a carriage window. It was twilight, and I was idly leafing through a book of sad tales, when I lifted my head to gaze at the white mist on the horizon, and wondered about the life of the man who wrote *Smoke* [Turgenev]. The twilight of the day, the twilight of one's life. Where was I going? What awaited me at my journey's end? I found the answer in the faces of my fellow-travellers in the carriage: those wrinkled faces deeply etched with weariness and grief, whoever shall quietly gaze on them a while must either weep or go insane. But, to the other side, was the silhouette of a beautiful young girl. The twilight made a soft backdrop. Then I said to myself, if there were no beautiful women, how desolate the world would be. Because from them, we can sometimes glimpse the face of Eve before the Fall. Then I gazed at the clouds on the horizon, and like the eighteenth-century mystic poet who claimed he saw angels and spirits, I 'held eternity in an hour.'"

"Where were you going then? What made you speak like this? I don't follow your line of thought."

"I very much prized my dreams then. I even wanted to paint their every detail."

"What kind of dreams were they?"

"At first I wanted to paint a round window. I used to pass the window every day, either at early dawn or late at night. I always looked at it, but although I often heard sighing like a white flower drifting down inside, I never glimpsed even a shadow. While I was hesitating the window would disappear. I would not be able to find it again. Later, a painted brush, probably in a dream, wrote down a line of characters for me: 'Clearly Prince Wen's dream that night / Is known only to the black round fan.' When I awoke, I felt unbearably melancholy, as if this had really happened. Since then I have liked wandering in desolate places. One summer when the gentle night was moving along the streets, I entered a graveyard. I suddenly lifted my head; it was a clear, moonlit night. It was such a scene as often appears in Ch'i Hsieh's tales of marvels. I sat on a white stone. My shadow looked like a black cat. I couldn't help stretching out my hand to pat it, ah! Then I thought it must be a belt left behind by the ghost of a grief-stricken woman, but when I picked it up, it somehow turned out to be a round fan. I took it home and treasured it, and when I felt in the mood for working, I took it out and painted my dream on its surface."

"And where is the fan now?"

"When I grew tired of my native land and went roaming by the sea, do you think I remembered to bring it with me?"

"So it is still in the land from where you come?"

"Not necessarily."

"In that case I shall spend the rest of my life roaming through every continent in search of it."

"In that case, I am afraid that when you find it, the shadow on the fan would have faded long ago."

Midnight, 22 February 1936
(*Painted Dreams*, pp. i-v.)

Dusk (*Huang hun*)

The sound of horses' hooves, lonely and melancholy, draws near and scatters on the pitch-black road like tiny white flower-buds. I stand still. A black, old-fashioned carriage, without a soul on board, slowly passes by. I suspect it carries dusk, casting its dark shadow along the road; and then it draws away, and disappears.

The street is even more desolate than before. Twilight descends, gently closing in; as if from silver-grey homing wings it drops a certain lassitude into my heart. Proudly throwing back my shoulders, I heave a long, mournful sigh.

A well-preserved palace wall stretches before me. Does it enclose dreams of ancient, ruined splendour, or the moans of imprisoned spirits: more than once I implored it with my eyes, and it answered my question thus:

—Twilight hunter, what is it that you seek?

The frenzied wild beast seeks the strong man's knife, the graceful soaring bird seeks a cage, the youthful unfettered heart seeks baneful eyes. And I?

I once had golden joys which deeply moved me, as when the March night air drifted into my dreams and drifted out again. When I awoke I saw the first dewdrops of love, shining and pure, soundlessly falling to earth. I have also had spells of quiet solitude, under the dark window, before the all-night brazier; I closed the door tightly, yet they still escaped. Can I forget melancholy as easily as joy?

As the darkening sky descends, the pavilion on the small mountain peak stands out rounder and higher above the forest green; from it came the disappointment of my hopes. In the far-off, distant past, when I still had beside me a beloved, quiet companion, we wandered at the foot of this mountain peak, and on a sudden impulse, we made a vow that one fine morning we would climb this mountain. But afterwards, also on an impulse, we abandoned the idea. This pitch-black street, since those soft footsteps are no more, every day seems more desolate, and I, now disappointed and despondent, let the pavilion hoard forever those untasted joys. I dare not climb alone the path which my imagination clothed with such delight.

[May 1933]
(*Painted Dreams*, pp. 18-19.)

A Record of painted dreams (*Hua meng lu*)

1. Ting Ling-wei

Ting Ling-wei suddenly forgot his tiredness, and his wings were fanned by a wind of pleasure; following his gaze, he swept down from the sky towards the city of Liaotung. The city was the colour of earth, encircled by a belt of rooftops and trees. At Linghsü Mountain, he had suddenly been troubled by worldly thoughts of his native town, so he had taken to the sky in the form of a white crane; with the sunlight caressing his wings, and the blue sky so soft and tender, his pleasure then had been something like his feelings at this moment. But now he was anxious to reach somewhere where he could alight.

Skilfully he came to rest on the commemorative pillar at the city gate.

A broad street ran towards the city gate; at this hour of the morning the wind was calm and the sand was still; empty of passers-by, there were only the curved shadows cast by the eaves. The shadow of the commemorative pillar broke in two at the side of the street and climbed up to the roof-tiles, with an image of the giant long-necked bird as its cap. These buildings and these houses had sprung up remarkably since the days he remembered, and he suddenly became conscious of time. Unable to summon the owners inside, Ting Ling-wei spread open his wings.

Only the low earthen wall remained the same: although it too had fallen down several times and several times been repaired, it still stood in the same position and looked the same as before. Looking down from the top one could see Peimang Mountain beyond the city, the aspen leaves quivering like gold pieces among the innumerable grassy tombs now added there. Ting Ling-wei stretched his neck to look, but all was silent; he was unable to ask for news of former friends. Those who are born to the earth return to the earth; may their eternal sleep be blessed: Ting Ling-wei closed his eyes and reflected. Did he have a secret regret at having studied how to become immortal in the depths of the mountains? But uppermost in his mind was the question:

"Why have I returned?" He opened his eyes to seek a reason for coming back: the small town was very desolate. He who has taken a long, long journey through time is like a farmer who has ploughed the barren land in winter innumerable times, but who, even in spring when traces of green are everywhere, cannot summon forth from the great earth a feeling of prosperity.

"But I should like to take a look at the present generation! How your unfamiliar faces will move me! From your faces I will see whether you are happy or sad, whether you have advanced or fallen behind. Come, all of you, come ..." As the thought gradually turned into sound, Ting Ling-wei was suddenly startled by his own crane language, and the shrill, harsh, long cry which welled up from his neck and burst out through his long beak was stilled.

But it summoned from the houses, narrow lanes and streets a crowd of people to welcome him:

"Ah, here's the first crane of spring returning."

"And it's even a real red-capped crane."

"It's very strange, a crane resting on this pillar."

And it didn't even fly away when it saw them. Among the sounds of talking, laughing and clapping, Ting Ling-wei felt extremely sad, gazing down with his crane's eyes on the half-circle of people, not moving, so that their curiosity changed into anger, and believing him an inauspicious omen, they waved their hands and uttered threatening noises to drive him away; finally one young boy suggested fetching his bow and arrow to shoot him.

The bow was a finely-constructed boxwood bow. When the boy drew back vigorously the bowstring and the tip of the feathered arrow flashed in the sun, Ting Ling-wei awoke from his trance and beating his wings flew away.

As the shouts of the crowd pursued Ting Ling-wei up into the sky, he flew swiftly, describing a circle around the small town. Before soaring even higher into the sky, he couldn't help uttering a few shrill, harsh, long cries. Translated into human language, they would probably go like this:

There is a bird, a bird called Ting Ling-wei,
Who left his home a thousand years ago and now returns.
The city walls are as before, the people are not so,
Why not study immortality as graveyards grow.

(*Painted Dreams*, pp. 44-47.)

2. Ch'un-yü Fen

Ch'un-yü Fen, bending down under the locust-tree, found at last a round hole among the roots which protruded like a range of mountains, a hole which could be blocked up by a pinch of mud the size of a finger-tip; turning, he informed the guest at his side, "This is the road the carriage took in my dreams."

Ch'un-yü Fen woke up in alarm on the wooden bed in the east wing; through the window gleamed the colours of the setting sun. He rubbed his eyes and made out the figure of a servant sweeping the courtyard steps with a bamboo broom. The wine-stained cups were still on the table. The other guest was washing his feet.
"Ah, I passed a whole lifetime in the space of a few minutes."
"You've been dreaming?"
"A long, long dream."
How he was welcomed into the Locust-tree Kingdom by two purple-robed messengers, wed the Princess Golden Bough, took command of the South Pasania-tree Prefecture, conducted a war against the Sandalwood Kingdom and was defeated; and how after the princess died he quit the prefecture and returned to court; and how he was slandered and subsequently escorted away by the same purple-robed messengers; all these things he related to the guest. Thinking back on them, he sighed. The guest said,
"Are you sure this actually happened?"
"I can still remember the road the carriage took in my dream."

Ch'un-yü Fen knelt under the locust-tree, among the roots which protruded like a range of mountains, and pushed the little finger of his right hand up the ant-hole; but it was full of twists and turns and he could not get through. Then he put his lips together and whistled, but the sound dispersed in the profound darkness without an echo. In there was a city with pavilions and halls, there were mountains, rivers, trees and plants—of this he had no doubts at all; he could remember the Divine Turtle Mountain to the east of the kingdom, where he had once enjoyed himself hunting. Perhaps his present awakening was really a dream? He stood up.
The locust-tree was very tall, with feather-shaped leaves clustered thickly on the branches which spread out in all directions, like the sky. The distant evening clouds gleamed. An ant, with tiny feet and a

slender waist, so weak it could not withstand the wind, wriggled in Ch'un-yü's imagination. Were it to climb up the cracked bark, how pitiful it would look! But comparing the ant to himself, Ch'un-yü Fen felt that he was even more insignificant. He forgot the distinction between large and small, he forgot the distinction between a long passage of time and a brief one, so that this afternoon's hangover did not seem like a matter of a few moments.

Ch'un-yü Fen had become very drunk at the party. This was not the first time he had become very drunk since he had lost both his position and his self-confidence after a drunken quarrel with his superior officer. But his body which had gradually grown weak and old was no longer able to support his reckless spirit, and he was carried back from the party by two guests who laid him down on the wooden bed in the east wing, saying to him,

"Go to sleep, we are going to feed our horses and wash our feet, you can go when you feel better."

Ch'un-yü Fen lingered under the locust-tree; the setting sun had already melted into twilight. He said to the guest beside him,

"In this dream kingdom I was very ambitious, but unfounded rumours made me depressed and unhappy. When the king finally urged me to return home, I couldn't remember that another land existed outside that kingdom. When he said that I had come from the world of men, I had to think for a while before I finally understood."

"You must have been bewitched by a fox or a tree-fairy. Let's get a servant to chop down the locust-tree," the guest said.

(*Painted Dreams*, pp. 47-50.)

3. The White Lotus monk (Pai lien chiao mou)

The White Lotus monk went out again tonight. The red candle burnt down one inch, two inches, three inches, forming on the tin candleholder on the table a small golden flower-bud which, still unopened, illuminated the four walls. Which road was the White Lotus monk travelling now? His disciple sat on the edge of the bed, obeying the order given on his departure, "Watch the candle, don't let the wind blow it out!"

The small flower-bud in the tin candleholder on the table opened, unfolding golden double petals, which dropped off one by one, while in the middle arose a black stone pagoda with a pointed roof, confining some spirit, perhaps. Suddenly, inexplicably, it fell down, soundlessly, and turned into a long road, a long road which made one sad just to look at it ... My dear child, don't fall asleep! The disciple woke himself with a start from his drowsing, stood up, and with a pair of scissors trimmed off half an inch of burnt wick.

Once before, the White Lotus monk had gone out, leaving in the room a wooden bowl covered by another wooden bowl, and on departing, had ordered, "Watch it, but don't open it to look!"

The magical arts of the White Lotus monk were famous near and far, and many pupils came to him. But when after a long time they had got nothing from him and could not get used to his unreasonable demands, they gradually fell away, leaving only this last disciple, a young man who had an earnest desire to study his arts. He knew that he must be patient and pass many tests, before being able to obtain his teacher's approval and inherit his skills. He sat on the edge of the bed, thinking.

"Don't open it to look!" This prohibition stirred his curiosity, and he opened it: floating in half a bowl of clear water was a small boat made out of straw, with sails and a mast, so fine and delicate that he felt an irresistible urge to play with it. Should he give it a push? It overturned and sank into the water. When he hastily rightened it and put the cover back, his teacher was standing beside him, with a wrathful expression. "Why didn't you obey my order?" "I didn't even touch it." "You didn't touch it! My boat just overturned in the sea, and I almost drowned!"

The red candle had already burned down by two inches, three inches, or even four inches, when on the tin candleholder on the table there appeared a tiny yellow bird, its beak raised towards the sky, flapping its wings as it awaited the wind. Where had the White Lotus monk gone? Had he walked to the end of a long road, penetrated a dark wood, reached the streets of a strange city? What kind of people were they, on the streets of the city where it was never night, what kind of clothes did they have, and what kind of pleasures?

Half a basin of water was for him a sea. Was that sea peaceful, or did it have violent waves? He had taken out a small boat all alone. The disciple thought: If I had such skills! If only I had such skills!

The little bird on the tin candleholder on the table beat its wings and flew away, and with it flew many birds of the same kind, forming golden circles whirling around, then joining to form a long upright ladder, reaching to the ceiling, climbing up step by step, a long road ... My dear child, you have dozed off again, now just lie down on the pillow for a moment! The disciple saw from a great distance his teacher's back, that slightly stooped back, going foɪward along that great road, not pausing for a moment, hurrying till he was exhausted ...

When he awoke in the dark, he immediately realised his error in dozing off; hurriedly he groped for the lamp on the table, took a taper and relit the candle. But his teacher, his back slightly stooped, had already entered, with a wrathful expression.

"I ordered you not to fall asleep, but you did anyway!"

"But I didn't."

"You didn't! I had to walk more than ten *li* in the dark!"

[between December 1934 and January 1935]
(*Painted Dreams*, pp.50-53.)

Lament (*Ai-ko*)

... Like the song of a woman from a misty clime, she sang an ancient tale laden with sorrow and love, telling of the misfortunes of a princess who was confined in a tower by her father because she had fallen in love. Adeline or Sylvie. Aurelia or Lola. The names of French girls are gentle and pleasing to the ear, evoking thoughts of long, slender bodies and long, slender hands. And the names of Spanish girls? Large eyes ringed with black, gleaming and mysterious. I cannot help feeling a mild resentment against this ancient country of ours: when I was trying to choose names for the three sisters in this lament, I thought over and over again but in the end left them as three nameless sisters. And then, why do I see a black shadow, and feel a slight chill? Is it because I recall those lonely childhoods?

Thirty years ago. Twenty years ago. Even up to the present time. Girls in the country are still confined to their own apartments, awaiting the command of their parents, the word of a go-between. In Europe, although there was a time when girls were also confined in convents, only returning to their families and society after having reached a certain age, it was still not the same as our old custom. Today, girls who live in cities already hold confused new ideas about love. We have already seen some brave ones who have engaged in unhappy rebellion. But the ones who move me more deeply are the young women who belong to the past, who without hope pass their days in silence, in darkness, a smile hovering on their anxious red lips. We do not have to refer to Spinoza or some mechanistic view of the universe; simply relying on our own impressions of human affairs, a few scattered thoughts, a kind of intuition—there is no doubt that we are quite powerless about our "tomorrows"; dark hands spin the net for us, hurriedly, but still with the plan fully worked out in advance; and who can see the other side, who can know the uncompleted picture?

When our grandmothers and mothers were young girls, they were unable to imagine anything like this, for imagination must rest on some personal memory. As for our sisters, they have come to a crossroads of illusions, just like ourselves. Those young, pretty aunts of ours concern us most. And their cloistered life, so soon to pass away. Ah, we have seen a pale face appear at the open window of her small apartment, looking towards the distant mountains, the blue sky, a white cloud; it was long ago. And we have also seen long, slender hands, fingernails stained with the red juice of the balsam flower, slowly closing the window in the twilight. Or, with head bowed, she sits on a small bench, welcoming the sunrays which fall through the window onto her embroidery, a pillow-case or a door-curtain, wearily yet carefully persevering with her trousseau. Her trousseau already fills several boxes. Beside these new boxes are some old ones, holding the trousseaux of her mother and her grandmother. Both the style of her grandmother's time, its foot-wide sleeves with broad edges of flower embroidery, and the style of her mother's time, its narrow sleeves with satin edging embroidered in tiny circles, are out-of-date. When she opens these boxes, she begins to laugh, a sound both happy and yet full of tears. Let us stop our imaginings. My memories of my aunts are extremely simple. Of the eldest and the second aunts, I can remember only that the former was rather slender, and often ill; I cannot further distinguish their faces, and as for happy or tearful laughter, I never heard any at all. I did see the garden at their house with clarity, a kind of misty clarity. A stone terrace, an earthenware basin, all kinds of flowers and plants—I could not give you their correct names. At that time, had you placed me alone among the orchid leaves like pennants, dishevelled lily fronds and coir palms, I would have howled as if I were lost deep in the forest. But I was fond of the pool in their garden. And the three-storied pavilion, rare in the countryside. How often it stirred my fantasy, the childish impulses of my mind, and yet I dared not cross the shadowy verandah and run up the winding steps to gaze into the distance. Did they often lean with lowered heads against the stone railing around the pond, looking at the water, and at the algae in the water? I never saw. Their family lived in the same old house as mine, but the stone step in front of the hall, which marked the boundary and which was very long, together with the well and the high wall which could produce echoes, all seemed to represent a kind of threat, a symbol. And news of the death of the aunt who was rather slender and often ill was communicated across that long, stone step.

Let us leave that large empty old house. An old house on the verge of decay is like an old man on the verge of decay, it has a queer, indefinable quality about it. We had already gone to a newly-built fortress. Our house was near the aunts' house. At the rear of the fortress, we could hear all day long the sound of pounding stones, the sound of men at work. We were building a stone watch-tower and a water-tank. In my grandfather's opinion, and in the opinion of his books—both the worm-eaten block-printed and the yellowing handwritten ones—we should not start building facing that particular direction and in that particular year, because it would cause three calamities. My grandfather was a man of considerable learning; he knew many curious things and he believed in them firmly. Anyone who doubts this ancient and mysterious knowledge should go and argue with him. However, late at night in front of the incense-burning shelf, he recited a kind of charm, taken from secret books, to ward off disaster. He did this for many nights. What confused us was that the charm did not work; first a stonemason slipped and fell from the rear of the cliff; afterwards, a two-year old daughter in my uncle's family died; and then my second aunt died.

As for my youngest aunt, my memory is rather distant but still very simple. With head bowed, tracing patterns before the window in her small apartment; or lifting a large, round key to open a box, a mournful smile accompanying her solitary words; or sitting with the old folk under the lamplight making playing cards out of paper slips, and yawning. She was confined in that fortress just as I was in my remote and monotonous childhood. A stone fortress perched high on a cliff brings to mind the ancient castles of France or Italy, inhabited by decaying aristocrats and golden or raven-haired maidens, whose eternal songs tremblingly ascend to heaven, laden with sorrow and love, telling an ancient tale. Far away, from the high steeple of the church floats a peal of bells, clear and deep; as if awakened from a dream it passes by. But our castle is pervaded by a desolation of sound. In the morning and at noon, a few long cockcrows. The green shadow of the eaves crawls up the wall, slowly; finally it reaches the top and falls away to the fields below the cliff. Then it is sunset. It is a very exact timepiece, telling me when I should run down to the stone tower to begin my morning and afternoon lessons, to study the ancient, mysterious books as our fathers and grandfathers had done before us when they were young. But my youngest aunt just sat there by the window in her apartment, wearily and yet carefully persevering with her trousseau. She had long been betrothed, on her parents' command and the word of a go-between.

Vanity of vanities; all is vanity. All things answer to the inscription on King David's ring. When we are sad that saying makes us happy, but when we are happy it makes us sad. Now we have already spent remote and monotonous years in a strange district. We have memories of other houses and other young women. Clinging to the rails of a swiftly-moving steamer, the river wind ruffling her cropped hair, a girl who has just fled from the village; or a girl with confused new ideas, who drifted overseas with someone and now returns home again. What can we surmise from their eyes, from their faintly-wrinkled brows? Do we think of those young, pretty aunts? It is already three years, four years, five years since we left home. After the fatigue of a long journey, we return to our native district. A fine, clear day. We are very surprised to find the woods, streams and paths unchanged. We reach the gate in front of the house. The gate creaks with old age. We enter the small reception-room. The polished laquer chairs are still arranged on either side of the table. On the table still stands a "burst gall-bladder" vase. The vase is still empty. It all makes us feel very confused. Have we entered "time past", or does all of this exist outside of time? Finally we see a few threads of silver in our mother's hair. From her excited and incoherent words, we learn that some old men have passed from long illness to their eternal rest, while others, still in their prime, have left this world after some unlucky chance. In this confused and emotional state, I hear the final news about my youngest aunt: she has married, and has also died. She has died, and has also been forgotten. But whenever her silhouette flits across our minds—it may not be as Azorin has said—we see a garden, a rustic grove, and the small trees obscured in ashes and dust, and the lamp hanging on the wooden post which the fierce winter wind has blown sideways.

16 January 1935
(*Painted Dreams*, pp. 54-60)

Magic plants (*Mo-shu ts'ao*)

Books on magic say there is a marvellous plant: no lock, however difficult, can withstand it. This saying stirred my imagination. In the depths of the mountain, the herb-gatherer seeks out this plant; it is green, but after several days shut tightly in a wooden box it turns dry and yellow; and still its magic power is beyond compare. For a long time I have been afflicted with a mysterious grief, I seem to have been wandering outside my own door, like someone who has lost paradise; sometimes I feel a strong desire to become a firewood-seller's child, that in the cold night, out-of-doors, I may strike a tiny golden spark as if opening a window from which to catch a glimpse of fortune's glow. Now at last I understand that the key for which I had been seeking was probably a plant, the traditional knowledge of which has long been lost to us.

Many marvellous arts have already been lost. When I was a child, I heard that in the small market-place near by, among families which had seen better days, and small traders after their ten per cent, dwelt a man with neither home nor occupation; wrapped in his tattered garments and shuffling along in worn sandals, he would spend the whole day strolling up and down the single street; with his right hand he would pick up the green copper coins from his left hand, and as he picked them up their number gradually increased. In this manner he obtained enough money for his daily needs. "Why is he still so poor, then?" I asked the barber or the shoemaker; both had praised this strange old man. "That kind of money can't be kept, you have to spend it as it comes." But why? Slowly I came to understand the reason. A man who studies magic must take an oath before his master that he will assume the handicap of some affliction as the price of obtaining these secret teachings: blindness, lameness, or childlessness. This explanation put a check on my fantasies at that time, giving me a dread of supernatural powers as well as a deep pity for my strange, impoverished friend.

But my inclination towards magic was not completely destroyed. Under the lamplight or by the fireside, I eagerly listened to strange tales and legends. A distant ancestor of mine more than a hundred years ago appeared in one of these tales as someone who knew many magic arts. At the Clear and Bright festival, I used to go and sweep his grave; the inscription on the granite steps and headstone was old and clumsy, unlike the other graves, which made me conscious of its great antiquity.

One skill I very much coveted then was a way of transfixing people: by some magic power you could induce in someone the obscure belief that he was at the edge of a cliff or surrounded on all sides by water, so that he dared not make a move. There was a story that when my distant ancestor went out for a stroll leaning on his staff, if some ill-mannered youth offended him, he would employ this magic trick and leave him gaping by the roadside; he would not release him until he saw another person approaching. He was very much respected by contemporary sorcerers. Once he went to a certain house to see some sorcerers performing their skills. These rascals, probably not recognizing the famous old man, were not very deferential, so he quietly retired outside; at the same time, two big stone drums leapt inside. They leapt into the hall and began to dance along with the sorcerers, who were thus shocked into a sudden realization of the identity of their recent visitor. But my ancestor did not at any time in his life have the handicap of an affliction. I did hear that late in life, whenever pigs were slaughtered for the family's New Year feast, he had to be sent far away to a relative's house; otherwise, when he heard the pigs squealing in pain, he would be so distraught that no more pigs could be killed. Perhaps this made him weary of his own skills. Yes, he must have often pondered on these matters, and undergone much secret suffering, for his skills were never passed on to anyone but followed him into the grave. But at that time I was a child and never wondered about such things. I only listened enraptured to the stories about him. Apart from this mystic knowledge, people said, he was also well-versed in the Classics. He had staying with him for a long time an old, impoverished scholar from another branch of the family, who had written a commentary on the *I Ching* (Book of Changes). The two old men frequently had heated debates in the study, rummaging through the books all over the desk. On long summer afternoons, a servant would send in some cakes, which they would dip into the ink-slab and eat, leaving aside the bowl of white sugar. This old gentleman who had been bewitched by the *I Ching* would return home whenever there was a marriage or a New Year celebration in his family, a bundle of books on his back and staff in hand. Reaching the shade of a tree not far beyond our gate, he would sit down to rest; he would open a book, read until it grew dark and then would have to come back again. The following day, he would set out again, this time in a sedan-chair. His commentary on the *I Ching* was eventually printed. And a distant descendant of his, who happened to be my first tutor, came to the capital to present this book; he could make divinations from tortoise shells.

I once caught sight of that book among the untidy heaps of books in our boxes (it may have been destroyed by now), but I did not pay it any special attention. What I was looking for was a book on magic. During all the confusion of those days, when the adults were constantly worrying about how to avoid the troubles, I was free to lose myself in weird, strange tales. I found a realm of fantasy and imagination. I very much desired a plant of invisibility I read of in one story: with a root of this plant at your side, no-one could see you at all.

Now, under the lamplight, on white paper, I write a heading: the origin of magic. With a kind of pessimism, I want to explain that the origin of magic is very natural, just like our dreams at night. The sage has no dreams; although this state of being is very bright and pure, ordinary people like us reject it as barren and desolate. But my pen suddenly stops on the white paper. "Ah, you have become distracted again. To what distant land have your thoughts flown now?" "Nowhere," I answer myself, "My thoughts are within the lamplight." The lamplight, like a white mist, describes a round borderline, resembling a circular grave. I put down my pen, and for a moment really believe that I am under a magic spell of the White Lotus sect: a bowl of clear water, a boat made of straw, and I am off on a trip across my sea.

19 March [1935]
(*Painted Dreams*, pp. 66-70.)

Lute-strings (*Hsien*)

Whenever I meditate sadly on man's fate, I think of lute-strings. Sometimes the links in our train of thought are very subtle. One afternoon, when I was walking alone in a garden, I wandered with my head bowed under the green shade of a tree, and suddenly thought of my native district; when I awoke from this dream, I was deeply surprised, for it was a very ordinary locust-tree, and there was no reason for it to have reminded me of my native district. Then I realised that it was probably because I was beginning to grow old that I had thought of a courtyard garden. Now I think of lute-strings. There was an old fortune-teller in our district; he carried on his back a blue cloth bag containing brushes and ink, and a three-stringed lute. When he sat in the courtyard to tell someone's fortune, his fingers drew from the strings a sound like striking jade, monotonous, fragmentary, just like the words of those magicians; but as a child, I loved that simple instrument, though I secretly thought to myself, why aren't there seven strings, if there were more strings it would certainly sound better. I am not sure whether the strings I am thinking of are those between the old man's fingers, or whether I am thinking of a more complex instrument; but I have already begun to wonder about the old fortune-teller's own fortunes.

If we grow up in lonely old houses in the country, then an old servant, a pedlar, a tramp who happens to come and beg a meal, are very dear to us. We grow near to them and then forget. One day, we return to that kingdom of our childhood, and are taking a leisurely stroll in the evening sunshine, when an old man appears along an old path. What are ten or twenty years to this old man, patiently living out his declining years, so we cry to him, "Do you recognize me, fortune-teller?" He pauses, raises his head and gazes doubtfully at us. "Don't you recognize me? You told my fortune once." We tell him our names. At first he is silent, a little embarrassed, with the gentle embarrassment of an old man, then he asks us a string of questions. Because we have just returned from a distant land. As for him, he has just come from a large mansion now on the verge of decay. It is in a neighbouring district, which we often visited as children; now we feel it is far away, and wonder whether or not we should pay a visit there. We think of the past as we walk along, talking with this old man, who himself seems like a ghost from the past. "Tell my future again tomorrow." "You scholars don't believe anymore." "No, I believe." How can we explain to him our pessimistic mystical tendencies? How can we convince this old man, who has lost faith in his own profession? Before, when people laughed at him, he used to say, "Master, fate is ordained by Heaven, there can't be the slightest doubt; we tell the future according to the book." He loved to tell one story: "In the book, it says that there were once two men, the eight characters of their destiny were exactly the same. But one became a prime minister, the other became a beggar. And why was this? Because one was born in the first quarter of the hour, and the other in the last quarter of the hour. There is that much difference in one hour." "Well, have you told your own future?" the mockers would say. "Master," he would sigh, "there is no need to tell our own fortunes." By this time, what hardships has he suffered, before what has he bowed his proud head? Does he have a family? Where are they? We want to ask, but in the end we do not. But without waiting to be asked, he rambles on about many of the things that have happened in this village, events often tragic, sometimes comic. But he does not talk about himself. Perhaps he wants to talk about that large mansion which he has just left, where a new generation has just been added; it is not as prosperous as it used to be; the lovely flower garden behind the house has become overgrown during a long period of neglect. That garden held our countless footprints, laughter and illusions. We wait for sadder news. But he stops, neglecting the piece of news which is nearest to our hearts, about the only daughter of that family, proud and melancholy, the princess of our childhood, who passed with us many hours of happiness, and who also often tortured our tiny soul. How is she now? Married or dead, the only alternatives that await a young girl, which do we wish to hear? We want to ask, but in the end we do not. We ponder over man's fate, as we walk with the old man, silently, along the old path in the evening sunshine. Then dusk closes in on all sides. Reaching a road, which branches off in two directions, we pause, and raising our heads, doubtfully gaze for a moment at each other. "Please go back, Masters." So we say: "Goodbye."

Goodbye: reaching a crossroads, how many friends have we said this to, warmly or in anger. Perhaps we have already said this to the dearest person in our lives, simply because of youth's arrogance, or boastfulness, leaving ourselves to pass alone countless long dark days. One day, when we are growing old, we may happen to recall those warm and distant memories, and become even more melancholy. Yet we still say that we have no regrets, and attribute all to fate. But what is fate? a trembling lute-string between the fingers of a man who is old or blind.

23 July [1935]
(*Painted Dreams*, pp. 78-81.)

Essays from *Diary of a Visit Home*

The first edition of *Diary of a Visit Home* consists of five travel essays plus a long introduction, "The Essay and I"; the essays date from December 1936 to early 1937, and the introduction was completed in June 1937. The outbreak of war the following month delayed publication until August 1939, and by making communication between author and publisher difficult resulted in some errors and omissions. Subsequent editions in 1945 and 1949 corrected and restored the text to some extent, but since the author then took the opportunity to revise in significant ways some of his material, I have translated the first edition only.

The Essay and I (a preface) (*Wo ho san-wen : tai hsu*)

How I came to write essays

If ten years ago some prophet had predicted that I would devote my life to literature, and had also stated that there would be no work more agreeable to me, more ideal for me, than writing away at my desk, I should certainly have burst out laughing. And five years ago, I myself could not have guessed that I would be wasting a great deal of time writing these compositions, neither short nor long, which go under the name of essays.

My life is full of chance.

What first tempted me into the path of writing was poetry. I wrote poetry for many years, and I wrote many bad poems; it was only in my third year at university that I suddenly realised my failure, that I was like a stream which had taken the wrong direction and could not find the ocean.

At university I studied philosophy, and this was an error of chance; earlier I had simply imagined that a knowledge of the origin and development of Western philosophical thought was essential to understand the basis of European culture; I did not take into account my own interests. Poetry and stories and graceful essays had so refined my digestion that I could no longer swallow coarse food, those dry and clumsy theoretical works. Immanuel Kant was a dull person, and his works are even duller. Our teacher told us that in his whole life he never went further than sixty *li*, and that he regulated his whole life like a clock, so that his neighbours could tell the time of day from his walks, meals and studies. In the class on Indian philosophy, another earnest, white-haired teacher lectured on the theories of the Vaisesika and Samkhya sects, while I gazed at the sunlight through the window, letting my imagination roam without restraint among tropical trees and flowers, exotic butterflies and huge elephants.

It was at this time I began to see a lot of two fellow-students. This for me is something well-worth mentioning. Because although my name was entered in the roll of this school which had more than a thousand people in it, my life was till then like an island far from the mainland, completely isolated from other people. And this was the chance which set me writing essays. One of these two students was translating with careful precision writings by Azorin, Gide and so on; although these people were not just essayists, it would be correct to call them prose writers. The other student was also very industrious; whenever I went to find him he would be at his desk translating a book he had not even finished reading, or spreading out white paper yet to be written on. Then I felt that after my solitude, idleness and secret extravagance, although I could neither keep on writing poetry nor attempt a different kind of large-scale work, still, like a craftsman who understands his own ability, I should sit down quietly, attentively, and slowly carve out a few small objects. So I began to write lyrical prose. And we often discussed this kind of miniature composition; we felt that among the branches of Chinese new literature, the production of essays could hardly be called barren or feeble, but apart from the theoretical, satirical or pedantic type of essay, lyrical writing was mostly channelled into narrating various personal experiences or the sentimental reporting of individual encounters. My intention was to show that with a little effort each essay could be a pure, independent creation, neither an unfinished novel nor the expansion of a short poem.

A little magazine published in the north was pressing me on. The first student was one of the editors, and he often came to my lodgings to take away the manuscript I had just completed; and for the sake of adding another item to the front cover to make it seem more lively, I had something accepted in almost every issue.

But before long the magazine ceased publication. I too left my university lodgings to learn a new lesson.

"A factory for the production of middle school students"

A new situation like an evilly-grinning trap appeared before me. Without the slightest hesitation I advanced towards it. For the first time I exchanged my own labour for bread, while my pride told me that among these people I should find not good fortune but suffering.

It was a hot and muggy day in August. I was put into a small room facing west; separated from me by a thin wall were the telephone, the electric bell and the workmen's quarters. And in the corners of the wire window-screen swarmed horrible black flies. Right from the start I began my struggle against these enemies who tried and tortured me: the sun, discordant noise and flies.

A close friend who had arrived earlier took me for a stroll that afternoon to view the local scenery: a stretch of marshland which received the filth and stench that flowed from the city.

At the edge of the marsh, a long bank appeared in the evening sun, arousing visions of the sea, sand and white waves. Alongside flowed a foul river.

As we strolled along the bank, breathing the fetid air, my friend told me that it was the custom here to dump in the marsh the coffins of the poor who could not afford funeral expenses; often stray dogs would tear them open and devour the corpses inside; and in summer, even more frequently, the poor people near by would sit there, resting their teapots on the coffins and chatting away as they sipped their tea. He also told me that along this path at dusk groups of young girls would return home from the factories; he frequently watched them, imagining their many sad stories.

We felt we were also workers squeezed for our labour, because where we lived was "not so much a school as a famous, privately-run modernised factory for the mass production of middle school graduates."

In this life I could no longer continue to have those beautiful and gentle dreams, nor the peace of mind in which to describe them. I fell silent. But the silence was not altogether due to being beaten down and oppressed by excessive misery; it was also the hesitation before beginning a new type of work.

Of course, it was also the case that my time was so exploited that I had little time for writing.

On moonlit nights, or when only stars were shining, I would often go for a leisurely stroll with my friend in a large vacant allotment, discussing many plans, many matters. But as for human injustice, at that time I still condemned it with the indignation of an individualist. I was planning, preparing to begin a rather larger work, a full-length novel as a defence of individualism. I had no further wish to write "essays". I felt that only by writing a novel could I accept my opinions on various questions, and relieve the depression on my spirits.

But because I had no spare time, I put it aside after only one-tenth of the projected work had been completed. In that year, I am ashamed to say, all I did was to collect these short compositions from the past into a slim volume, *A Record of Painted Dreams*.

"A Record of Painted Dreams" and its preface

Between the first essay in *Painted Dreams* and the last there is a distance in time of more than two years. Therefore in both style and atmosphere these short pieces are by no means all of a kind; strictly speaking, many should not even be regarded as essays. For example,

"The Grave", the earliest one, was written after reading several short tales by Villiers de l'Isle-Adam; when I wrote that, I had not even thought of the word "essay". And with "Soliloquy" and "After Dreaming", although they are not written in verse form, they are obviously a continuation of my poetic work, because they are too condensed and lack the connecting threads which essays should have.

"Cliffs" was the starting point of my deliberately-composed essays. The beginnings in any new work are generally rather clumsy, and so I wrote very stiffly and obscurely. Gradually my ability to control my writing increased, and I became able to tell my stories calmly and concisely; they were not as pretentious or laboured as in the beginning. However, I was just starting to achieve some skill when my small book came to an end. In fact, I wrote too little.

As I said above, I was seeking a new direction for the lyrical essay. I hoped to create with very few words a new atmosphere: sometimes by relating a small tale which could set the imagination free, sometimes by a wave of emotion accompanied by a profound thought. Just as bewitched as when I used to write poetry, I was seeking a pure harmony, a pure beauty. To complete a two or three thousand word essay would usually cost me two or three days' anxious toil: almost each word would have been fondled by my spiritual fingers. Therefore, when I read in an article criticising *Painted Dreams*, "However, there are people who seem to enjoy the assistance of Heaven, whose achievements do not cost them any effort at all. Perhaps Mr Ho Ch'i-fang has not taken very great pains, ..." I could not help feeling astonished. Fortunately, there was still a "perhaps". At this point I realised that apart from one or two very intimate friends, few people knew how slow-witted and deficient I was.

It is not my intention here to explain my former self, particularly in regard to those subtle and even fragile emotions, thoughts and sensations. Because by now I have developed a state of mind which may be described either as desolate or as healthy: although the old dreams still exist, I have no wish to revive them again. A year ago I said sincerely, "Sometimes I loathe my own refinement." "Because this refinement," as was said in the criticism mentioned above, "if we look at it from the bad side, is only another face of decadence." This proposition is correct, and I feel we may even omit the conditional phrase. Although I have never boasted of my decadence like someone who shows off his infirmities, yet I do not lack a little self-knowledge, and I realised very early that I was a restrained decadent.

Or should I say an armchair pessimist? Because the origin of this kind of pessimism did not arise from a long life full of adversity (when you are struggling to keep afloat you do not have the time to sing songs of fatigue), but from solitude. The truth is, solitude was my sole companion at that time. I remember how I chanced to read in some book then a remark by a Hungarian thinker to the general effect that there are two kinds of people in the world, one kind bores other people while the second kind bores himself; the former are unbearably vulgar people, the latter for the most part are thinkers and artists; this moved me very deeply. It seems from this time I had one resolution:

> I would like to live in an utterly desolate land, covered with ice and snow, and tend sheep for nineteen years, to prove my faithful heart.

Faithful to whom, this faithful heart? To life. I was in fact filled with a passion for life, filled with desire; and because the wall of solitude cut me off from the world, I "wept for its cold indifference."

In life, I want now to say loudly, there are in fact things I love and things I hate. It is by no means as I said in the preface to *Painted Dreams*,

> The only thing that moves me in life is its appearance.

I wrote so recklessly and bravely because of pride. At that time I was at the student-factory described above, and for a long time I had not written anything. One midnight, I suddenly took up my pen again; I felt extremely wretched, and quite simply wanted to turn my back on the whole world. On an impulse such as comes in writing poetry, I scribbled down that disturbing and rambling dialogue. Not far from the end it went:

> I found the answer in the faces of my fellow-travellers in the carriage: those wrinkled faces deeply etched with weariness and grief, whoever shall quietly gaze on them a while must either weep or go insane.

This was another completely contradictory attitude towards life. I could turn my back on good fortune and human happiness, but in the face of suffering and unhappiness, my pride had to lower its head and dissolve into tears of indignation and sympathy. Last year I came from that city overflowing with filth and stench to the countryside, where the open spaces, fresh air and reality lashing my body like a whip all made me grow stronger; no longer did I mournfully crane my neck to look at the sky or dream on walls. Now, what I care about most are human affairs.

Concerning "Diary of a Visit Home"

I came to a small district in the Shantung peninsular.

Leaving my second home, Peking, and going alone to a remote, out-of-the-way land, I almost felt the chill of exile; but like the lucky encounters in story tales, each new environment has helped me to mature, so that I discovered there a new continent of the mind.

Formerly I was like a kingdom in an age of decline, its borders daily contracting. Now I am gradually expanding again.

Because now I am not only concerned about myself.

Because now that I look at these countless people trapped between death by starvation or death by exposure, I have forgotten individual joy and sorrow.

The life of country people is harsh. Every day when I talk enthusiastically with sincere young people from the countryside, I cannot help thinking sorrowfully of the future stamped on their faces: poverty and ceaseless toil. At the same time, I also think of people who live in cities and of people who have the strength to work but do not:

On the one hand, strenuous work,
On the other, lewdness and depravity.

These two iines are like whips. And they are lashing across my shoulders. In those long years now past, what have I done apart from wandering, seeking a road? And now? I remember guiltily the novel I planned, yet I hesitate to take it up again. I do not want to play the role of a defender of individualism, a twentieth-century Don Quixote.

At this point a friend who was editing a magazine in the south wrote to me and asked if I could write some travel essays for him, because during the summer vacation I had gone on a visit home. This suddenly provided me with the opportunity for some short-term work, so that after doing my lessons and correcting, I could describe in a few leisurely articles a corner of my native land.

This was *Diary of a Visit Home*. Even more the result of chance.

When I read them over one by one as I wrote them, I was quite surprised. Quite beyond anything I could have expected, my sensibilities had coarsened. How different these pieces were to the ornate and fanciful things in *Painted Dreams*! It is a good thing to have become coarser, I then said to myself, it is quite unnecessary to confine your feelings as narrowly as the waists of beautiful maidens in ancient times. So I kept on writing. But then I also discovered that my knowledge of my native district was pitiful; in my fortnight's stay there I had not grasped many new things, so that a true description of the various aspects of that corner was beyond my reach. I was only copying down memories of the past.

Writing down these ordinary, unremarkable memories was not very exciting or interesting and soon I lost my initial enthusiasm. I still wanted to complete them, not for pleasure but to fulfil my promise to myself.

Therefore, this small project eventually tied me up for a year. A year is very long, and meanwhile the longer work was also maturing in my mind. I wanted to let the character in the novel who was most strongly opposed to suicide finish up by throwing himself into the sea to end his life, because a true individualist can only cut short his life by his own hand, if he is not to abandon his individualism.

"To live is in the end admirable"

Now let me repeat what I started off by saying. If ten years ago some prophet had predicted that I would devote my life to literature, and had also judged that there would be no work more agreeable to me, more ideal for me, than writing away at my desk, I should certainly have burst out laughing.

Ten years from now? In the same way, it is impossible for me to imagine.

Nevertheless, I certainly intend to go on living with courage and determination. To live is in the end admirable, because one can work.

Laiyang, late at night, 6 June [1937]
(*Visit Home*, pp. 1-9.)

The sobbing Yangtze (*Wu-yen te Yang-tzu-chiang*)

It had been raining for a long time. Each time I have passed through Hankow I've encountered continual, dismal rain, because it has always been in summer. But this time it was particularly depressing. For three days we had been waiting for the direct boat to Szechwan, for three days we had been listening to the rain.

Through the monotonous sound of the rain, suddenly the voice of someone singing a vulgar, cheerful and brassy song drifted from the gramophone in the Kwangtung wineshop opposite over to the upstairs room where we were staying, producing in me a sensation like handling a live fish with a strong, rank odour. I looked down from the side window, but a bank building blocked my line of sight. The air was very damp. In air which is saturated with so great a percentage of water, people accustomed to the continental climate of the north feel very uncomfortable. And although it was raining, the room was still stuffy. So I put on the small electric fan which was standing on the floor.

My young companion was nursing a silent resentment against the transportation in our country. She was longing more keenly than I to return soon to our native district, and to meet again the people at home. We both forgot the hardships we suffered on the Peking-Hankow train. One morning the train had suddenly stopped before a small station in Honan, because a coal-train had overturned ahead. We stayed there until late at night. The June sun which turns to gold the rice in the paddy fields inflicted on the innocent passengers for a whole day the ancient torture of being bound to red-hot pillars. There were electric fans even in the third-class carriages, but probably they were designed only to look impressive and to act as an advertisement, as they were not very often switched on, and as soon as the train stopped they were immediately switched off. My travelling companion blamed heaven and man alike with childish impatience. I thought of a satirical story by Zoshchenko, which described very bitingly the transport system in imperial Russia. I related the story to her. It was also on a train, and the passengers were looking out of the window at the scenery when they suddenly discovered that the train was going backwards; it seemed that the guard's hat had been blown away by the wind; when they reached a clump of trees the passengers disembarked and went looking for the hat. They searched for a long time before finally they retrieved it from the branch of a tree, and then everyone got back on and the train continued its journey. At least we can be grateful that in our country, I concluded with a smile, we are a little better than that. In the end we continued our journey too. It was just that when we reached Hankow we were eight hours late, the special express train having become a specially slow train. But not only did I not use this natural disaster or man-made calamity to attack the rail transport system, but I began to praise it, saying,

"Little sister, do you remember how you were complaining on the train? I said then that the railways were the most advanced form of transport in our country, they have a definite schedule and a definite timetable; if the Yangtze boats were the same as the trains, wouldn't we be almost home by now?"

I was a little inconsistent.

I was angry, angry at what the man at the inn reported when I asked for the boat timetable. He said there was a direct boat today from the People's Life Company, but there were no tickets, as they stopped selling tickets two days before the boat left Shanghai. Because there was some kind of inspection team going to Szechwan, the boat was full. I suddenly thought of the current slogan, "Szechwan is the foundation of the national renaissance". Too bad for the natives of "the foundation of the national renaissance", I said to myself, you are walking right into a trap.

"I hope our family keeps out of their way," I said aloud.

The boat we finally took was both small and dirty, but it went directly from Shanghai to Chungking and so it was also crowded. Fortunately I had bought a cabin ticket in advance, so I saw my sister settle down in a cabin which already contained a woman with three children, letting her listen to the "*wa-la, wa-la*" sound of the Shanghai accent, and smell that rank odour peculiar to human beings. Then I went to the main dining room, because the steward said my berth was there. When I reached it, I learned from the other travellers that this area, which was called a *Saloon* but which was neither spacious nor clean, was a place where many other people were sleeping at night, using the tables and chairs as beds. One of the passengers, a thin, tall young man with high cheekbones, struck up a conversation with me; speaking quickly and not very clearly in the standard colloquial but with a Kiangsu accent, he told me that being in the main dining room was much better than on deck, there was no worry about it raining. While he was speaking I watched the white spittle which issued from the corner of his mouth, then turned my gaze to those people and the sleeping berths with beds made out of wooden planks, which were crowded on the deck. Frowning, I fell silent.

But then he introduced me to his companion, a man of the gentry type, with elegant manners and a tendency to stoutness. He spoke slowly and with a Kiangsu or Anhwei accent, and I could understand him easily. They were fellow-students, this year's graduates with B.A.s in education, on their way to work at the Popular Education Institute in far-off Kweiyang. When they questioned me, I only gave them the name of the school which I had left the previous year.

We talked about the transport system in Szechwan and about school conditions in Kiangsu, but when the conversation turned towards conditions in the north where I had come from and the student movement, I found it difficult to say anything. I said a few stupid things and then fell silent again.

They turned away and talked with some other people. I still sat there at the dining table, but gradually the conversation of the others which sounded in my ears lost its meaning, and I became engrossed in deep thought. During the years I had spent in the north, I had locked myself up in solitude and become indifferent to worldly matters, like a character in a Turgenev novel—"Except when I sneeze, I never look up at the blue sky". Only with me, for "the blue sky" read "real life". I almost began to write a book to prove that plants have a more beautiful and freer life than mankind. However, as I have written elsewhere, "A storm cast me upon this desert island," and I entered a new environment; rather than call it a school, it would be better to call it a famous, modernised factory run by private interests, since its major product was middle school graduates. Every day I would look at these children, who came from places as far away as Kwangtung, Nanking and Honan, and feel that I was an accomplice aiding and abetting the deception. I was utterly passionate and utterly indifferent at the same time. Then the so-called student movement came along, and we turned into an obscure "third force". But in actuality there was no such thing as a genuine "third force": when the students went on strike and we still went into class to the sound of the bell and talked to the walls, we were under orders to appeal to the students by our dull and pitiful state, and when the military police surrounded our dormitories for two days and two nights, and there was no way in which we could even send a letter outside, we were then fellow-criminals with the students. And yet now people ask me about the student movement in the north ...

These memories were making me feel rather depressed, but just then a strong young man came up to me:

"Excuse me, do you know how the buses run from Chungking to Chengtu? Do they run every day?"

"I'm not sure. It's been many years since I was last back home."

"I haven't been back for a long time either."

From his voice I could tell that he came from my native province. From his clean-shaven head and his khaki army trousers I could tell he was a soldier. Afterwards he told me that he was a second lieutenant.

Somehow or other we also got on to the subject of transport.

"You could say there has been considerable progress now," he said. "They have already built a great many highways, and they're about to start work on the Chungking-Chengtu railway."

"I feel it's still not good enough. For instance, this national transport route, this Yangtze River, we can't even use it properly."

"There has been a lot of progress here, too. A lot of progress. We know that in Szechwan waters the People's Life Company boats are considered the best, and in rivers below Ichang the state-owned Commercial Company boats are also in very good order. If I wasn't in a great hurry to get back to Chengtu I would never have taken this broken-down foreign boat."

When he spoke his confident manner made me think of the youth of Germany or Soviet Russia. Soviet Russian youth on the Trans-Siberian line urge people to study philosophy and go to their country to study, not to Germany. And German youth take part in the government's book-burning campaign, singing songs in defence of German womanhood. I did not feel happy, nor yet did I feel sad; it was only that because of my own premature aging I find this optimistic attitude somewhat remote.

"I am not trying to say that there's been no progress in our country. There has been obvious progress in every direction, it's just that it is much too slow. For example, take the Yangtze transport. There should be at least one national line going to and fro every day, with definite schedules and definite timetables like the railway." I paused for a few minutes. "This time I waited in Hankow for four days for a boat. I have only got one month, I was prepared to spend a fortnight getting there and back, and to be at home for a fortnight, but now I am afraid I can only be home for ten days."

"I've only got a fortnight's leave altogether, and I'm going from Nanking to Chengtu. If I can't extend my leave, I'll have to turn back when I'm only halfway there."

"Is it hard to get an extension?" I hadn't expected him to be more pressed for time than me.

"If there's no other way then I'll extend it."

He sighed gently. At the time I thought it strange that such a delicate, melancholy sigh could issue from the mouth of a soldier.

Our conversation ceased and I turned around to look at the people talking so intimately in twos and threes; they came from different places and spoke with different accents, but in a brief space of time they had become close friends, although a few days later when they were back on the ground they would be as aloof and indifferent as before.

I went to see my sister. Even she was frowning only slightly now, she wasn't in any mood to complain any more. It was very hot. Passengers were packed in like goods in a shop. I thought that at least those third-class railway carriages were fairly neat and clean, and in retrospect they actually deserved praise. But I spoke patiently. I said that the sooner we embarked then the sooner we'd reach our destination, and that anyway the boat would set out this evening.

I once wrote in a short story:

"Do you think I am telling a story? In stories we say there is too much chance. In human life we say there is too much mischance." Below I lightly added the line, "How many possibilities are there in a second?"

My dear friends, let us discuss this matter of chance or mischance some other time; on the second night after this small and dirty boat set out, within that damned second of time, we lightly sailed right into a sandbank. We ran aground. The next morning I awoke from my dreams or should I say from the four chairs that I was using as a bed, only to discover that our boat was like a dead grasshopper pinned by a schoolboy in his specimen case. We were midstream in the Yangtze with not a person in sight and on either bank were tall green reeds. They said we were probably about halfway between Hankow and Ichang.

Everyone aboard cursed the pilot. But the stewards then said that he was a "first-rate, experienced pilot". Then one steward produced the reason for our trouble, saying that the pilot had quarrelled with his wife before he embarked at Hankow.

We suffered for two whole days from despair, irritation, confusion and the sun, and then on the third day a boat owned by the same company in the Ichang area arrived by chance, so we all transferred to this boat with our luggage, and when we reached Ichang we changed to a Szechwan boat. After the trouble and fatigue of these incidents, we were no longer in any condition to complain about anything. We were simply exhausted, as exhausted as a quilt which has been thrown around and trampled on over and over again.

However, when finally we awoke after a full night's dreamless sleep on the fairly large and clean Szechwan boat, the fresh morning river breeze, the green mountains on either side, and the joy of soon arriving home revived our spirits again.

The boat reached Hsiling Gorge.

People from other provinces who were entering Szechwan for the first time were amazed at the steepness of the mountains.

The tall and thin Kiangsu man studied a map all the way along and asked the names of places; sometimes he wrote something in a pocket diary, and would then lean on the railing, sighing incessantly.

"This is really magnificent. Magnificent." It provoked my fellow-provincial, the second lieutenant, into smiling:

"In a short time you will see the Wu Gorge, what will you have to say then?"

"You can't mean it's even higher and more dangerous than this?"

"I certainly can. Let me tell you. It's really as steep as a cliff, the clouds and mist start halfway up the mountains, and above the clouds and mist there is still more mountain, you can't see the sky without craning your neck."

Never-ending mountains. Monotonous mountains. The travellers' looks of surprise and delight gradually changed into boredom.

The Kiangsu man with the tendency towards stoutness turned the topic of conservation to another matter, which he thought would provide an interesting discussion for Szechwan people: a woman who had married a Szechwan man had written a few travel sketches about Chengtu, which were published in a Peking magazine. She made some derogatory remarks about Szechwan, which first aroused the indignation of a Nanking newspaper; afterwards a Chengtu newspaper responded, making the woman very angry and distressed. In short it was a thoroughly boring business from beginning to end. But nevertheless he brought it up, meaning to get the views of myself and my fellow-provincial.

"I haven't got any feelings about the matter," I said. "I haven't even seen the travel sketches, I don't usually read magazines of that sort. As for the Nanking attack which stirred up the trouble, I heard someone mention it recently, but to me it's still news."

"She said that Szechwan eggs don't taste like eggs, is that true?" the tall, thin graduate in education said with a laugh.

"I have no opinion on that point; although I lived in the north for five or six years I only remember that Szechwan eggs were a little bigger than in the north." I laughed too.

"Szechwan and Szechwan people are certainly not without their shortcomings," my young fellow-provincial said in a resolute voice, "but she did not mention any of them. Without even going into the ridiculous things she said, if you just analyse her psychology you'll see that it is completely inferior. She regards herself as a woman of position and reputation, who is undergoing hardship in some wild and remote district; she has not become quite used to her surroundings and so she loses her temper. She is simply acting like a spoiled child towards society. But unfortunately society isn't a woman's husband. Therefore I can assure you that Szechwan eggs taste like eggs and Szechwan fruit also tastes like fruit. These famous Chinese scholars are a pitiful lot. Look at her—she has only written a trivial vernacular history of foreign countries for senior high schools, which actually left out America altogether, but when she goes to Szechwan she is made head of the history department."

"But her article about middle-school students impressed educationalists so much that the ministry of education issued an order reducing the number of class hours in junior middle school," said the graduate in education with the tendency towards stoutness.

"Therefore I say she is acting like a spoiled child towards society."

At this point I couldn't help addressing a few regretful words to my native province, for having become indifferent to it. Or I should say that I had almost forgotten it. But if you ask me to criticise my fellow-provincials, it's not that I have nothing to say; I feel that we have one great strength and also one great weakness. In seeking and pursuing vast horizons and a bright new atmosphere, we are invariably determined and steadfast. As for the shortcoming, I can explain it with one small example. Previously, before there were proper law courts and lawyers, cases were settled by the district magistrate, and the opposing parties involved in the lawsuit usually resided together in small shops around the magistrate's office. The two parties would talk and joke together and sometimes invite each other to eat at a restaurant, but once they were before the district office, even on the following day, they became quite vicious towards each other, and very cunningly tried to construct capital crimes around their opponents: skill in diplomatic speech and the social graces seem to be natural talents of the Szechwanese. But unfortunately I've lacked these things all my life; if I don't lapse into a very clumsy silence when I am with people, so that I'm mistakenly regarded as cold and proud, then I'm pouring out my most intimate feelings in front of total strangers, so that people laugh at me behind my back. So I can't help feeling that the blunt and frank temperament of the northern continentals is very appealing and likeable. I am not trying to say that northerners are absolutely honest; for instance, Peking servants rarely go out shopping for their masters without retaining a little money for themselves (that would be sufficient reason for dismissal in my native district), but their technique of deception is so clumsy that it is as attractive as Dostoevsky's "An Honest Thief". I don't know when I began to feel remote from my fellow-provincials, but now, when this young man spoke so vividly, his eyes shining with sincerity, I couldn't help placing complete trust in him. Perhaps this generation of young people no longer has these shortcomings. My native province, I am looking forward to seeing you.

The boat had reached Wu Gorge.

Again many passengers came rushing from their cabins to the deck in admiration.

I was six or seven when I first passed through Wu Gorge, and it left me with a memory of desolation and melancholy. I wanted to know whether people lived in the mountains there, what sort of place it was. Later the geography I learnt in school gave me my answer. It is a very barren place, a place of starvation, a place which has never seen the light of good fortune. And yet it is still a place where man lives. So on this occasion I regarded the travellers' enthusiasm with a cold, satirical and even angry gaze. I said to myself, if they had to live for a single day on these mountains they admired so much, they would curse and moan and perhaps become a little more intelligent about the place.

Then I heard from the rapid current in this narrow gorge a sobbing song, a song of life and death, a song awaiting freedom and happiness.

That evening the boat stopped overnight in Wushan district.

At four o'clock in the afternoon of the following day I saw the lighthouse below Wanhsien; my sister and I quickly collected our luggage, hurriedly, restlessly, waiting with a mixture of joy and distress for the boat to stop.

From Peking to Wanhsien it had taken us altogether fourteen days.

Laiyang, 29 September 1936
(*Visit Home*, pp. 20-39.)

Sad and lonely, I returned to my native district.

I say sad and lonely, because to me that small district town was as coldly indifferent as if it had been some foreign land. Had I not been depending on the kindness of a friend from the north, who had written beforehand to tell his family to take in this native son with nowhere to lay his head, I would have had to go to an inn and keep a whole night's lonely vigil. My family lived in the countryside some fifty or sixty *li* outside the town. Owing to the rugged and dangerous nature of the mountain ranges, it was a good half-day's journey away. The place where we used to stay previously when we came to the district town, a medium-sized house where an old aunt lived alone, had been sold to a company, and now the roofs, walls and dilapidated wooden gate were being demolished.

When shall I be able to demolish these ancient, dilapidated childhood memories, since they prevent me from building anew?

I no longer remember clearly how old I was when I first came from the countryside to the town; we were going to visit some relatives and passed through on our way. Only the high town gates made a deep impression on me. Apart from this, I can still remember clearly the white-painted boats in the river and the dark waters slowly flowing by; my mother and I were sitting in the sedan-chair, and asked someone to throw some copper coins into the river. I'm not sure whether it was to pacify the river god or for some other reason, but in any case, when I think of it now, it makes me feel very melancholy. But this has nothing to do with the district town.

When I was six or seven, the eastern part of Szechwan was overrun by bandits, or should I say soldiers turned bandits. In Wanhsien, which was popularly known as a well-off, first-rate district, the more worried citizens either hid themselves in fortresses or fled to other regions. Before my family moved to Hupeh to avoid the troubles, we lived for a little while in the district town. This was really the first time I tasted town life. The house we rented adjoined a French Catholic Church, but at that time the clear sound of bells was absent, and so was the sound of hymn-singing: a regiment was stationed there in place of the devout monks. It was a quite famous regiment, because of the peculiar method it had of paying its soldiers. It was said that the commander of the regiment had laid down a procedure for payment by turn. Each company, when its turn came, would change into civilian clothing (though keeping its weapons), and descend on the countryside, seizing people to hold for ransom. And this holy place, dedicated to the worship of God and his Son, was their common lair. In our house, we would overhear the low moaning of the prisoners, or a clear sharp clinking sound of silver dollars being counted. This frightened us into silence—we did not dare say anything, we did not even dare tread heavily.

And this was the first memory I have of town life.

In Hupeh we spent two years wandering around, and then, as the local troubles subsided a little, we returned. We stayed on in the district town. Although robberies and so on were still frequent in the town, prosperous families in the countryside were more likely to attract the attentions of bandits. In town, the population was greater, so that the really wealthy and the comfortably-off could be inconspicuous. This time we did not rent a house, but lived in a coir-fibre factory, jointly owned by my grandfather and a merchant. Now a coir-fibre factory, with huge bundles of coir-fibre heaped up everywhere, is quite different to an ordinary dwelling-place. I lived alongside those clumsy, silent bundles. A child of around nine of course does not realise that lack of warmth and happiness can cause illness, but at that time I seemed to feel that I was spiritually undernourished, like a small plant which has never seen the sun. I was so miserable, so disheartened.

So, while this district town may have been lively, enormous, or even joyful to other children, to me it seemed totally gloomy, confined and desolate—a desolation without sound or colour.

While I was visiting in spirit that desolation in my memory, the dusk had quietly flowed in like a melancholy river, submerging the district town. I was standing irresolute in a street. On disembarking, after I had taken my luggage to my friend's house and before resting a while, I went out for a walk, not to buy anything, nor to visit anyone, but simply because I wanted to take a look at this district town and its streets. When I lived in that great city in the north, at dusk and late at night I often liked to linger alone in those long, straight, main streets. I felt they were the pulse of a great city. I listened to their beating. I would imagine the different kinds of people who passed along those streets in the daytime and at night, and choose certain characters out of which to compose a tragic tale; slowly I became affected by this imaginary plot, and finally I felt that I myself had become a character in the story; then I would sigh and wonder why the world was full of misfortune and suffering. And my bosom seemed to fill with a passionate love for mankind.

But now, as I stand irresolute in a narrow, winding, uneven and broken cobblestone street in my native district, I seem to be entering my childhood, my head hanging and my spirits low.

This is a true story.

This is a humble, insignificant story.

When I was fourteen, I entered the first grade of the district middle school, that is to say, I returned to the district town after four or five years in the country. At that time, people were still suspicious and contemptuous of the school system, particularly country people. They believed that this turbulent, emperor-less period would soon pass away, and that the traditional examination system which lay firmly embedded in their minds would soon be revived. So they stubbornly shut up their children at home, reading the Classics and Histories, awaiting the "Great Peace" of their imagination. It was not an easy thing then for me to leave the family school for the school in town. However, thanks to an uncle's help and my own determination, in the end, with a kind of confused hope and timid joy, I entered for the first time a strange new social life.

The school was on the site of a former district examination hall. On each side of a long wide stone path stood the two-storied dormitories and classrooms and a few lonely *wu-t'ung* trees level with the tiled eaves. This was my new world, just as confined, gloomy and desolate. In this mass of almost two hundred people, I felt as lonely as before.

One month later, something happened that only increased my feelings of loneliness, new arrival that I was.

At that time, the school was already proceeding with the new educational system, but there was still a great variation in the ages of the students, which probably ranged from thirteen or fourteen to twenty-three or twenty-four. In my dormitory, two or three students in the higher grades were already adults; they were very kind to me, but because of my extreme youth, they tended to overlook my existence, and did not entirely conceal from me matters which should have been kept secret. They were conducting a kind of campaign. They had joined in with some people outside the school to attack the present headmaster, and had also discussed supporting a certain person on his dismissal. At that time a petty warlord had stationed himself in our district, and the district education office was completely under his control. All the headmasters were hired and fired by him. It seems that these secret campaigners had not only written a petition, but had been to see him once in person in the capacity of student representatives. Subsequently the headmaster, who was in the habit of pacing the floor slowly with both hands behind his back, was dismissed. The person appointed as his successor, however, was not the one they had proposed, but a third man.

In our district there was a normal school as well as the middle school. Those who came from the two different schools connived and struggled against each other as if they were political cliques. The new headmaster unfortunately was from the normal school, and so with this as a pretext, the people who had secretly attacked the former headmaster united together with his genuine supporters to retain him, and they caused a terrible disturbance.

I don't remember whether it was in the morning or the afternoon. The new headmaster, accompanied by the district magistrate, had come to take up his appointment. As they walked along the wide long stone path into the rear courtyard where the headmaster's rooms were located, from the dormitories on both sides a crowd of warriors suddenly burst out, yelling and cursing, and set out wildly after the two men, chasing them up to the rear courtyard where they milled around for a long time. Finally the unfortunate headmaster escaped through the school gate, his face and lips smeared with blood.

I did not go to savour the climax of this military drama. The unexpected explosion in fact rather frightened me. For the first time I saw how insane, how terrible, people can become.

This terrible insanity continued even after victory had been won.

The warriors were yelling and laughing raucously; emboldened by their recent success, they besieged the confounded headmaster in a room, and threw a dumbbell in through the window.

Next the belongings he had left behind became the objects of the crowd's hostility. His boxes were broken up as if they were so many chestnuts. His straw hat with its top torn off landed high on a banana-tree, and his white silk gown, ripped down the middle, hung on a branch of a tree for public exhibition. A large, wood-block printed copy of *The Book of History & The History of the Han Dynasty* became countless white butterflies, drifting across the courtyard and coming to rest on the grass.

Encountering an event like this with the mind of a fourteen year old child, although at the time I did not make any outward show of indignation or hatred, nevertheless increased my awareness of human cruelty, which in turn increased my awareness of my own isolation. I began to observe adults very early in life, silently and dispassionately; I tested them and found them untrustworthy. But this indeed was a brand new lesson.

And this brand new lesson was not finished yet.

At nightfall, the school was besieged by a few dozen soldiers flourishing fixed bayonets. This resulted in the capture of a mere eight or nine new boys who had not yet escaped, so they were locked for the night in a small room. The soldiers on guard terrified us by saying as a joke that the next day they were taking us to be interrogated by their commander, and that we might have to be flogged. We were only children, after all, and after discussing what our answers would be the next day, we went to sleep, quietly huddled together.

The next morning it was raining heavily. A young brigade leader came to give us a lecture and then released us. Braving the rain I ran to my old aunt's place; I was so drenched I nearly turned into a fish.

And this was the first memory school life gave me.

The soft night started to move along the street. The dim street lights cast a yellow circle of light. Where was I going, anyway? Did I walk down this narrow, winding, broken cobblestone street, and then cross the bridge, just to visit my old school? It had been pulled down a long time ago. The dilapidated building had been sold to a certain bank, and a new school built on another site. I could no longer view the lonely *wu-t'ung* trees level with the tiled eaves. I could no longer mount the rickety, creaking wooden steps, wearing the homemade blue cotton gown which was always too big for me. Right now I am facing a squalid street. It is the anaemic pulse of a small district town; the people passing by me, heads hanging, spirits low, bereft of hope, must nevertheless still bear the burden of toil and strife.

This is my native land.

This is my sad and lonely native land.

As for my former schoolmates, although I have just recalled their brutal rioting, I do not really blame them. If I were to meet them now, here on the street tonight, I would certainly stretch out my hand to them, as an unexpected pleasure. I would discover again their virtues. Even recalling them as they were then, I remember honest ones among them. Moreover, rather than blame them, I should blame those petty educationalists who lived parasitically like bacteria in the district town. The headmaster who was always striding up and down with his hands behind his back, I hear, holds the position of district education officer now, while someone else from the same clique who

From *Diary of a Visit Home*   101

later became our headmaster, I also hear, has lost his job and become a loafer. If I were to meet them now, here on the street tonight, would I generously stretch out my hand to them? No, I still have an irrepressible hatred for them. Although I should add: I do not blame them, but society.

This society which man has created is really a dark, vile, miserable hell. I would almost like to write a book to prove that other animals lead a more rational life than men.

Ideals, love, virtue, beauty, happiness, all these things which comfort us when we are sad and make us weep when we are happy, are easy to find in books but in real life rarer than precious gems. It was in books that I first encountered these sweetly-sounding names. They were so new, so strange to me that I only dared whisper their names. What the real world taught me was completely different. When I was a child, I was thoroughly accustomed to darkness, cruelty and squalor. I thought that this was man's only diet; although I found it coarse, bitter and hard to swallow, still, with the patience and courage it takes to become a man, I took it for a long, long time. But afterwards books opened up for me a golden door of illusion, and from then on I strenuously rejected and even despised the reality of this world. I lived in stories, in books, in my own daydreams; I was intoxicated, lingering in a non-existent world. But even in dreams, there comes a time of awakening, and I awoke too soon. What should I believe in now? Should I place my hopes in the unknowable future of mankind? Can I decide that in the future of mankind there will surely be a rational and happy life, where men will no longer need to open those pitiful books, and read those endless lies? Even if it were certain to happen, what has that to do with me? Must I repay man's indifference with love, passion, sincerity and generosity?

For man, love is a subject for study, a difficult subject in which it is easy to fail.

I repeat my words.

All words are nothing but empty sounds.

Again I stand irresolutely in this second narrow, winding, uneven, broken cobblestone street. The night and my dark thoughts remind me that I am lost myself. Where am I now? Is this my native land? Or is it not my native land? I must find a go-between to prove my connection with this district town. I must find an acquaintance. A rickshaw passed alongside. I tell him an address whose whereabouts I do not even know, and climb in.

Finally we arrive before a large gate.

It is a primary school, I have an acquaintance who lives there. But he may have already gone to the country for the summer vacation.

The two great wooden doors are sternly closed. At first I tap the door knocker lightly, then bang it with both hands, then I start shouting. Finally, I bend down to listen: inside is as still as night. I think that a school would surely have a gate-keeper. I think there might be a gate-keeper's lodge, but when I ask some passers-by, they say no.

Then, as if to shatter all my heavy thoughts, I beat the door with my fists, with all the strength I can muster, and start shouting at the top of my voice.

I grope for the luminous watch in my pocket: eight o'clock.

Night, 15 October
(*Visit Home*, pp.40-56.)

The scenery of the district town (*Hsien-ch'eng feng-kuang*)

The district towns along the upper reaches of the Yangtze River use the mountains as their town walls. On the lower slopes which jut out like gigantic feet into the ever-flowing waters of the river, the encircling walls, constructed out of rocks heaped one on top of the other, are set down on the narrow end of the slanting foot; from the river they look like armchairs. Had we not been turned into dilettanti of scenery, stuffed full of odes to nature by past writers, we might experience a kind of sadness when we gaze on the small towns crawling up those natural giant feet, that we are insignificant beings who are still unable to tame nature with all our science, civilization or manpower. These mountain towns for the most part still retain their ancient primitiveness. Three years ago, when I was similarly on my way home, I entered "K'ueifu's lonely city, as the setting sun slants"; the "sad and bitter" poet of the T'ang dynasty, Tu Fu, spent two years in this place. Its narrow, stone-paved streets, its dwellings with their stunted walls and low eaves and its desolation made me feel that I had entered the mediaeval age. I could not resist buying several boxwood combs. This crescent-shaped comb is the only local speciality of this mountain town, and also it calls to mind the black tresses of women in ancient times, cloud-like, and long enough to reach the ground.

But going upstream, from the Wu Gorge to Wanhsien, my native district, we can breathe out; both the eye and the mind experience a feeling of unbounded space. The mountains on both sides of the river banks have humbly retreated, leaving rather more level ground. Faced with such natural benevolence, we feel that it would be very possible to organize our manpower to develop a large city here. And thus, thirty-four years ago, the foreigners demanded that it should be developed into a trading port, so a red anchor-shaped mark appeared on the map, and among those broken-down houses appeared a church, propagating the Europeans' moral code; then, ten years ago this district town and its residents were bombarded by warships of the British Empire.

The district town was on the north bank of the river. Set around a mountain stream, we could describe it as "impressive", with its administrative quarter to the east, and to the west the commercial quarter. In former days only the eastern section was walled. The southern bank of the river had a more level and extensive embankment, and people had prophesied that with the development of trade in the district town, it could be opened up into an even more flourishing market. Nevertheless this prophecy had not yet been fulfilled; separated by a vast river and by white waves poised to swallow up junks, from a distance we still see no more than a small stretch of scattered houses sheltering in the densely-wooded blue foothills, like ants that have crawled on to a bear's hairy paw. This is Turquoise Screen Mountain. A lovely name, it is listed as the first among the "Ten Scenes" in the district *Gazette*. When we studied *The Scenery of Wanhsien* at middle school, I could recite these "Ten Scenes" off one by one, but now, forgive my indifference, I have forgotten them. But I still remember one of those forgotten things, the first, Turquoise Screen Mountain. Then to the west of the town was T'aipo Cliff; there was a tradition that Li T'ai-po had once built a hut there so he could live there as a hermit, but in fact there are only a few temples along the cliff-face, and a few monks and nuns; there is no evidence at all of any relationship between the mountain and the drunken poet of former days. When I was in middle school, on our spring and autumn outings I often climbed up the several hundred steps of the winding rocky stairs after my fellow-students, and later in the suffocating atmosphere of the incense-heavy temples we would eat our three or four cakes provided by the school. Although then I didn't despise famous landmarks or scenery, they didn't give me any pleasure either. At the foot of the cliff, there is a Floating Cup Pool; in this case there is a stone tablet as evidence. On this tablet, which is becoming indecipherable because of the ink-rubbings which have been taken from it and from the effects of the wind and sun, we can still read an inscription made by Huang T'ing-chien, which says that he once passed through here on such and-such a day, that the prefect here accompanied him on an excursion and feast, and how pleasant it was. In front of the tablet was a large stone slab, with a carving of the curved Floating Cup Pool. Afterwards when I was at the Flowing Water Sound in South Lake in Peking, I saw a much larger curved pool, and it occured to me that this landmark in my native district was probably made by well-meaning people simply to give the ancient tablet additional interest.

Let me forget these places now. Let their names stay buried in the wood-block printed district *Gazette* where no-one will excavate them again. However, apart from the "Ten Scenes", there was one place which adults find beneath their interest, but which I find hard to forget: its name is Red Gravel Bank.

Going eastwards downstream on the Yangtze, we discover when we are not far from the town but beyond its noise and bustle a bank of gravel seven *li* long and three *li* wide, covered with pebbles of every shape and colour. White goose-eggs. Cornelian-red pearls. Turquoise ear-drops. And other gems impossible to compare or describe. What child would fail to find this place an exciting treasure-mountain, what child going past would fail to pick up in his tiny hands a few pure and flawless joys. And he will take them back home and treasure them, as the relics of dreams, and these gems will always cast their beautiful light in his dull, grey childhood, as if they were the sole favour given to children by Mother Earth, though they are nothing but cold and silent pebbles.

Because my family lived by the upper reaches of the Yangtze, as a child I rarely had an opportunity to go to this bank of gravel. And even on these few occasions, because the adults were always in great haste to continue their journey and would not wait, I always left that treasure-mountain with a feeling of sadness; my sense of tragedy and hardship was like that of an unfortunate ruler banished from his kingdom. I often consoled myself with thoughts of pleasures to come; I thought when I grew up I would hurry down there by myself and play to my heart's content for one whole day, or even two.

However, when I returned home this time I did not go to fulfil this childhood wish. It was not that I feared that my adult feet stained with foreign mud would shatter these fragile dreams, nor that I believed that this gleaming, solemn, strange place would have changed through the erosion of time into a barren wasteland. This time I was in a hurry. Haste—is this the reason, which is no reason, that we mistake, lose or drive away so many joys? Why do we press on so urgently along this short path, this grey and lonely path which stretches towards the eternally silent darkness?

I could only stay in the district town for a day and a half, as my family in the countryside were anxiously awaiting me. It was June, and it had not rained for a long time. The fear of drought weighed heavily on the local people. The depressed state of the market told me how trade had fallen off.

I could not bear this spectacle of misery and trouble on every face. Although I had not held excessively high hopes for this town, I was still prepared to see some changes, because I had heard over three years ago that it had been freed from warlord rule. However, let me touch on a rather delicate matter. I have long suspected our race of something I find hard to explain. In plant life there is a flower called the poppy; when we see it in the fields, with its beautiful, smiling, large red and purple blossoms, we are full of praise, ah! But over the last few decades many of our countrymen have developed a craving for its juice, against which legal prohibitions are powerless. And their way of administering it, their attitude towards it ... I cannot describe it except as "wine must be enjoyed sip by sip", a saying which admires "the art of living" our countrymen appreciate so deeply. I cannot say how widespread this addiction was in our district, but when I was a child, I often saw it in the homes of some older relatives. They were recluses unconcerned with worldly affairs. When they fondled the small objects on the lamp tray they were like antique collectors, and when their minds were full they became "pure talk" philosophers. My grandfather was a very strict abolitionist. Even then I often wondered why these people put themselves on such intimate terms with an enemy who would destroy their health and strength. Now, in the name of national unity, I said to myself, this ubiquitous evil habit may have been wiped out completely, or at least be on the decline. However, opium shops were readily seen in the streets. Besides—and when I was told this in lowered voices, I seemed to glimpse an invisible, gigantic and terrible spider's web—an even more terrible white crystalline powder, known to science as heroin, had reached this small town, and was circulating surreptitiously. They say that this drug is often dispersed through families in small paper packets attached to the gartered thighs of women. But where do these honeybee legs get them from? Why are these imports, which have never before appeared in our mountain kingdom, suddenly available here? I could only gaze with cold and suspicious eyes at the sternly-worded "Anti-Drug Regulations" displayed on the walls.

But what was even more confusing and difficult to understand was that these small townspeople, who were complaining about the falling-off of trade, were now thinking back longingly to the petty warlord who occupied this town ten years ago. He was a very notorious warlord, and many exaggerated events and stories were associated with his name.

Soon after he arrived in the town, he pulled down the old stone wall around it, and with money forcibly extracted from the people and pretended "engineers" who came from heaven knows where, began to build macadam roads which swallowed up the homes of the poor like a snake. At that time, no-one even dreamed that there could be such a thing as compensation for resumed property. The poor could only watch as their homes were bulldozed, bewailing their unhappy fate. But those with money bribed the engineers to alter the routes on their plans, with a slight curve here or a bit of an angle there, or even to find a new route, in order to protect their homes and ancestral graves. As a result, we now have a road which climbs up and down and veers from left to right. When we take a rickshaw, it is like being on top of a high mountain; we suddenly climb up and the rickshaw man pulls slowly with bent back, and then we are rushing down and he cannot stop, as if he were under a spell.

Nevertheless, I remember that at the time, the rich were also pulling faces, sighing and complaining. Although they were well able to use the privilege of offering bribes, the bribes cost money, and so did the taxes for completing the road. The road tax at that time was a very heavy imposition. Had it been less heavy, I am afraid that after the distribution of "expenses" at each level, there would not have been enough left over to take the road even a foot longer.

I mention this matter not to blame this warlord who has now fled into exile in a remote corner of Szechwan, but to explain that by comparison with militarists of that period, he could be regarded as a reformer. Not only did he pull down walls and construct roads wherever he went, but he even had a respect for scholars. All university students who returned home from outside the province, regardless of whether they had really been to university or not, had only to go to see him wearing Western clothing and he would give them the title of private secretary. His concubines at various times numbered more than ten, and his secretaries I am afraid numbered more than a hundred. Apart from the secretaries who had other important duties, most of them received no salary; but they could always ask the ordinary soldiers to take their hurricane lamps into the camp and fill them with kerosene.

He built a public park and a library to adorn this small town. The library proudly occupies a very lofty position, and to get in you have to climb dozens of steps which leaves you sweating; hence, the library was as deserted as an ancient temple.

He was an ambitious man. He established a political training school, as he wanted to "systematize" the area under his control. That is to say, all his officials employed staff who had been trained by him. He often held "morale-booster talks" with these future magistrates, local educational officers and militia chiefs, saying that his first step would be to unify Szechwan, then the lower reaches of the Yangtze River; then he would extend his rule over the areas north and south of the Yangtze and unify all of China. This was no doubt the reason he respected scholars. He liked people to wear Western clothing; it suggested mental alertness. In order to make people of every sort in the town wear short jackets, he initiated a "scissors policy": he instructed the police to stand at the crossroads armed with scissors, and when they saw someone wearing the long gown they cut off the "floating panels" at front and back. I do not know why it was so difficult to put this new policy fully into effect, but in the end, the "plantain flower has its brief moment of glory, and then fades."

However, it was already quite enough to make the townspeople pull faces and sigh and complain. As long as I can remember, the people of my native district have always gone around with long faces and doleful sighs. Nevertheless, it is true that in those two or three years the tax burden was the heaviest, and in addition there was the mental burden of their stubborn opposition to such new arrangements as building highways and so on.

So why do they now look back to that time with the greatest nostalgia?

Yes, at that time trade flourished in the town. But those who flourished most were gamblers and prostitutes.

I have to provide my own explanation: men are pitiful creatures, who find it easy to forget. When we are not satisfied with the "present", we frequently dwell on the "past". It seems that times were better then, though in fact they may have been just as bad or even worse. And so we continue to live. And such is the history of mankind.

Now let me walk once more down this road with its sudden ups and downs and sudden swerves to the right or left; let me enjoy once more this human scenery. Among the old, rickety houses with their crumbling walls there are newly-constructed tall buildings; modern goods from Shanghai are on display in the shops where trade is slack; the children who roamed the streets ten years ago have become merchants or tradesmen, but now their children roam the streets, just as undernourished, just as grubby. To endure the suffering of the "present", we must forget the suffering of the "past". Fortunately we can forget.

Ten years ago the cannons of British gunboats delivered death and destruction to this town, but who still thinks about it now? Even my own personal experience of it is now a little blurred in my mind.

Let me conclude our tour of the district town with this memory.

It was a very hot afternoon in September, and I was returning to school after enjoying the Sunday holiday; I had just put my foot on the steps outside the school gate when I heard a burst of repeated gun-fire echoing across the river. The school was situated near the river bank. We already knew a little about the recent diplomatic clash. When I entered the dining-hall, the tables had been laid for dinner; suddenly there was a roar of cannon-fire which shook the walls and roof-tiles and we all ran out by the back door. We took shelter in a low ditch at the foot of an overhanging cliff. The sky was such a peaceful blue, but uninterrupted thunder reverberated from valley to valley. We saw the soldiers move a rusty cannon to the river, and a little while later saw them carrying back the wounded. I cannot remember how long we were crouched there before we went back to school. But after the sound of the cannon had stopped the town was still in flames, the huge red blaze menacing the mute heavens. Only a few walls in the school had been destroyed. The terrible sulphur bombs hit the stone foundations of the walls but were unable to penetrate as far as the inner school buildings.

The next day I went out with some schoolmates to see a whole street reduced to ashes. I cannot describe what a deep scar this insane act of the white man carved on my youthful heart.

However, we have seen new buildings arise from these ashes, and gradually everyone has forgotten the great conflagration, just as we forget any accidental fire. Because fire-fighting is not properly organised, fires large and small often break out in the town, and the merchants have a saying that the more fires there are the more prosperous it gets. The number of people killed on this occasion received less attention than the number of houses destroyed. This animal known as man is really far too prolific; natural disasters and man-made slaughter are so common that no-one bothers much about them.

This town was the setting for the famous play *Cry China!* Now it sits quietly on the bank of what Tretiakov called China's Volga.

Night, 1 November [1936]
(*Visit Home*, pp. 57-72.)

I am now sitting comfortably at home. I am sitting in a rattan chair in front of the house, facing a mass of green orchid leaves in the courtyard, recalling the earliest memory I have of this old house. At the time I would not have been more than three or four; I was sitting in the same courtyard, my short arms resting on the arms of the small wooden chair, while the drifting gold of chrysanthemum blossoms filled my gaze. This old house is more than a hundred years old, quietly falling into decay, but like many customs and rules in this district, although the process of disintegration has begun, it will yet stand firm for many years to come. I think it was my grandfather's grandfather who bought this house from a relative—at that time it was even considered luxurious, the floors inlaid with tile patterns and with more than ten courtyards. But now, there is only an air of coldness, desolation and decay.

The protruding staircase led to the abandoned upper stories, all hung with cobwebs. As a child I never dared climb up there alone, because it was said that at night you could hear the lonely footsteps of a woman's bowed slipper on the stairs.

I am aware now that this old house was really built in an old-fashioned way, occupying a very large area but without any bright or comfortable rooms. What annoyed me most were the pitifully small windows. Whenever I was sitting in one of those rooms full of darkness, unable to see sun or sky, I would plead for the windows to be made a little larger, but my brother told me that grandfather had said that in that direction no work could be undertaken this year because it would not be auspicious. My grandfather was a man of learning and ability, and in the district he had a name as a skilful geomancer and eye-doctor. He diagnosed my hereditary short-sight as an enlargement of the pupil, and made up prescriptions for me— ah! how often did I take his bitter medicines!

But this is a very good example: there are difficulties even in the matter of enlarging windows.

This dark and damp old house was an ideal breeding-ground for infection, and my visit home this time happened to coincide with an epidemic of malaria. In village lore there were two kinds of malaria: the ordinary kind came from eating and drinking, especially from eating a lot of fresh fruit; but the more serious kind was caused by evil spirits. My youngest brother, who had just completed his second year in medicine, had been seriously ill for rather a long time from this epidemic, and I heard that he had taken strange drugs, called in a sorceress, and had even borrowed a jade bracelet which had been buried with a corpse and was said to be able to expel evil influences, and wore it on his wrist for several days. But all these proved ineffective, and in the end some anti-malarial sulphate of quinine pills cured him. I wanted to tease him by asking where his studies in physiology and hygiene had disappeared to, but then I thought that although he knew the cause of malaria, he was not after all a doctor, and besides, when someone is ill, he will grasp at any expedient that might make him better.

Even prevention was difficult. Everyday at twilight, huge mosquitoes would begin humming in chorus before setting out on their rounds of the old house. I still remember how much I used to enjoy killing with my tiny hands the mosquitoes which stopped to rest on the walls. And at night, inside the mosquito net, catching them and burning them in the lamp with two glass sides and a round door on the third side, made me even happier. And no-one even suspected that among these blood-sucking insects with their irritating whine were a more evil kind, with brown speckles on their wings, back legs haughtily poised, plotting to inject malaria germs into our bloodstreams.

Following the malaria epidemic into our village came a Chinese-style doctor. This was not simply a concrete and inevitable manifestation of the people's belief in Chinese medicine. At a time when scientific institutions had not yet reached as far as the villages, sick people had no other recourse than to trust themselves to ancient medical practices. Even in the district town it was difficult to find a doctor who had received proper professional training, while bogus hospitals similarly deceived people.

People who live in the country are naturally stubborn and conservative, but looking back over a period of time, we may say that they are slowly giving way before the intrusion of new things. Ten years ago, private family schools were still extremely common, because people believed that the district school was part of the educational apparatus of a rebel administration, and that the system which had been overthrown would soon rise again. They kept boys at home reading the Classics for the same reason that they continued to bind girls' feet: they were afraid that when all the old ways were suddenly restored, people who had boldly unbound their feet would suffer ridicule and hardship. At that time some busybody issued a prophecy based on the design on the reverse of Szechwan silver coins: having very carefully counted the small rings which surrounded the seal character for "Han", he said that the Republic had only a life expectancy of eighteen years. A few of the local children who went to the district school developed a taste for the pleasures of town life; they were talked about in an exaggerated fashion in the countryside, and someone who gambled was said to have lost half the family property in one night; this provided an excuse for preventing children from going to the school. But now, the eighteenth year of the Republic has long since passed, and the people who trusted the prophecy have forgotten it, and those who opposed state education allow their children to go to school. The village primary school has now replaced the private family school. Girls go to school now, although the older people still have their doubts: what's the point of sending girls to school? But it isn't a very solid opposition, because everyone does it. The future they were expecting has not come, and now fashions and events they cannot understand keep on developing in the countryside; they cannot help feeling thoroughly confused by this age and this world. But why should we laugh at that? No-one has taken the trouble to explain things to them carefully and systematically, and their knowledge is limited to past experience.

Here we see the complex nature of each problem. Even if primary school education has spread through the villages, and small children all go to school, at home you are still forbidden to eat fruit after dinner, and if you want to build a window into a dark room you will still run into trouble.

Besides, even if the adults in the villages have some scientific knowledge, when they or their children fall ill, all they can do is trust Chinese medicine and swallow the bitter juice of poisonous roots and leaves, because hospitals run by foreigners exist only in a few big cities.

Country people live surrounded by superstition and rumour.

It is very difficult, I am afraid, to eliminate superstition in human society. How much of our behaviour, how many of our revered customs and laws are based on reason? But we go on living in obedience to them without any doubts at all, even to the point of stoning any disbeliever who should appear among us.

Rumour springs up more often in cities and also spreads faster there, yet we still feel that village rumour is completely ridiculous.

One evening at the dinner-table, my grandfather mentioned that he had heard that they were using many new weights and measures in the district town, then angrily and yet enigmatically he spat out,

"Who knows what will come of all this?"

Father as usual sighed by way of agreement. I raised my eyes to look at my brother who sat opposite me. I felt obliged to defend those innocent weights and measures.

"Probably the government wants to unify the system of measurements throughout the country; our weights and measures here are not the same as the standard."

His expression clearly showed that grandfather was not inclined to agree with my explanation, so I did not continue. As I resumed eating, I wondered why grandfather was so angry and mysterious. The so-called "legal currency" regulations were generally disliked in this part of the country. People here looked at things in a simple way: the bright shiny coins were gone, leaving them only with indecipherable paper notes. At this time, too, the terms "inheritance tax" and "income tax" were bedevilling the minds of the country people. Perhaps grandfather imagined that the new weights and measures were somehow connected with taxes. Or perhaps he thought that the government was afraid that people were dishonestly understating their annual harvest and wanted to use new measures to re-estimate the taxes. But what could the new weights have to do with it?

A simple piece of news which has passed through several mouths can turn into something quite extraordinary. There are also people who deliberately manufacture rumours. In town I had already heard vague conjectures of local unrest, but in the countryside it became quite openly a matter of political discussion; the main import was that the former provincial armies were to unite and expel from Szechwan all outside authority.

One day I heard a rather more knowledgeable peasant talking; he believed that the troops from outside provinces would be expelled before long. He also said that a certain disgruntled army man had already come back to Szechwan; I had to cut short his pleasure by giving him the true picture.

"It can't be successful," I said.

"If all the local armies join together, they can certainly drive them out. Outside armies have never been able to remain stationed for very long in Szechwan."

"Now things have changed. Now that they're in, they won't go away."

What else could I do except try to explain in over-simple terms like this? Could I tell him that the province where we live has now had the honour and glory of becoming "the foundation of our national renaissance"? Could I explain clearly that narrow provincial thinking had to be replaced by national thinking, and that we ought not to discriminate against troops from outside provinces? The race, the nation—these terms have no meaning for country people. They have no way of imagining how much bigger Szechwan is than Wanhsien, and how much bigger again China is than Szechwan, and they have even less chance of understanding their relationship to each other; people from other provinces and people from other lands are to them simply people from far away.

I cannot help wondering about the basic reason for their dislike of outside authority. Perhaps it was the large numbers of new programmes. Whenever government officials undertake any kind of new programme, they never require the people to understand it, and it is still compulsory even though no explanations have been made to the people. Therefore, even plans for their own benefit are still opposed and misunderstood. For example, the land surveys were regarded as being for the purpose of confiscating inheritances, and the population census was regarded as a device for conscripting young men into the army.

Again, the recently-enacted *pao-chia* training has not been welcomed by the peasants. I have heard that in the beginning, they all had to go and perform exercises every morning; later, because it was affecting their farm work, it was changed to one day a week, but for the greater part of that day. If they cannot manage to be well-fed and warmly-clothed after toiling all year round, how can they raise an interest in military know-how? This kind of training, with its "Attention!" and "Stand at ease!" cannot produce an extra bushel of rice from their fields, it is only a waste of their time.

The life of the peasants is harsh.

In this district, the conditions are not the same as in the north, for very few peasants here own their land. The majority of those who make their living from the land are tenant-farmers. When they want to work the land of a landowner, a contract is drawn up as surety, and a certain amount of cash is given as a deposit. They then take their families to live in a cottage attached to that piece of land. If it is a large piece of land, the peasant himself will hire labourers, but if it is only a few *mou*, then he relies on the labour of his own family: rising at dawn, going to bed at sunset, ploughing in the spring and weeding in the summer, until harvest-time, when he hands over to the landowner the amount of grain specified in the contract. From the remainder, he must feed and clothe his family. They say that formerly it was the custom for the landlord and tenant to divide the produce of the land evenly, but now in good years, at the most the tenant keeps only one-third. In bad years, he would ask the landlord to make an inspection and reduce the rent according to the severity of the troubles.

The life of the bigger tenant-farmers may be fairly prosperous. Those who till only a few *mou* are thankful that the land can produce different kinds of crops, for to fill their bellies they must often squeeze various green vegetables, sweet potatoes and beans in between the rice.

Both the high land and the valleys in this mountainous area are irrigated, and the main crop is rice. The fields on the more level ground are comparatively fertile, but those on the mountain slopes are both stony and terribly dry: even a few days without rain in June and July makes the farmers wrinkle their brows and sigh. The hardworking peasants toil, live and breed like ants whether their land is rich or stony. The son of a peasant will always be a peasant, unless he leaves the land and fortune favours him.

The landowners' main task is simply collecting rents and paying land-tax. After "rendering unto Caesar the things that are Caesar's", the landowners live off what is left. The whole purpose of their lives lies in amassing money and adding to their lands, to make an inheritance for their sons and grandsons.

Big landlords are very rare in this district. If families with middle-sized properties have many children, the land will be divided and eventually they will sink to being as poor as the peasants. Those who grow up in leisurely and comfortable surroundings, cannot, for the most part, work as hard as the peasants, and in the end they are forced to sell their inheritances.

Peasants and men of the landowning class can be distinguished by their physical appearance; the landowners are either thin and weak like consumptives or white and obese like prisoners who have been confined for many years, while peasants in the prime of their lives are very strong. In the fields they look like statues from the hand of a master. But those arms, straight as an arrow, will slacken and wither from the miserliness of the earth, and those bronzed shoulders will become bowed with the too-heavy burdens of time and misfortune; in the end, those honest, strong heads will be pillowed in eternal rest, peace and dark, as they sleep in their graves.

One afternoon, when the blazing summer sun was already sinking towards the west, my young brothers and sisters and I set off from our old house to visit our "fortress", one *li* away, that fortress perched high in the mountains, which imprisoned us as children. The fiery heat settled over the road; there was not a breath of wind. We walked up to a stone bridge beside an old temple, but even the shade of the bamboos and the still green waters offered us no relief. In the fields sited on level ground, thanks to the thick mud or the stored-up water in the dikes, the tall rice stalks still stood up straight with full ears, awaiting the golden ripening. But the rice stalks on the sloping fields higher up were already bowed down, and the grain, not yet ripe, was white and useless. Some ears of grain were so dry that it seemed as if they had been burnt.

There had been no rain for a long time. This year had seen yet another drought in the mountain country. As long as farming continues with old-fashioned agricultural methods, there is no way of avoiding natural calamities. In this district, people believe at one and the same time in two superstitions about drought-breaking: on the one hand, the slaughter of cattle is forbidden at the markets, with the idea that refraining from killing animals will move or please Heaven; on the other hand, they hold processions to drive away the drought demon. It is widely believed that there is a drought demon, covered all over with white fur, who inhabits mountain forests and can stop the rain falling. Those who can read say that he is mentioned in books, and peasants pass around stories that someone saw him in the branches of a tree; no-one doubts his existence. So they all form into bands, equipped with home-made bird guns, to drive away this product of their imagination and exhaust their strength. But still there is no rain.

The dikes have all dried up; in the creeks the dry white pebbles lie exposed.

When we had almost arrived at the foot of the fortress, we saw that some peasant men and women were in the fields reaping the early rice. The grain in the ears had mostly turned white; with their backs bent in silence, and streaming with sweat, they gathered, with their hands and their sickles, these crops which they had nourished with hard work, though they had been cheated of the proper harvest. We exchanged a few simple words with them. While silently climbing this hill, I vividly remembered the curse on Adam in *Genesis*, when Jehovah drove him from the Garden of Eden:

> In sorrow shalt thou eat of it all the days of thy life; thorns also and this-
> tles shall it bring forth to thee; and thou shalt eat the herb of the field; in

the sweat of thy face shalt thou eat bread, till thou return unto the ground; for out of it wast thou taken:

These sentences simply and powerfully describe man's life. But we should cast aside the curse, cast aside this accursed man-made Jehovah, cast aside all religions which teach us to swallow bitterness, suffer all our lives, and go to our deaths without a single murmur. If men desire a paradise on earth, they must build it with their own hands. If men have already lost paradise, they have destroyed it with their own hands.

However, I still have doubts: do I want to enter a paradise built on corpses? Can paradise be built by bloody hands? Can hands which are not bloody build anything at all?

Dusk has come; it seems the whole world lies silent.

25 November
(*Visit Home*, pp. 73-90.)

Standing outside the gates of our family house, you can see a walled fortress made of stone jutting out from among the trees. In fact it is perched on top of a small hill, or perhaps I should say, a high cliff, but from a distance it looks as if the misty green of the dense trees lifts it high into the sky.

Like a square grey tower rising straight up into the sky. But that is only the side view. In fact it is tall and narrow. At its foot, several hundred paces away, a stone-paved road down the cliff slope leads to the district town. Before, many people used to take this road, and as they lifted their gaze to the fortress, they liked comparing it with a steamship; but this fortress was taller and larger than the steamers navigating in Szechwan waters.

Inside there was room for six households.

It was built by my grandfather and five of his close friends. Twenty years ago, our district was plagued with bandits, and to avoid danger people fled to caves or stockades. By caves I mean the natural cavities halfway up the face of a cliff, with a containing wall added for protection; although they had this natural barrier they had to beware of a protracted siege, since they were completely cut off from food and water supplies. And if a cruel enemy tried to smoke them out like rats, they were in a hopeless position. The stockades, whether large or small, were really miniature towns. Several dozen households might live in the large ones, but not only must it have been difficult to have been squeezed up together, there was also the chance that when bandits attacked there might be traitors inside to help them. So that we six families built a small fortress like this.

This fortress was really very confined, with only four rooms to each house. Behind was the cliff face, and in front was the wall. The only road inside the fortress was a small passage between the wall and the houses.

I was shut up here for five or six years altogether.

The cold stones; the small windows; the long, lonely years.

But how vividly do I still remember those years, those petty incidents, not worth recounting, the wall I ran along countless times, the pond, and the fortress gate, reinforced with iron and hides. I can still recite by heart the first three lines of the inscription carved on the stone wall inside the gate, with not a word out of place:

Amid the marshes and hills, only this mountain is perilous; should you go from the mountain foot to its very peak, and lean over to look down, the distant valley below plunges thousands of feet, to unfathomable depths ...

Below, after the words "Composed and written by" is inscribed the name of one of my uncles (my father's younger brother). The last line records the date: such-and-such a day and month in the sixth year of the Republic [1917]. This uncle was regarded in our family as an excellent writer, and was well-known for his mastery of the principles of composition. Formerly, whenever grandfather mentioned his name, he would sigh over the abolition of the examination system. But my mother's brothers, who shared a taste for Taoist philosophy and literary criticism, took great pleasure in discussing him in front of me, ridiculing him, pointing out his mistakes, and turning the whole thing into a joke. At this point I should explain that the rear of the fortress, although on the top of a cliff, was only forty or fifty feet high, while the steps down to the gate had only an incline of ten degrees: talk of "a distant valley plunging to thousands of feet" was really a little exaggerated.

Memory is a strange thing. It is like a loosely-woven net, sometimes it only catches a few drops of water. I cannot now remember what season it was when we moved into this newly-completed fortress, nor what impression it had on me; my earliest memory of the fortress is the noise of the stonemason's chisel, the shouting of the workmen, and the tall building-frame constructed out of timber.

(*Visit Home*, pp. 91-94).

The Laiyang poems

Between November 1936 and June 1937, after an absence from poetry of more than a year, Ho suddenly produced a number of bitter and violent poems. Five of these form the third and final section of *The Prophecy*, and mark the end of his early work.

Funerals *(Sung-tsang)*

The white waxen candle burning in the silence
Is a sigh pressed from my bosom.
This is the age of funerals.

I have heard the splenetic Lord Byron
Reciting in an icy voice: "Gold.
Icy gold. But it may be changed for happiness."

I have seen Nerval leading on a blue silk sash
A lobster, holding the secrets of the sea, through the streets.
And with the belt from a woman's skirt
Hang himself outside the door of a doss house.
The last of the peasant poets just now in the hotel
Is slashing the blue veins in his neck.

Never again shall I sing of love
As the summer cricket sings of the sun.

Adjectives and metaphors and·artificial paper flowers
Blaze up just once in the fireplace.
Caterpillars which silently nibble the pages of books
Are busily making their cocoons.
This is winter.

Among the long, long file of mourners
I bury myself
As if scattering the mythical dragon's teeth
Waiting for them to grow into a troop of warriors
And engage in mutual slaughter
Till finally only the strongest remain.

8 November 1936 (*Prophecy*, pp. 77–79.)

Mr Yü Yu-lieh *(Yü Yu-lieh hsien-sheng)*

Mr Yü Yu-lieh is a strange person.
One afternoon I met him alone in a field,
His hat off, bowing to a clump of tulips.
The sunlight was shining on the yellow, white and red flowers.
"Plants," he said, "have a beautiful life.
These small flowers use scent and colour
To attract bees and butterflies to propagate their species,
And the lofty willow by the riverbank perpetuates its kind
Again through wind, through birds, through water.
A plant's reproduction is its preparation for death,
There is no birth control, there are no obstetric wards."
Slowly he walked over to a pot of sensitive plant,
His finger tips brushed its feathery leaves.
Those green eyes opened and closed again,
Its whole stem like a weary head drooping in sleep.
Mr Yü Yu-lieh is a strange person.

10 November (*Prophecy*, pp. 80–81.)

Sound *(Sheng-yin)*

Fish have no sound. Crickets sing long with their wings.
After our ancestors learnt to walk upright
They responded to happiness with shouts and songs,
Venting that joy or sorrow which chokes the throat,
In the same way red flames warmed them,
As they feasted at night in chilly woods,
Their hands dyed with the blood of wild beasts
Or tightly grasping their stone axes and swords.
But who created the ingenious bow and arrow,
Shot a reindeer
Then turned round and shot his brother through the forehead?

Now there are great cannons, ten storeys high,
Threatening the peace of the sky,
Their creaking iron wings scatter seeds of fire
Burning the skeleton of a whole city: steel and cement.
In the face of man-made death, alas,
Mankind loses its voice
Like fish
In a black net.
While the long list of casualties keeps on growing
Those to die later still scavenge silently in their panic for food
A slice of potato, an egg.

And silently those insane gamblers
Take, with their plump white fingers,
Man's fate and in a single throw
Slap it down — all or nothing!

(*Prophecy*, pp. 82–84.)

Let's get drunk *(Tsui pa)*

To those who are gently singing

Let's get drunk. Let's get drunk.
The true drunkard is blessed,
Heaven belongs to him.

If wine and books
And honey-dripping lips,
Cannot conceal human grief,
If I come from dead-drunk to half-sober
And then completely sober,
Do I still tilt my cap,
Half-close my eyes,
And play a life-long role of slight intoxication?

The fly, trembling in the cold wind,
Flutters its wings against the window-paper,
Dreaming of dead bodies,
Dreaming of water-melon rinds in mid-summer
Dreaming of a dreamless emptiness.

In the ridicule of my last words,
I hear my own shame:
"You too buzz buzz buzz
Like a fly!"

If I were a fly,
I would await the sound of a fly-swatter
Smashing down on my head.

(*Prophecy*, pp. 85–87.)

Clouds *(Yün)*

___

"I love those clouds, those drifting clouds . . ."
I am the stranger in Baudelaire's prose poem,
Mournfully craning his neck
To look at the sky.

I went to the countryside.
The peasants were too honest and lost their land.
Their households shrank to a bundle of tools.
By day they seek casual work in the fields,
At night they sleep on dry stone bridges.

I went to a town by the sea.
In the wintry tarred streets,
Row upon row of summer villas stand
Like modern prostitutes in the streets,
Waiting for the happy laughter of summer time,
And for the lewdness, the shamelessness of big-bellied merchants.

In the future I'll insist on expressing my opinions:

I want a thatched roof,
I do not love clouds, I do not love the moon,
I do not even love the many stars. ·

(Prophecy, pp. 88–90.)

Prose from *Sparks*

The essays or reports in *Sparks* are divided into three groups: (i) satirical essays (*tsa-wen*), written in Chengtu between March and June, 1938, three of which are translated here; (ii) reports (*pao-kao*), written from notes made between October 1938 and September 1939 on Ho Ch'i-fang's journey to Yenan and his experiences as a front-line reporter in Shansi and Hopei, three of which are translated here in full together with two of a series of five letters; (iii) essays written in Yenan after his decision to stay and work there. Of these only the autobiographical "An Ordinary Story" has been translated here.

Sparks was first published in 1945, but was subsequently revised several times before and after 1949, the date of the edition I am using here.

On work (*Lun kung-tso*)

Last year, I taught at a district normal school. Once the school received orders from above to organize a wartime reserve service brigade. That would be good, I thought, everyone could do a little work outside the classroom, and didn't both teachers and students feel it rather boring to spend their whole life inside the classroom? I suggested that the work should be organized as far as possible by the students themselves, and that we teachers should limit ourselves to being observers or advisors. We should find one or two students at the very least to share part of the responsibility for each group within the brigade, in the capacity of secretary for instance. It is my general belief that when students take the responsibility to carry out voluntary work, they do it very well. Besides, the students constitute the main body in any school. But it was like talking in a vacuum; no-one paid any attention to me, no-one supported me, no-one even explained why my suggestion would not work.

However, this service brigade eventually came into being: the headmaster was the brigade leader and certain teachers were the leaders of the various groups; the remaining teachers were group members. The students were also group members, each being selected and put into a group. And their work? Not so fast—they still needed training, four weeks of training.

And who carried out the training? The teachers as usual, but they only put in a few hours after classes. Needless to say, it was the students as usual who were given training. Presumably people believed that being a teacher of Chinese necessarily implied that you were literate, and that being literate implied that you could write propaganda—anyway, I was sent to join the propaganda group, and was instructed to train the other members of the group as well. I attended only one hour of these strange training sessions and thereafter failed to carry out my orders. The "training" I gave began like this:

Today I thought that I would say a few informal words to you. According to school regulations, this is called training; however, in reality, it is only an informal talk. Because if it comes to training, I am afraid that it is you who should be training me. Because I have almost never carried out any propaganda work before. However, the school was ordered to form wartime service brigades in the interior*; we must obey the order to provide training, you must obey the order to carry out propaganda. In our country, work carried out under orders is generally poorly done. Our enemy has held us up to ridicule as a "literary country". Now that I have returned to Szechwan, it has occurred to me that the enemy's sarcastic remark was not severe enough; it should have been a "statutory country". All we see are statutes here and statutes there; other forms of writing have almost disappeared. Nevertheless, I still hope that you will take this opportunity to carry out in all seriousness some piece of work, not thinking of it as an "order" but as a voluntary undertaking. Also, I hope that by the end of the four weeks, you will have trained yourselves through practical experience. That would be a useful kind of training. That would be a genuine kind of training ...

The four weeks passed very quickly. What sort of training the others had, I do not know. I only know that when the four weeks of training were over, everything was over. That is, no further work was undertaken at all. This was something I had not expected.

Orders from above, to do this and to do that, came endlessly; some wanted the school to perform some task and report back, others only required a public announcement. Once we received an order for the teachers to go out and do three days propaganda on "conscription for the protection of the country". The school authorities decided that this should be reduced to a day and a half's work, to be carried out on a Sunday morning. On this occasion I did not go. I thought I too could make a reduction and not do anything at all. In the first place, I felt that I just could not go and say to the peasants in the market-places, "Go and be soldiers, go and die, let us enjoy reserved occupations as teachers in the interior." Secondly, I doubted that propaganda which was delivered lecture-style, from benches in the tea-houses or even from tables which were higher than benches, could achieve anything at all.

The whole situation regarding work in the interior left me feeling very dissatisfied.

For myself, I felt that the word which best described my state of mind at that time was simply this, dissatisfied, but others jokingly called me a pessimist. What they seemed to be implying was this: "You are dissatisfied with this, dissatisfied with that, if that's not being a pessimist, what is?" Their attitude more correctly identified was this: the situation of the country at present is not very good, but it will certainly get better; at the front we will of course suffer defeat,

* in the unoccupied areas of China, such as Szechwan.

but victory will come; in the interior at present there are of course many shortcomings, but we can't do our best because we are limited by circumstances. I was not very pessimistic about the future of our country and the War of Resistance, but unlike the others, I believed that we would have to suffer great, and probably prolonged hardship before we achieved the progress we wanted; it would not be as simple as saying a few comforting phrases. At the same time, the hardship should be borne just as much by intellectuals like ourselves as by our brave soldiers. We should strive to the utmost to perform work which is directly or indirectly of use to the War of Resistance, no matter whether at the front or in the interior. But it is not good enough to be dissatisfied with this and that and yet still not carry out any work; similarly, it is not good enough just to say "the final victory will be ours" while sitting back and refusing to extend one's clean white hand to do this sort of work.

I was depressed. I was dissatisfied with myself. It seemed I belonged to the first category of people who are not good enough. But the depression and the dissatisfaction, whether directed at circumstances or at myself, were both good. A further step forward should have been to do some serious work.

At that time, there was a continuous stream of news from the front lines: Taiyuan had fallen, then Shanghai and Nanking as well. Then the people who had held me up to ridicule as a "pessimist" became pessimists themselves, and their faith in the War of Resistance began to waver. Then it was my turn to speak. I said, "When you become pessimists, then I become an optimist." This was not just a joke; what I meant was that when everybody realised that it was not good enough to sit by and wait for the final victory, then perhaps everybody could look one step further and carry out some work useful to the War of Resistance.

However, I still kept hearing this complaint: we are limited by circumstances.

The objective limitations of circumstances cannot be wiped out. Yet there are many kinds of work and many ways of working; this reason alone is not sufficient excuse for laziness, false security or oriental-style individualism, because a tree which has been forced to bow down can still grow. I often think of what a friend told me just after I arrived in Chengtu: "Work is not a matter of locality." This was the title of a forthcoming article. In principle I agree with this. However, he was not really pointing to those who were able to work but did not do so; he wanted to discuss the young people going to north Shensi* over the last six months. He also added that he knew rejected lovers were going to north Shensi. Here I must put forward an objection. According to my information (my information is, of course, limited), the majority of people going to north Shensi want to be trained; they realise that ordinary schools will not assume the responsibility of training them, and that ordinary training is not suitable for their immediate needs, so they resolutely set out to attend school somewhere else; there is nothing wrong with that. Whether they went because they had failed in their professions, or at school, or in love, or whether they had failed in anything at all, does not need going into. Take the rejected lover, for instance, surely he shows more strength of character in going to north Shensi after being unsuccessful in love than if he were to kill himself, ruin himself, or play the fool?

At the same time, we who regard ourselves as not needing or not wanting training of any kind should ask ourselves this: what really have we done, what are we doing now, and what are we planning to do?

Or let us narrow the field of reference a little, to people who ordinarily devote themselves to literary work. The first question which faces us is whether or not we should abandon literary work for the present. Secondly, if we do not, what should be our attitude to it?

In my opinion, if we have the opportunity to do something more immediate, more effective, and more useful to the War of Resistance, it should not be difficult to give up literary work. We are not so crazy as to believe that the great literary masterpiece of our nation's future must come from our hands. On the contrary, we believe that a work of literature which is separated from life, from the age or from the masses who are suffering, struggling and dying for the freedom of our race, cannot be a masterpiece, no matter what its form. We are not so hopelessly insane as to hold the views of defeatist bureaucrats, such as, for instance, a statement made to students by a certain professor at Wuhan University as reported in the small magazine *Cultural News*, "You must keep on studying with a quiet mind; after your country has been defeated you can all be Tagores." It is the other way around: a free and independent country is worth a thousand Tagores.

However, and this is again my individual opinion, there is no necessity to abandon literary work while we have no other weapon at hand to replace it. We should shoulder more earnestly and

* Yenan

enthusiastically the responsibility for wartime literature. Here there is the question of attitude. In wartime, literary workers have two quite different alternatives: concern themselves passionately with the war and with the masses who are doing the fighting, and exert themselves to the utmost for the sake of the age; or, keep their eyes closed, pretend to be deaf and continue to devote themselves to what they regard as imperishable artistic creations. As an example of the first , we may cite Romain Rolland. Although he cried, "Au-dessus de la mêldé!", although he took up residence in Switzerland, he still maintained a deep concern for the war and the people fighting in it. Not only was he constantly writing articles which courageously opposed the "unjust war", but he was also in constant touch with the men at the front and in the interior. Of course, the Great War in Europe and our present war of national liberation are two entirely different kinds of war, and our attitudes to these two wars are also entirely different. Nevertheless, our attitudes to war, our passionate concern for the war and the people fighting in it, our efforts to devote our individual strength to the age, are the same. We can also give an example of the second alternative. For this I am obliged to Mr Liang Tsung-tai, whose critical biography informed me that in the France of Romain Rolland there also existed the last of the symbolist poets, Paul Valéry. During the war in Europe, he was a government official writing his long poem of over five hundred lines, *La Jeune Parque*. After the publication of this long poem one critic wrote, "Our country has just given birth to a phenomenon even more important than the Great War: that is Paul Valéry's *La Jeune Parque*." It is not my intention here to attack Valéry. I only want to say that either that critic was as ignorant as an eighteen-year-old boy in his first year at senior middle school or else he was completely shameless. During the Great War in Europe, thirty million people died; not just five hundred but even fifty million lines of poetry cannot be measured against thirty million human lives. It is not good enough to produce brilliant lines.

But at that time I had only spent one year at senior middle school, and after little more than a month at university, I dropped out of school altogether. Mr Liang Tsung-tai's biography was the first step in my infatuation with the works of the French symbolists. At that time I was utterly ridiculous: I could not even read French and yet I was very much attracted to French literature.

When was that? The September 18 Incident [1931] had occured. Then Jehol was captured, and Yükuan. But I was still dreaming "beautiful, distant dreams", or to put it more clearly, I passed my days in confusion. Then in my second year at university, with the worsening situation in the north-east before the Tangku Truce [31 May 1933], General Ho Ying-ch'in was making ready to defend the city, and the schools ordered the students to leave; and even on the first evening that I left Peking, I could still write in a small inn the essay "Dusk" from *Painted Dreams*:

The sound of horses' hooves, lonely and melancholy, scatters on the pitch-black road like tiny white flower-buds ...

To mention these things today makes me feel very ashamed. But what else could I have done, when not one of my friends would criticize me properly, and everything I read was in this vein?

We are always under some kind of influence in our work, whether great or small. Therefore we must never fail to be on our guard.

Chengtu, 5 March 1938
(*Sparks*, pp. 1-10.)

On basic culture (*Lun pen-wei wen-hua*)

In the March 12 issue of the *New News* there was a report of the after-dinner speech of a certain gentleman at Sullivan's in Chungking.* Firstly he said that the shortcoming of traditional Chinese education was its loss of self-confidence; his concluding remarks were on the rebuilding of the original culture of China; in between, he talked of China as an agricultural society, where fathers, sons and brothers worked together, and where there was no class distinction, with the result that fathers were benevolent and sons were filial, brothers exchanged affection and respect, husbands led and wives followed; while Europe and America were industrial societies, which took the individual as the unit, so that the bonds between fathers and sons, brothers, husbands and wives, became distant and shallow, which marks the beginning of a cultural collapse, because no-one can rely on anyone else but oneself, and nothing is desired but money, with the result that individual freedom and a materialist view of history flourish.

This reminds me of the first night after I came to Chengtu, when I stayed with an old school-friend whom I had not seen for many years. We talked so late into the night, touching on basic culture among other things, that I had a cold for a week.

Basic culture, or original culture, although explained in various ways by its different adherents, generally refers to the culture developed over the last two thousand years in our country, under the influence of Confucian thought. I am not prepared to discuss non-original culture, particularly Western culture, because I am not too clear about it, having only read a little simplified world history and a few foreign novels. But I do have opinions on the subject of original culture. I am Chinese, I have personally experienced it, I have had its bounty fully bestowed on me.

At this point, I would like to say that for a long time I have felt that a very great defect of our culture is that it lacks the concept of "man". We have not had a real period in our cultural history corresponding to the European Renaissance; and "the individual" is also basically neglected in Confucian thought.

---

* Sullivan's was originally a famous European confectionary shop in Shanghai. After the fall of Shanghai, some Chinese businessmen set up a confectionary shop in Chungking under the same name. Attached to the shop was a small dining-room.

Our tragedy as a people is double: on the one hand, sincere intellectuals have already, like Romain Rolland, become deeply aware of the shortcomings of individualism and its weakness; on the other hand, Confucian thought, which inhumanly despises the individual, is still very strong. The Confucian concept of human relations is always expressed in terms of oppositions, noble to lowly, old to young, rich to poor. In court one is either ruler or minister, in the family one is either father or son, elder brother or younger brother, husband or wife. People are the same, but everywhere they are divided into superior and inferior. Human feeling is one thing, but everywhere it is divided into many different things. These divisions necessarily give rise to falsehood and tragedy, but these falsehoods and tragedies are simply ignored by reactionary Confucians, for the rulers of history have seen that these theories of separating men and dividing emotions are useful in training people to be submissive. Each successive dynasty since the T'ang has been worse than its predecessor, because the power of Confucian thought was strengthened by the contributions of the Sung *li-hsüeh* philosophers. The Yüan, Ming and Ch'ing dynasties are simply like a "dark age".

Today, don't we want the people in the occupied areas to arise and resist the rule of the enemy and the Chinese collaborators? Don't we bemoan the apathy of the people? We should put the blame on more than one thousand years of training the people into submission under a totalitarian system. People who have been trained into obedience in their families will still be obedient under enemy rule.

Therefore if we want to promote basic culture, or original cutlure, we should at least seek out its defects, and cut them off as we would gangrenous flesh.

How much, in fact, of the culture which exists in a real "agricultural society" is completely basic? Apart from things like ancestor worship, concubinage, parents beating their children and wanting them to grow up to be officials and make money, brothers quarrelling and going to law over inheritances, husbands treating their wives as slaves, and old women maltreating their daughters-in-law, which we can count as pure products of our original culture, most of the thinking of our so-called agricultural society is Taoist or Buddhist. Although Taoism is quite primitive, it could be counted as original culture if the Confucians did not object on the grounds of orthodoxy. But it is really impossible to introduce Buddhism as the glory of our race, unless we say generally that it is the original culture of the East.

But east or west, man is always man, and there should be a

"culture of mankind". That is, the cultures of each race should hold in common some basic spirit; if great differences still exist, we must be more progressive or else we shall surely slip backwards. Therefore I do not support the all-round promotion of original or basic culture.

27 March 1938
(*Sparks*, pp. 11-14.)

On saving the children (*Lun chiu-chiu hai-tzu*)

About twenty years ago, Mr Lu Hsün made this appeal: "Save the children ... "

But even today we still hear children crying, and adults swearing at them.

I do not know how others feel about it, but I believe that hitting children and abusing them is the wickedest kind of human behaviour, because it is clearly a case of bullying the young who are unable to fight back or even defend themselves. As for holding that one has the right to chastise them because they are one's own children, this is even more despicable, though it can be said that it is very old moral concept and is based on social custom.

Last winter, *New Youth* wanted me to write an article, but I was very hesitant; what could I write for a magazine which was read by children in upper primary and junior middle school? In the end, after some time I sent them "Private Tutors". At the time I thought that life in the old private or family schools would be curious enough to interest the children of today. Also, it might benefit them to learn about it, so that they could say to themselves, "Thank goodness our generation is much more fortunate than previous ones. Let us work hard." But it had not occurred to me then that although primary schools are now established everywhere and the majority of primary school teachers do not use the whip, children have still not escaped from beatings and abuse in their own familes. Having lived in schools for a long time, I had almost forgotten the treatment given to children at home.

When I returned to Szechwan I was often invited into true Chinese homes. Every time I sat down at table, the husband and wife would offer me dishes and press me to eat while at the same time abusing their children which made me so upset I began to suffer from indigestion.

The facts tell us that children are still objects for adults to vent their feelings on. In this society, adults for the most part live in misery and suffering. Even in a family not troubled by "economic crises", the adults may have a toothache or some such minor ailment, or may have lost money at mahjong, or the husband may have fallen victim to his superior's bad temper and the wife to her husband's, so they abuse the children. It is hardly necessary to say that both adults and children in poverty-stricken families lead "inhuman lives".

It has always filled me with a complex emotion, a combination of indignation and distress, to walk down a street or through a village, and see all around children wearing tattered clothes, with yellow, skinny, wasted bodies, growing up in poverty, sickness and neglect, and without any education at all. I have often wanted to cry:

"People, don't boast so brazenly about the size of our population. Rats are more prolific than people."

At the same time, I think that many people are like rats, digging their holes in the ground, or, to speak without metaphors, they establish a secure niche for themselves in society, then find a wife, have a few children, and that's all.

I find it strange that people can be so short-sighted; they can't see things even a short way ahead, and can't understand matters that are even slightly complicated; and also, that when they become adults themselves they are so forgetful and look down on or even ill-treat children.

Apart from the abuse they have always received at home, children do not necessarily receive a rational education at school. I am most familiar with slightly older children, we should perhaps call them adolescents or youth; let me explain what I mean with a few examples from Chinese Language and Literature, the subjects I have been teaching.

Last September, I went to a certain district normal school to teach classes in three different years, and was confronted right from the beginning with the problem of teaching materials. Textbooks were unobtainable because of the war, and we had to compile our own. Although I don't know much about science, I believe in science and the scientific method. I wanted to draw up a plan for compiling material. I believed this would be of some benefit to the students. Afterwards a student happened to say in conversation with me that he had already studied some pieces of classical prose five or six times; the selection chosen by the teacher in primary school had also been chosen by the teacher in the first year of junior middle school and then again with other teachers in the second and third year. There was almost nothing of the new literature in the school library and the books laid down for vacation reading were *Mencius* and *The Family Correspondence of Tseng Kuo-fan*.

Even when I came to Chengtu, I heard some strange things: the Chinese textbooks from primary school to university level were for the most part selections from *Excerpts from the Classics, Histories and Philosophers* and *A Treasury of Classical Prose*, and if you wanted to do well at senior middle school or university examinations, it was best to use the classical language; the primary school teachers of the future, students in the normal schools, were studying the ancient characters and writing classical prose ...

It was in this sort of atmosphere that the graduating class of the senior middle school in which I was teaching, demanded with great courage and on their own initiative the new literature, while at the same time the second year of the junior middle school almost failed to get even the texts prescribed by the school, because they said they already had copies of *Selected Classical Prose*. These *Selected Classical Prose* addicts would write in their compositions things like "Attack the islands of Japan and take alive the Meiji Emperor", or "After Italy united with Austria, the Powers began to organize the League of Nations". There was even one student, who worked very hard at classical Chinese and was fairly proficient, who wrote, "The Records of the Ancient Emperors of our country, our Classics, Histories and Philosphers, are the wellsprings of world literature, the basis of all progress in the West." But when it came to writing in the vernacular, it stuck in his throat like something indigestible. He was a frail, docile child, only fourteen or fifteen years old.

If we want children to grow up strong in mind and body, we must realise that this heavy emphasis on resurrecting the past is harmful. In Hunan, after the outbreak of war, the *National Weekly* reported that the evil influence of General Ho Chien's promotion of classical education had been completely exposed when some senior middle school students were tested, and revealed their total ignorance of current affairs; they confessed that they had not read a newspaper in more than a year. This deserves our attention.

The above is only a side issue in school education. At the present time, when the war of national liberation is proceeding with great vigour, the young people in the interior are even more depressed and troubled: they are longing to arm themselves at great speed in both spirit and knowledge, and at the same time exercise their strength directly by devoting themselves to work which would help the War of Resistance, but neither the education nor the training they receive can satisfy this longing.

This is the whole problem of wartime education, but it can be resolved. It is a fact that there do exist schools which are quite well-adapted to this period of resistance. Nevertheless it is equally true that some schools still prefer to resurrect the past and uphold the conventions; for instance, the people who run girls' schools still advocate the Three Obediences to father, husband and son and the Four Virtues in behaviour, speech, appearance and housework, and concentrate on training the students to bundle up quilts and to wax floors so that they might win a word of praise from observers and school inspectors.

Too much concentration on the past can numb the brains of children, while a preoccupation with the conventions, so that things should look good on the surface, although it can deceive the foolish, cannot hide its foxtail from people whose vision is clear. Thus on Children's Day this year, a primary school in Kwangan wanted the students to put on a performance of guerrilla warfare, which resulted in a girl's arm being shattered by a bomb. It is a terrible thing to shatter someone's arm with a bomb, and everyone was very quick to criticise the person responsible. Yet the brain is more important than an arm, and work which numbs people's brains is still going on, but no-one seems to take the slighest notice.

I must cry out over and over again: "Save the children!"

Although the sound I make is tiny, if it reaches the ears of a few people it may make them uncomfortable, because this sound of mine, like a mosquito, disturbs their complacent dreams of reviving the past, or their ambitious dreams of achieving individual prosperity or even the "winning hand" dreams of the mahjong table. Surely it will. A friend has written to me:

" ... When the staff of the provincial normal school saw the article you wrote in *Work**, they were very displeased, and denounced your errors to the students. But after you left, the students didn't want the teacher who replaced you, so they engaged another who though accepted was not very good either. Recently for some reason or another a student was given a box on the ears as part of his moral training; this provoked general opposition which was not resolved for four or five days. Several students from the girls' school ran away to north Shensi, and now whenever the girls go down the street, someone always goes along to watch them. A lot ran away from one school, and a few also from another middle school. Lately the headmasters have been blaming the students' disobedience on their military training, saying that they have been badly trained, and so as soon as there is any trouble they rush to the district office for instructions. One school asked a special officer to go and expel a dozen or more people, at first they wouldn't go, finally they were frightened off by the

---

* A magazine which Ho helped to publish in Chengtu.

troops. A while ago there was a headmasters' conference, where they decided they must supervise the students more strictly and not let them take part in so many group activities. This is what it's like ... "

I couldn't help doubting the truth of these things, because I only left there a little over two months ago, and I wouldn't have thought that so much trouble could have occurred. But the letter lay clearly before me. Reality is cruel.

Morning, 28 April
(*Sparks*, pp.15-21.)

Notes on the Szechwan-Shensi road (*Ch'uan-Shen lu-shang tsa-chi*)

A night at Tzut'ung

Tzut'ung. A small district town in northern Szechwan.

There are no newspapers. There is no middle school. The population of the whole district is seventeen hundred thousand, about eight thousand of whom are opium addicts. They say that every month the local government has to forward more than thirty thousand dollars from the open sale of opium and in lamp-tax from opium-dens.

Guests at the inn can freely buy opium paste for smoking.

One evening, I retired to sleep very early. After I had to gone bed, I heard people in the next room talking in a Shensi accent and smoking opium. As I listened, I heard a low female voice press them, "Have a smoke", or "Have one more".

From her disconnected words I guessed that she was probably an opium addict who had sunk into poverty and then became a prostitute. Doubtless she had now been summoned to accompany the opium.

The Shensi voices, which were partly unintelligible to me, were talking about the "Three Advantages Market"; this was a peculiar bazaar in the busiest street in Chengtu, Ch'unhsi Road, which had a theatre, a teashop, a barber and a public bathhouse . "Once I went there for a bath," one of them related in a loud voice, the kind which carries overtones of laughter and abuse. "I said, send in a masseur, and mother's*, in came a woman!" Another spoke of a masseur boy, also in a very indecent way. He said that the son of a rich man who went there to bathe once gave a certain masseur boy sixty dollars.

Later, it seemed that the woman who was preparing the opium wanted to go, and was haggling over payment in a low wheedling voice. "Give me another twenty cents." Her attempts to arouse sympathy seemed to achieve their object. Then the man who was paying said cheerfully, "Stay the night and I'll give you fifty cents." "No," the low voice answered. "Sixty cents?" "No." "Seventy cents?" "No." "Eighty cents?" "No." ... Jokingly, as if singing an extremely simple and also extremely vulgar song, he kept on teasing her, until

---

* A favourite Chinese swearword.

in her low yet clearly audible voice, she wound up her plea: "Give me two dollars."

The woman finally left. The two or three men in the room exchanged a few remarks in their Shensi accents and then fell silent. I heard the last two sentences quite clearly. "Really, it's sad and it's funny, too," one said. "She must be over thirty," said another. "Even for two dollars it used to be no."

The night was quiet with sorrow.

The following day, I tried to guess which were these Shensi men. There were quite a few Shensi people staying at the inn: some were on business, some were wearing splendid yellow army uniforms. They all had solemn adult faces. There was no way for me to tell.

Two interludes on the bank of the White Dragon River.

The White Dragon River was in flood.

The bus which had been carrying us and several dozen containers of petrol came to a stop on the bank of this tributary of the Chialing River, at a place called Kuochia Ferry. Because it had been raining for several days, the river waters had risen unexpectedly quickly, and were running very fast.

The highway should have crossed the river, but there was no bridge.

The gentlemen from the Szechwan Department of Highways are very clever, and use wooden boats as a substitute for bridges: the car or bus goes on the boat and can thus cross to and fro over the river. A boat can't go by itself: it needs artificial legs of wooden oars, a rudder, a pole and a boatman's arms. On the White Dragon River we must also add a towrope-puller. Because the current of the river is so swift, you need several towmen to drag the wooden boat upstream first with the towrope, and then paddle it obliquely across to the opposite bank.

Today, a boatman was swallowed up by the White Dragon River. When our bus arrived at Paolunyuan, we were confronted with this tragic news : today a man had been drowned. When we reached the river bank we found out that he was a towman.

We got out of the bus and stood on the bank looking. The river burst out in front of the mountain gorge to the left, and following the mountains, it suddenly made a ninety-degree turn and rushed straight towards another gorge. As it dashed against the hidden and exposed rocks along the river banks, it uttered a sombre roar.

Three cars loaded with antiques from the Palace Museum in Peking were parked on the opposite bank like three stupid crabs. At the part of the bank nearest to us a long, narrow sandbar lay passively upstream, stretching into the water.

Today, the unfortunate towman, in order that a car loaded with antiques should cross the river, had shouldered the towrope and gone out onto that sandbar, going further and further out, until he lost his footing and fell into the depths of the river. The river, which was flowing swiftly, carried him away, and he was not heard of again. They did not drag for his body.

He had elderly parents. He had a wife and a child. When the unhappy news reached his family, his father beat his head against a stone, and his wife ran crying towards the river, to throw herself in.

The other towmen related this to us, simply and haltingly; their hearts seemed to be filled with grief and anger. They must have been thinking of the tragic nature of their profession. Their monthly wage was from seven to nine dollars. The compensation for drowing was thirty dollars per man. Each was wearing a blue cotton shirt, and on both sides of their chest were six characters made of white cotton, three to each side: "Boatmen of the Chaohua Bus Station".

One small chap swore coarsely, saying that today they had been too busy to have their evening meal, and that when the dead man's mother had brought his lunch, he only had two mouthfuls before putting it down, and then went to tow the rope and die.

It was getting late. From the distant mountain gorges, the twilight slowly unfolded like a blue mist.

Our bus was still parked by the river bank. Across the broad expanse of the river, we gazed at one of the cars laden with antiques crawling like a stupid crab onto the boat, while the towmen bent their backs, shouldered the towrope and walked out onto the sandbar; then the wooden boat finally entered the swift current of the treacherous broad river and crossed obliquely over to the ferry station on this side.

I was thinking of a news item in an old copy of the Chengtu *New News*. It was about the plans for the distribution of the English Boxer Indemnity Fund for the current year. In it was an item that more than six hundred thousand dollars had been allocated for transporting the Palace Museum antiques.

Our bus decided to return to Paolunyuan for the night. Paolunyuan was ten *li* from Kuochia Ferry; on the Shunpao map it is marked as Paoningyuan. In front of the bus station hung the sign: "Szechwan Department of Highways, Chaohua Bus Station". But the district town of Chaohua was still many *li* distant.

The White Dragon River was flowing sombrely.

While I was sitting by the lamp jotting down the day's events, old Yang called us to go and watch a "rapping god".

The entrance to a house not far away was already packed with people. We looked inside over their shoulders. In the room were two square tables; the one further inside was set up with a statue of a god in a sitting position, with its big fat arms and legs outstretched like a big fat man; on the outer table sticks of incense and candles were burning. To the right of the tables a man was celebrating a Buddhist mass. He was wearing blue cotton clothes, and was dressed just like an ordinary peasant except that on his head he had tied together with a red cloth several trembling pieces of white paper, like a wreath. With his head lowered and his back arched, he was shaking, uncontrollably, frighteningly. He went on shaking for a considerable length of time, and then struck the table with his fist, shaking the "Buddha circle". Then grasping the right foot of the god, he rubbed it with his face while continuing to shake, after which he jumped a few times and began to sing in a strange, utterly incomprehensible voice. At the side, another person was interpreting, saying that he was giving the reason for the sick person's illness.

After we returned to the inn, a waiter told us that a child in the family had become ill, so they had asked the "rapping god" to come and cure him. "The 'rapping god' can prescribe medicine", he said. "Once, the medium who asks the 'rapping god' questions was holding the god's foot and prescribing medicine, when a soldier came in to watch. The soldier suddenly gave him a box on the ear and shouted, 'Let's see if it still moves when you're not holding it!' Now really, how could it move by itself?" He said that this person relied entirely on the "rapping god" to eat. For every invocation he earned twenty or thirty cents. The "rapping god" is made of wood, with movable hands and feet.

It made me think of Ivanov's "When I was a Fakir". The hero in this story was performing in public for the first time as a sword-swallower; when the sword passed through his throat the pain was intense, but when the ringmaster said to him, "Why aren't you smiling at the audience?" he bore the pain and smiled.

I set foot on Shensi soil for the first time.

My country which embraces a vast area, my country which although the enemy has penetrated into your bosom still embraces a vast area, today for the first time I set foot on the soil of your province called Shensi.

Yet after I took my first step on Shensi soil, something happened that made me feel ashamed.

Ningchiao Bus Station. We got out of the bus. I opened my hand luggage to let the military police at the inspection post examine it. A military policeman wearing a steel helmet first took out a book from my case. It was a very thin book, costing only ten cents, *On Concepts*. A philosophy book. Very intently he leafed through it, then rolling it up he kept it in his left hand and would not give it back to me. With his right hand he picked up the other book which lay upside down in my case. He turned it over to look. As if disappointed he quickly returned it to its original place. It was the second volume of *Journey to the West*, which Pien Chih-lin had bought at Kuangyuan greatly reduced. There were only these two books in my hand luggage. Finally, when the inspection was over, he said with contempt, "I'll take that book." The miserably thin book *On Concepts* stayed unmovingly rolled up in his left hand, and from his manner of speaking it seemed that he was borrowing it from me to read.

Next he examined someone else's luggage. "I make clocks and watches for a living," the man said. He did not even begin to look through it, but just asked him to shut his big leather suitcase.

We went to look for an inn. The road where the bus station was located, outside the town, was very dirty. The inn wasn't very clean either.

In the evening, two other military police from the inspection post came to check the inn. After looking at our passports and luggage, one particularly asked me whether I had any books. This made me regret that I hadn't earlier asked the military police, "Why are you taking it away?" Although I knew very well why that small book had been confiscated; it was because of a line of small red characters printed on the cover: Encyclopedia Publishers, U.S.S.R. His answer to my question would have been interesting, I thought.

Someone else later told me what the interesting answer was.

"These books are sold openly everywhere, why should you confiscate it?"

"If you can buy it openly I can confiscate it openly."

(*Sparks*, pp. 49-57.)

I sing of Yenan (*Wo ko-ch'ang Yen-an*)

The town gate of Yenan stands open all day long, and all day long young people from every direction enter through this gate, bearing their luggage and fiery hopes. To study. To sing. To spend their time being busy and joyful. Later, group by group, wearing their army uniforms and with burning enthusiasm, they pour out again in every direction.

In the mouths, ears, imaginations and memories of the young, Yenan is like the first note of a famous anthem, a ringing, moving melody.

What meaning does this simple name hold in its two short syllables?

It takes in three mountains: West Mountain, Cold Mountain, and Pagoda Mountain.

It takes in two rivers: the Yen River and South River.

It takes in between its three mountains and two rivers an ancient town and its people.

It takes in history and legend: a border town in the Sung dynasty, governed by Han Ch'i and Fan Chung-yen; before the Ming dynasty, it was fairly prosperous, but after the Muslim Rebellion it declined ... Should you visit the sixty-year old ancient on Cold Mountain, he can still pour out an uninterrupted torrent of words about events from the last century down to the present, even though he lies on a sickbed. But let me keep to the present.

Yenan takes in the Shensi-Kansu-Ninghsia Border Region Government, the United Popular Front of Anti-Japanese Resistance, the Communist Party and Comrade Mao Tse-tung.

It takes in several schools: the Anti-Japanese Resistance Military University, the North Shensi Public School, the Lu Hsün Academy of Arts ...

It takes in uninterrupted progress:

Two years ago, before the Red Army arrived, this was a desolate, poverty-stricken town, and yet the people were bowed down under heavy taxes; every month, every family had to pay out three or four dollars, sometimes even thirty or forty. Now trade flourishes, and there are more than thirty thousand capitalist businesses.

A year ago, when the Red Army became the Eighth Route Army, the population was only four or five thousand; there were only four or five restaurants, using plates carved out of wood and chopsticks fashioned out of bent branches; the shops had no signboards, and if you bought the wrong thing it was difficult to find the original shop to exchange it, because every place looked equally dirty, old and broken-down; there were no benches in the main assembly hall, and on the platform there were only one gas-lamp, a dozen or so wax candles for "foot-lights", simple dances and "living reports". Now, the population has increased to over ten thousand; the streets are filled with foodshops, and these are stocked with "honey mumbles" and "three-won't-sticks"*, specialities of Yenan. All the shops have put up signboards with white characters on a blue ground and light blue shopfronts, as if changing into new, well-fitting clothes; at the main assembly hall they have put on three-act plays and shown silent movies, Chaplin and *Lenin in October*, and the audience sits down at the seat numbers shown on the door-tickets.

Two months ago, wide-eyed I entered this town on a truck ... even in these two short months there has been so much change. Instead of an earth road which became impassable after a fall of rain, a splendid paved road goes from the south gate right through the drum-tower in the centre of the town and stretches a little further on; soon it will pass through the north gate.

Like a living person, this living town is growing all the time, and all the time changing its face.

"What is there to write about in Yenan? Yenan has only got three hills ...", the great leader of our people, Comrade Mao Tse-tung, wearing a blue cotton uniform and sitting before a small white table in a cave, said to us with a humorous smile, when we told him that we wanted to write about Yenan. But he went on to add very seriously, very firmly, though still courteously, "There are a few things to write about."

A few things? From my understanding of two months, and in my honest opinion, the right way to describe it would be "very, very many". I am full of impressions. I am full of emotions. But what I want to celebrate first is the atmosphere in Yenan.

An atmosphere of freedom. An atmosphere of tolerance. An atmosphere of joy.

As soon as I entered this town, I sniffed, inhaled and drank in this atmosphere to my heart's content. There are no such things as school drop-outs here, or people out of work. There are no beggars. There

---

* A kind of pancake which "won't stick" to the pan, plate or chopsticks.

are no prostitutes. As for those deeply prejudiced people on the out-side who specialise in manufacturing rumours and slander, popular usage here has an extremely generous designation for them: "reactionary elements".

Do you think it is too tolerant?

"Yes, it's too tolerant," a woman writer who spent ten years in Paris says in a loud voice. Because she is very concerned about Yenan. Because she has heard that a Japanese newspaper has already published a photograph of the base hospital here. Because she believes that there are some very suspicious reporters here who should have restrictions placed on them. Because they have cameras worth over a thousand dollars which can take night photographs.

But it does not represent irreparable damage to Yenan that the enemy directly or indirectly has purchased photographs. The enemy's Special Service has covered the whole of north China, the enemy has bought masses of topographical surveys of north China, but it cannot buy the greater masses of people in north China; after the occupation of a large number of towns in north China, we are still continuing to establish a large number of guerrilla bases.

Do you still believe that we should limit the number of people coming from the outside?

"No, we do not want to make any restrictions," one comrade doing high-level work said at a meeting. "We believe that the intelligentsia who come to Yenan are the finest flower of our race. If ten thousand scientists and engineers come to Yenan, we will dig five thousand caves for them to live in." He spoke of how, after all the places in the Resistance University had been filled, all the electricity poles from here to Sian were stuck with signs saying, "No more student admissions at Resistance University", but, nevertheless, many young people made the journey on foot; and when they came they were given the opportunity to study or work, and not a single one was turned away. He spoke of how in getting to know a person you cannot only look at his faults, and besides, his faults can indicate his strong points: a proud man has self-confidence, for instance, and can carry out work which has already been planned in advance, while timid men are cautious and can do the planning; happy-go-lucky types can be socially very active; and people generally regarded as having mixed backgrounds are for the most part rich in experience, and knowing as many theories as they do, will undoubtedly be able to get at the truth and acknowledge it.

And yet, surely this atmosphere of freedom and tolerance can't be reflected in the discipline of work or the seriousness of life?

"Yes, the border regions talk about both democracy and centralisation," an observer from a friendly area asked the head of our North Shensi Public School, Comrade Ch'eng Fang-wu, "but why do our schools fall into confusion and find themselves unable to centralise as soon as they start to practise democracy?"

"I know the border regions develop work efficiency through shock brigades and competition," another observer, a high-ranking political worker in a friendly army also asked, "but why is it that when we adopt these methods in our army they don't work, and besides, everyone believes that airplanes and tanks are just toys that only children would be afraid of?"

"Probably so, probably so," answered Comrade Ch'eng Fang-wu, who wore a cotton uniform and hemp sandals and sat upright in front of a table, "because the Communist Party operates in the border regions. When there is a call, party members immediately set to work, without question."

To prove the correctness of this explanation, one comrade told me the following anecdote:

It was autumn. The weather was already getting cold, and they were in the process of building a motor road which had to cross a small river. The workers stood on the river bank, looking at the clear, cold water. There was some hesitation, and then the political worker jumped in barefoot, and waded along saying, "It's not cold." Then everyone jumped in. Then everyone worked in water up to their knees. When they emerged, the skin on some peoples' feet had broken open and was oozing blood.

This was a moving example. But, speaking generally, when it comes to difficulties in work, it is not necessarily the communist who jumps in first with everyone else behind. Many non-communists are working just as hard.

And shortcomings, what about shortcomings? Surely there must be some shortcomings?

"I still haven't discovered any shortcomings. I've only been here two days. Breathing in the air here I can only feel happy. It seems as if I have always been dreaming of a good society, a good land, and now it's as if I am living in that dream."

Two months ago, when I finished my humble talk at a discussion meeting of the Lu Hsün Academy of Arts with these words, one comrade from the literature department who had studied for two years in the Navy stood up:

"Our life is not completely without its troubles. We have no tables to write on, only a wooden board placed across our knees. In rainy weather, the road downhill from the caves is extremely slippery, and you keep falling over, and getting covered in mud. On winter nights the pen-nibs freeze, you have to put them in your mouth and blow on them to write ..."

Two months later, as I sing so simply and plainly of Yenan, I acknowledge that our life is not entirely without troubles. But compared with last year our material life in general has progressed tremendously, and the whole day we work hard and joyfully; the few, minor difficulties in our material life are like a handful of dried peas which have been placed under three eiderdown mattresses; I suspect that only the princess in the fairy tale would toss and turn and find it uncomfortable.

Therefore, this cannot be counted as a shortcoming in Yenan. This can't satisfy in the least the deeply prejudiced "reactionary elements" who specialise in manufacturing rumours and slanders. Because they don't believe their eyes, they don't believe their intelligence, they only believe their own weird fantasies. While the Eighth Route Army was establishing, consolidating and developing large numbers of guerrilla bases in north China and while the soldiers of the Eighth Route Army were shedding blood in the front lines, these people in the rear were saying to each other sneeringly, "The Eighth Route Army uses hit-and-run tactics, only it runs but it doesn't hit." They are extremely sharp-witted, as soon as they hear the term "Eighth Route Army" by immediate association they think of "Communists" and then by further association they think of their bank accounts.

And mistakes, what about mistakes? Surely someone must have made a mistake?

"Mistakes can't persist for long in Yenan," a poet comrade told me. "This spring, a troop from Resistance University were having a competition to keep the living quarters in order. Because the bed quilts were so thick, it wasn't easy to fold them so that they looked properly squared off. Someone discovered a way in which he could chew the fold into a straight line with his teeth. And others copied him. This made me lose my temper and I wrote a letter to Chairman Mao, saying that if Yenan produced Stakhanovites who chewed bed quilts with their teeth, we would not only be the laughing-stock of China but of the whole world. This mistake was very quickly corrected."

Therefore I say that this name Yenan takes in uninterrupted progress.

Therefore all day long we work, we smile and we sing.

Therefore a young electrical engineer said in a dissatisfied way, "These people waste too much time singing, but it isn't time for singing now!" A year ago, when I was on the outside, I came across this honest man in a small book about Yenan. I smiled, liking him for it. At the same time, I thought the people in Yenan probably like singing so much because their lives are so harsh. But I was mistaken. On the contrary it is because life is so joyful.

Yenan, at night, 16 November 1938
(*Sparks*, pp. 58-66.)

A Taiyuan primary school boy (*I-ko T'ai-yüan hsiao-hsüeh-sheng*)

Name, Age, Origin

Han T'ien-wei, he wrote down his name as Han T'ien-wei.

True age: thirteen years. But he was as tall as a boy of fourteen or fifteen.

He can be counted as being from Taiyuan (though he said he was actually from Wenshui, a nearby district), since his family had lived seven or eight years in this Shansi capital city which is always enveloped in the wind and dust of the great northern plain. His father still works as a doctor at an English missionary hospital there, and his whole family is still living in the hospital staff quarters.

His elder brother had been an assistant at F'ingyao Station and Hsinkou Station and the stationmaster at Yungk'ang on the Tat'ung-P'uchou line, and now, since Shansi's special narrow-gauge railway was seized by the enemy, he has become an unemployed young man leading a leisurely life at home. His sister-in-law, who had received a middle-school education, became his mother's assistant with the washing and cooking. His two elder sisters were studying in the missionary school attached to the hospital, and the whole family was dependent on his father's monthly income of sixty dollars. They lived the anxious and troubled life of people who have lost their motherland. As a rule no-one mentioned the Japanese, as if " that business" had never happened, and were happy to survive from one day to the next. But when a few of his brother's friends from the Eighth Route Army paid them a visit, the atmosphere in the home vibrated, smiled, reverberated, like a pond over which a gust of wind has passed. These adventurous friends were really like a wind which leaves no footprints, they came suddenly and suddenly they went again. They could tell it was the Eighth Route Army but outsiders couldn't. After their visit, the family would talk of where the Eighth Route Army had won another victory, and how many Japanese they had killed ...

Almost the whole family were Christians. "The Chinese people are suffering because they have sinned," his mother often said with a sigh. He did not believe. "What will become of you if you don't believe?" his mother would scold him. "I don't care," he would say. He would not go to church with them. At mealtimes when they said grace, he would take his bowl of rice and eat somewhere else. They told him stories about Jesus but he would not listen. He disliked all the fuss and bother it involved. He and his eight year old sister were the only ones in the whole family who had not been baptised.

The battle which was raging on Chinese soil changed many things.

His school, the first experimental primary school, became the first "new citizens" primary school.

The owner of the Hengteli watchmaker's shop in Taiyuan, a big fat fellow, became the magistrate of Yangch'u, the district around Taiyuan.

Ten days ago, he was still a schoolboy in the first year of upper primary school, and now he wears a grey cotton uniform, around his right arm is an "Eighth Route" armband, from his waist hangs a revolver, and he is standing in a room of a divisional intelligence section in the Eighth Route Army talking to me.

He talks to me in embarrassment, in a low voice. His head is down, and his hands play unceasingly with a brass zipper on his colourfully patterned shirt. His bashful eyes are fixed on that zipper, and his face is suffused with a red colour often found in healthy children. If it weren't for his very thick black eyebrows which barely curved at all, everyone would have taken him for a girl. He was never a particularly lively child. At home and at school he was very well behaved, neither mischievous nor fond of talking. Premature loneliness had given him a tendency towards quietness and thoughtfulness. But when he had a definite opinion or wish, he would stick to it stubbornly, or would bravely carry it through.

First interview

"In November last year," he said, "the Japanese attacked Taiyuan all through the night. In the dark the sound of bombing was terribly loud, our whole family hid in the cellar, we slept underground. The cellar was built out of bricks, it was big enough for two rooms, but no-one slept all night ...

"The next morning, we heard people walking in the street and so we climbed out and went upstairs to have a look: the street was a mess, covered with carts, boxes and clothing; animals ran around loose, and the doors to each house were tightly locked. First we saw the Japanese soldiers coming to reconnoitre, then afterwards came the troops, their leather boots thudding heavily, the sheep and horses, the cannons, the tanks, and the armoured cars, passing by unit by unit. I thought to myself, if they come in we are as good as dead. My home was in the eastern section, on a main road ... that part of the street is all residential ... the Japanese soldiers entered from the north gate, and many people were killed in the northern section, I heard they actually intended to kill their way down to the bell-tower ...

"In the courtyard opposite were a dozen or so street cleaners who did not run away, they were all bayoneted to death.

"Many neighbourhoods were looted, in some cases the locks on the main doors were forced open, and the houses entered. Some had secret locks, and were not broken into ...

"This is how the Japanese entered Taiyuan."

Second interview

"Do you think Taiyuan is any different now from what it was before?"

"It is not as easy-going, not as free; if you aren't careful all the time, you risk getting beaten up by the Japanese."

"Have you ever seen a Japanese beating up a Chinese?"

"Yes. Once I was riding my bike to school, and in the street I saw a little boy using a stick to chase away a pig that belonged to a Japanese. The Japanese hit him and kicked him and broke his arm. He ran away and I ran away too. Another time, I nearly ran over some Japanese soldiers. They were strung out across most of the roadway. They were drunk, their faces were red and they were talking. I quickly stopped the bike, got off and ran for cover. Those drunken devils for no reason at all started slapping a policeman across the face who was standing at the side of the road."

"Have people moved out?"

"They will let you into town but you can't leave, or they will let people leave as long as they don't take any furniture with them."

"Are there many Japanese in the city?"

"A lot. They've opened up Japanese restaurants and brothels. There is also a Japanese primary school, with forty or fifty Japanese young devils."

"Do you get into fights with them?"

"Mm, once I was going to buy some vinegar, and on the way I met four or five Japanese young devils carrying wooden sticks and knives. They blocked my way and hit me, but I managed to get past them. They're very bad. They often fire brass-barreled water-guns from doorways at Chinese in the street, aiming at your face or body. After they've hit you, they hide inside the doorways. Another time, three or four schoolmates and I shot a sparrow in the park with a bow and arrow, two Japanese young devils wearing short yellow pants wouldn't let us get it, we knocked them to the ground, and hit them with half a brick until they began to cry and yell. Then we saw some grown-up Japanese coming and ran away."

"What changes have there been in your school?"

"The headmaster's been replaced, and all the teachers too. There are tests all the time, the standards aren't as good as before, and the Chinese readers have been changed, too. We have *The New People's Principles* [a Japanese "version" of Sun Yat-sen's *Three People's Principles*] as a textbook now, but we don't pay much attention to it. When we are in class we write and draw what we like, we pass notes and draw pictures of everybody, we don't learn anything all day though we have more than ten lessons a day. They teach us Japanese songs, which we can sing but we can't understand them. The classes are less strict than before, and we are always having meetings and pasting up slogans. If we don't go to them we get caned."

"You don't get up to any trouble?"

"Nobody dares, the teachers are always saying, 'You be careful! Have you been bad? If you've been bad, the communists will get you!'"

"What subjects do you do for composition?"

"Once we had 'How to wipe out communism'. I didn't do it, I didn't want to because deep inside I knew that the communists were Chinese and were working for our national salvation. Another time, the Japanese primary school sent our primary school two clay puppets, a man and a woman, dressed in Japanese clothes. They were over a foot high. The teacher set us the subject 'A Letter to our little Japanese friends'. He told us to write 'Dear little Japanese friends, since you sent us the puppets, we have been wanting to repay your kindness. After we arrange something, we shall send it to you ...' Everyone wrote like this. Afterwards the school actually bought a lot of toys, dolls, steamships, cars, cannons and tanks and appointed a delegation to go with them."

"When you were writing, didn't you think of the Japanese young devils who bullied you?"

"When I was writing , I didn't dare think of their faults. I was afraid that if I thought too much about it then it might come out in what I wrote and spoil everything."

"Tell me how you escaped."

"My friend got me out ..." From the simple way he spoke you would take him for a much younger child. He had a friend who was fifteen, a former classmate; two months ago he went into an ivory shop as an apprentice, as his family were poor. One day after school, he bumped into this friend in a side-street. Nearby was a stretch of wood where some time ago a cave had been dug as a shelter against the enemy. When the enemy entered the town, they had discovered some people hiding in this cave, and had smothered them to death under dry grass and horse dung. Now the cave had been sealed off with earth. When they saw each other there, they talked about the wickedness of the Japanese. His friend told him that recently he had come across an old friend who also used to be an apprentice and who had recently joined up with the Eighth Route Army. Sighing with admiration, he said, "He was carrying two Mausers." Finally the friend invited him to come to the wood the next morning and escape with him, and he agreed immediately. The next morning he left home on his bike, his family thinking he was on his way to school.

"Didn't they have any suspicions at all?"

"I always went to school, I haven't ever run away from school before," he said with a smile. He seemed both proud and embarrassed about being such a good boy.

The story of his adventure was very simple.

The war which was raging on Chinese soil changed many things; it changed many peoples' thinking and feelings.

The whole city suddenly fell into the hands of the Japanese bandits, and remained under Japanese rule for one long year; for a thirteen-year-old primary school boy, this was education by negative example. Now he had passed these difficult examinations and had escaped.

He told me the story of his adventure in embarrassment, in a low voice.

One morning ten days ago, he said, he and his friend got on their Chrysanthemum brand bicycles and sped towards the new south gate, the only city gate which was open. ("Did they only leave one gate open in Taiyuan?" "Yes, ever since one wild soldier from our guerrillas made a bet with someone, and one night he dashed into Taiyuan, cut off the heads of several Japanese sentries guarding the gates and came back," a comrade from the intelligence section answered from the side.) Two Japanese sentries and two puppet policemen were inspecting from either side the traffic going in and out. The bicycle wheels lightly slipped through down the middle. In a short time five *li* had gone by. The Fen River bridge lay ahead, a Japanese soldier was relieving himself by the side, and the bicycle wheels lightly slipped across. In a short time, more than twenty *li* had gone by. They could hear machine guns up ahead. A few people who were carrying kerosene or cotton on bicycles got off and hid in a broken-down mud hut. They also got off and hid there. About twenty *li* away a convoy of Japanese vehicles had stopped; some carried people, others were covered with calico. The sound of the guerrillas' rifles could still be heard, but gradually the sounds became fewer and then ceased. After waiting for the Japanese to move off, they emerged from the broken-down mud hut and looked for a small track. They knew that the guerrillas were in the mountains, and when they had come to a place where the road ran out, they saw a sixteen or seventeen year old boy wearing a grey cotton uniform. "Where are your troops?" "They have gone back." "Where are you going?" "Back to the troops." Then: "We are comrades," he and his companion said together. Then: they came to the guerrilla detachment. Then: they stayed with the company for a few days, then he came to Lanhsien with our comrades from the intelligence section.

What could be more simple than this?

"Your friend?"

"He stayed in the guerrilla detachment as an orderly; he can't go to the front and fight, and he's not very happy," he finally said.

Written on 15 July 1939 from notes made at Lanhsien in December the previous year.
(*Sparks*, pp.77-86.)

The common people and the army (*Lao-pai-hsing ho chün-tui*)
(From a series of five letters describing conditions at the front).

The third letter

Have you ever heard the sound of machine-guns firing ten *li* away? Lately I have been hearing it all the time; I feel that this sound is much more unpleasant than the thundering of cannon. A metaphor comes to me: like a man in a fever, his teeth chattering.

We still hadn't recovered properly from the fatigue of our long march when we were encircled by the enemy. One brigade, which was our main force, fought on two fronts, east and west. Moreover, this was guerrilla warfare in open country, which simply means that fighting continues stubbornly all day and all night long. Because I was thrown from my horse and injured my arm, I did not go to the brigade to bring "comforts". But it occurred to me, what comfort could I offer them? A few empty words? It makes me feel ashamed to think that I carry neither guns nor grenades with me, but only a fountain-pen.

The comforts offered by the common people were more useful to the soldiers. During the fighting, the inhabitants of the nearby villages were quick to send steamed buns, griddle cakes and millet porridge, and some of them even insisted on taking them personally right on to the battle-field. When a soldier is wounded, they bring stretchers. When the battle is over, they bring even more comforts to the whole brigade, in the shape of carts laden with pigs, sheep and towels

"We must get some rest, we need at least a week's rest," said a senior officer at headquarters.

At the moment we are really having a rest. Probably the Japanese troops, retreating after their failure to encircle us, are pleased to rest too. Now the scale of the common people's comforts becomes larger, even reaching us non-combatants in the political section at headquarters, with woollen caps, stockings and shoes. There are even a few anecdotes about the shoes we have been wearing. When the people in the mass organization were collecting comfort items in the nearby villages, a beggar even donated a pair of shoes, and someone passing by quickly took off the shoes he was wearing and went home in his padded stockings; we told him not to send them until after he got home, but he insisted ...

The fourth letter

... You want to know about our daily life. I'm afraid people in the interior find it difficult to imagine guerrilla warfare, particularly guerrilla warfare on the plains. In the vast open plains there are roads everywhere, roads along which the enemy can bring its tanks, cars and cavalry. What can we use for cover? We rely on the people as mountains, on the villages as forests. The villages here are as tightly packed as a forest of trees, and as for the people, they not only act as guides and bring us news, but even dig ditches in the main roads and highways. In the battle near Hochien, before the enemy emerged from the town, the people had first sent in someone to spy out the situation, and he ran twenty *li* without stopping for breath back to our troop to report on the enemy's plans and numbers. And in areas under the enemy's control, the peasants are forced to work all day repairing the main roads, but at night they voluntarily come out and break them up. We simply have no way ourselves of destroying roads in the open. On our expeditions we rely on the dark night for cover. We have become well acquainted with the Dipper, and how the dark night gives way to dawn.

I live together with a few people from the editorial committee of the political section. And recently, a young companion has come into our lives. A "young devil" who has only just arrived. He was one of the Eight Route Army soldiers on active service, and at the same time one of the common people who supported the army. His father fried wheat-cakes for us, his brother served the food, and his own domestic duty was to gather firewood. Last year he supported a local guerrilla troop. He fought in one battle. "That time I just escaped with my life." He finished his story in this way as if rejoicing in his good fortune and also showing his complete indifference to danger and death. He was eighteen years old, but so small and thin he looked only fourteen or fifteen. When he first came he said he couldn't read, but we have discovered that he knows several characters and can sing quite a few songs; he can even caricature the way other people talk. He was always thrusting his hand into his cotton uniform to catch lice. "Do you have many lice on you?" one comrade asked. "Not too many," he laughed in reply. Recently we put pressure on him to take off the sweat-shirt he wore underneath and wash it in boiling water, and he finally agreed. When we saw how many eggs there were in this one piece of clothing we cross-examined him again, but he only acted the complete, happy-go-lucky optimist: he burst out laughing as if to say that these tiny insects couldn't possibly harm him.

Last night, our host came to while away the time; our young devil started discussing local affairs with him, and also talked about the support he had given the army. Our host was also an optimist. He was in his mid-twenties, the leader of the village self-defence brigade and he owned an earthen hut and a dozen *mou* of land. After listening to the young devil's tales, he gave an account of his own political beliefs. "There are too many Chinese, the Japanese haven't got a chance." He said that the Japanese were conscripting soldiers from the age of twelve or thirteen up to the age of forty-five; if all Chinese between the ages of fifteen and twenty-four supported the army, the Japanese would surrender without a fight. I smilingly corrected him: "Even if they did fight it wouldn't matter." He said that two months ago, they heard that the Eighth Route army was coming, but although they kept watch for a long time they couldn't see it; then one night he went out to relieve himself and discovered many troops, cattle and pack-animals filing past; he quickly returned to the village to report, and also said that each soldier was carrying a straw mat on his back; everyone said, "It must be the old Eighth Route," and became very elated. "You Eighth Route people are really like ghosts," he concluded. "One night I went to the village up ahead,and on the way I heard someone call me. It really gave me a start! I looked around everywhere but there was no one in sight; it turned out that you had climbed up the trees to keep watch."

I asked him what the army had been like before the War of Resistance. "Not too bad," he said simply. But our young devil had a different opinion to offer. "Not too bad! But they were very keen on beating people up and swearing at them." "Did you ever get a taste of their bullying yourself?" "I didn't, but I saw it happen to others." He had seen one soldier slap a shopkeeper across the face a couple of times just because he had refused to lower his prices, He had seen another soldier buying things with banknotes which were no longer in use, and even demanding the change be made up in ready cash. He had seen a soldier order someone to pull out a nail from a wall, but he wouldn't let him fetch a pair of pliers and made him pull it out with his hands. In the end, the man's fingers were streaming with blood and the nail still hadn't been pulled. Our boy cheerfully related these stories from the past, and imitated the soldier abusing the unlucky fellow who couldn't pull the nail out with his hands: "I'll bash you, you filthy pig! You grandson of a turtle!"

Finally we talked about a famous man who in the past lived in this village. He was a third-ranking graduate in the final military examinations. Our host told us many strange and wild stories about this man, just as many places have their stories about the not-too-distant past. When he took his leave to go to sleep, he invited us to come with him the following afternoon to see the great iron sword which this officer had used, which weighed over fifty *chin* ...

(*Sparks*, pp.96-101.)

An ordinary story (*I-ko p'ing-ch'ang te ku-shih*)

In answer to a question from the China Youth Society, "How did you come to Yenan?"

I came to Yenan. Surely this doesn't really require explanation?

On the hillsides where many new caves are being dug, on roads, at assemblies, I am likely to run into young intellectuals like myself. There are too many, I am already lost among them. Granted that each person who comes here has his own story, why should I be anxious to discuss mine, when, like they, I am busy studying and working?

Because I wrote *Record of Painted Dreams?*

This is not a good reason. That slim volume, that pitiful small volume, was only a plaything created by a lonely child for his own amusement. A very great distance separates it from Yenan, but that isn't to say that there is no road to bridge the distance.

Perhaps because I came rather painfully and late? Yes, I often feel that people a little younger than I are more fortunate than I. I look back on my past: it really was a long, lonely road. The companions of my childhood, those children of petty landlords, now for the most part lie at home smoking opium, eating up their inheritance and breeding children like rats. My fellow-students from middle school for the most part are exhausting their mental and physical energies in spying out, struggling for or maintaining some minor position. The ambitious scholars I encountered at university for the most part liked to dream of leading comfortable lives, and are now probably striving diligently in that direction. I walked and walked among these people, always with the cry in my heart, "I must set an example." I felt extraordinarily lonely, extraordinarily desolate. When I came to Yenan, I often used to hear the current expression, "to act as a model." One day, I suddenly realised that the meaning of this corresponded to my own phrase. Except that when everyone said it, it conveyed not melancholy but a happy, positive significance.

When I related my gradual awakening to a comrade who had taken part in the December 9 Movement of 1935, he said:

"It was different for us. Our road was very easy, it was as if we came here as a matter of course."

Yes, they came here in groups and bands, while I came alone, bearing dark memories.

I don't really think I understand things very easily, and I think I'm not really a rebel by nature. As a rule I only understand something after I have experienced or felt it repeatedly, and I only begin to rebel after unbearably heavy oppression.

I often use the words "silent" and "lonely": ever since I can remember, I have been only too familiar with the feelings, circumstances and the things they represent. I suspect that when I was a child I was dumb, for it seems as though I never talked at all, even to animals and plants as children do. When I was eleven, I finally began to talk to books, to some old novels. Often I stood irresolute beneath the window of a relative's house nearby, not daring to utter a sound, nor to express my wish to borrow a book. While I suffered bitterly through my inability to obtain new books, I would seize hold of them in my dreams at night. But just when I joyfully leafed through the rich list of contents and started to read, I would wake up and the book disappear in my hands. I had no conception at all of the positive side of life, of people—I thought that this was the whole world and I could not imagine it as being any better than this. I fully accepted it.

When I was twelve, I was still studying the old literary texts in the family school—they were all it had. One of my younger uncles told me a truth that he had heard passed around, that the world is a sphere. I did not believe him. My reasons were quite ridiculous. I thought to myself, "The books I've read don't say that." When I read the *Ch'ü Rites* and the *Descendants of King Wen* in the *Book of Rites*, I thought that being a son was a very troublesome business. I did not go so far as to wonder whether the rites were good or bad, or whether they should be continued or not; I was simply grateful that now people did not behave as the books indicated. I was already thirteen when, crying like a baby, I demanded to be sent to middle school. I was not at all clear about why the new-style schools should be better than the family school, it was just because of a vague desire, or a natural thirst for new surroundings.

A great period in Chinese history had begun. Because of our geographical isolation, the first great revolution in China (the Northern Expedition of 1926-27) hardly made any impression on me; the only clear recollection I have is that the five-coloured flag of the Republic was replaced by the Nationist flag, a white sun against a blue sky; the name of the local troops was also changed, from

"United Bandit-Suppressing Army" to "National Revolutionary Army", and red paper handbills were sent to our school by relatives of students killed in the uprising after the Chungking Governor had been assassinated. Apart from this, I had my own experience of loneliness. This made me behave like a hedgehog; whenever I was threatened by something I would curl myself up. The prickles I used in self-defence were solitude and books. Hans Andersen's "The Little Mermaid" was the first story to move me deeply. I very much liked the two foreign words used to describe the youngest princess: "BEAUTIFUL" and "THOUGHTFUL". Her unhappy end made me understand self-sacrifice for the first time. I did not know whether these three concepts (beauty, thoughtfulness and self-sacrifice for the sake of love) just happened to suit me, or whether they started off something inside me; and I, in my bitter poverty, seemed from this time on to have gained a few precious things. I would almost say that it was only because of these three concepts that I was able to finish this long, lonely road of mine, this road which has ended in Yenan. But they also restricted me, making me dislike emotions and behaviour which I felt to be vulgar. For a long time, I was therefore indifferent to politics and struggle and cut off from the masses. I was so perverse that I disliked whatever was popular, what everyone believed in, even in matters of greatest importance. When I lived in Shanghai for a year, I hated physical exercise, I didn't see a single film, and just because books on the social sciences were then very popular, so that almost every student had one or two on his desk, I did not so much as open one. One night, I wrote a short poem: I said that I liked small, delicate things, and that I wanted to be a small, delicate person. I rather regret that I later burned those youthful writings, for now I would be very interested in examining them, just to see how immature my expression of my immature thoughts was in those days. I was seventeen then.

My immaturity lasted a fairly long time, until I was twenty-one, that is, until I was in my second year at university. During this time, I created for myself a beautiful, peaceful, small world, filled with a lonely joy; my materials were gentle poetry and essays, the ruined and colourful background of the city of Peking, illusion, youth, and—let me ridicule myself a little—the not-so-beautiful allowance my family sent me nearly every month. I lived in this small world; and yet I felt dissatisfied. As I have written elsewhere, "Every night I was silent unto death." As well, "I rejected the masses, and then felt the sorrow of being rejected by the masses." I wrote some short poems and essays, and hoped that lonely children like myself could find a little happiness and consolation in them, like a piece of candied fruit in a bitter and harsh life. I thought that this was the only contribution I could make to man and the world. I had no greater ambition, no greater desire, for I was like an ignorant child; in many things I had no sense of responsibility.

But in this life, a new way of thinking had begun to grow; although it was still unhealthy, almost nihilistic, yet it was at least new to my thinking. One gloomy afternoon, I was walking along a secluded street by myself, when an eleven or twelve-year-old newspaper boy ran out in front of me, trailing a bag full of papers and miserably crying out newspaper names. As I looked at him, I suddenly thought of my young brother at home. A complicated thought seized hold of my mind: I thought that the paperboy was just a child like my brother, why should he have to cry out on the street like a beggar; I thought of how selfish and greedy mankind is; I thought how I couldn't just ignore him, simply because he wasn't my brother, and let him run off again. I suddenly decided to buy a paper from him, it seemed a way of easing his burden a little. He took a paper from his bag to give me, and because I had no small change, I gave him a dollar. When he went into a shop along the street to change it, I suddenly thought again, surely I don't really want him to give me back the change. Then I slipped into a lane, and ran all the way back to where I was living. A deep sense of disquiet was pressing on my heart, and for a short while I wept. When I regained my calm, I began to blame myself for being a fool, because I realised that this honest child would be looking for me in the street, anxious and fearful. For a long time I was depressed. Afterwards I thought of writing a story to explain a new thought which was beginning to grow on me. A wayward young man travelled for many years in foreign parts, and finally in one city he became seriously ill with consumption. His family, on receiving the news, hastened from afar to look after him, shedding secret tears on his behalf. But he was not at all grateful; on the contrary, he seemed to become enraged: "Just because every mother loves only her own son, and every man helps only his own brother, people have become unfeeling, so that everywhere I have encountered cruelty and indifference, so that I have become seriously ill and shall soon die." My life prevented me from being more progressive. I did not realise that the reason why people did not love each other was because the social system was so unjust; I did not realise that we will have to change society before mankind as a whole can be changed; and that in carrying out a change in society, a part of mankind have already changed themselves. And I was so humble, or should I say so timid, that I did not realise that I should shout aloud what I felt: "This world is unjust." Even less did I realise that my voice could also become a force.

But finally I lost my immaturity and became an adult. I lost my small world filled with a lonely joy. I spread my wings. I fell from heaven to earth. The colour of my evening dreams also changed: before, a white flower shining with a soft radiance, a stream flowing through green meadows, or a young girl in clothes the colour of swallows' wings; now, an empty room, the rainy weather of a man in sorrow, or a long grey road, a road which I had to travel even past the point of exhaustion.

I have previously compared this change to the travels of the Hindu prince. Between these two periods, I really did go on a journey. But I realise now that this journey did not teach me about human misery, because it did not bring me into contact with anything special; it was the accumulation of my experiences since childhood which suddenly changed me at this time. I am not after all a thinker; my experiences and emotions of ten years or so seem to be worth less than another person's one-day journey. The whip of reality had been beating me continuously, but because the beatings were light, the young Don Quixote that I was could continue for a few more days with head held high. In those years in Peking, the reality I was in contact with was very narrow: the home of a petty official, a deserted young woman, a few lost intellectuals. What penetrated more deeply into my life, bringing only unhappy shadows, bringing tears, was love. I do not exaggerate, nor do I underestimate, the effect which my first love had on my thinking. Love, which sounds so gentle, so happy, in reality is far from perfect beauty. To a young illusionist, it was even almost a violent shaking, or a beating. I was like a wounded beast, weeping and furious, because I didn't realise what it meant. (It was not until later that I found the source of human misery, and realised how difficult the fulfilment of love is in an unjust society.) But, in another sense, it educated me. Only someone who has himself encountered unhappiness can fully understand the unhappiness of another, and an intellectual, I would like to say in all sincerity, is not really open to a sense of shame at all: misfortune must touch him personally before he realises how heavy it is. Before, although I always felt that I could sacrifice myself for another, at the very most I refrained from actively doing harm, by not being selfish or greedy: I was still not in the least concerned for my fellow man. After this, as I have written elsewhere: "On human happiness and good fortune, I turn my back; in the face of human misery and misfortune, my pride could only lower its head and dissolve into tears." My favourite reading changed from the poetry of the symbolists and gentle stories in the French manner, to the hopless dry words of T. S. Eliot, and the moans of Dostoevsky's troubled souls. Nevertheless, the things I wrote were still far from reality: like the wife in Hauptmann's *Einsame Menschen* who lost her husband's love, who suffered to the extent that while telling her mother-in-law about her girlhood dreams she pricked her own finger with a needle without feeling the pain; and also like the woman visitor who, out of sympathy for the wife's suffering, decided to abandon her love, and, facing the lover she was soon to leave, picked out a melancholy tune on the piano in the twilight.

I went to teach at a middle school in Tientsin. Life was even gloomier in the teacher's dormitories there than at the university lodgings. That place was full of angry, yet feeble and ineffective discontent; everyone was unhappy about the factory-like control and exploitation, but could go no further than mere discontent. I began to feel the fearfulness of life: at times, it can drive men to insanity. A bachelor said to me at dinner, with a sigh, "We are too saintly, when the time comes we shall not be able to enter heaven." He actually could have worked somewhere else, but he did not want to leave the city with its cinema, skating rink, tennis court and flushing lavatories. Because one colleague fell sick, another teacher who was considered relatively healthy burst into hysterical tears. Watching the children of the rich arriving at the school in cars in the mornings, he often told me, "I'm sure they think we are lower than their family chauffeurs," or "One day we shall be crushed to death beneath their cars!" He was my only friend in those surroundings; we influenced and encouraged each other alone. At dusk, gazing at the distant chimneys and watching the young women returning from work as they walked along the banks of the foul river which flowed through the heart of the city, we began to talk of the evils of capitalism. In my class, a compradore's son listened all day while I taught composition in the vernacular, and in evenings returned home to study the ancient Classics with the family tutor. Gradually, I became ashamed of my work and my life. It seemed that I was looking at my imminent destruction. Then the student movement arose. It placed us in a very awkward and uncertain position, between the students and the school: we were a pitiful, indeterminate third force. On the twenty-eighth of May [1936], a band of demonstrators burst like a storm into the drill-yard outside our dormitories, inviting the students of our school to take part, enthusiastically holding meetings, and shouting slogans; it was as if a red fire had suddenly burst into flame, brightening the shadowy darkness of my life. Yet I could only look at it from my distant, cold corner, because despite the fact that I was as young and passionate as they, I was no longer a student but an employee.

I have always recalled with gratitude that small district in the Shantung peninsula where my thoughts of resistance ripened like a fruit. At last I clearly realised that a true individualist had only two choices: either to commit suicide, or abandon his isolation and indifference and go to the masses, to join in the struggle. At last I firmly realised that the greater part of human misery was created by man himself, and therefore could and should be destroyed by man himself. In that area, which was known as "model district", the peasants were so impoverished that almost half of the produce of their land was paid over in taxes. The young people who grew up in the villages, those teachers' college students with only a post in a primary school before them, an allowance of twelve dollars a month and hopeless lives ahead, lived as a rule off millet, fourth-grade black bread and sweet potatoes, and yet they were still so enthusiastic about knowledge, like young soldiers studying different kinds of weapons and their use. They were also so involved in politics: some had been arrested for spreading national salvation propaganda in neighbouring districts. Alongside them, I felt I was no longer alone. Like them I was full of faith and hope; my feelings became less refined, and also stronger. I saw the peasants who had lost their land driven from neighbouring districts with their bundles of tools to work as casual labour during the harvest, standing at dawn in the fields, like slaves at market waiting for their employers; I saw them with no money for lodgings, sleeping at night on the stone bridge outside our school gate. Then when I went to Tsingtao and saw the rows of summer villas locked up and empty for the winter, I felt with extreme clarity the significance represented by this comparison. I wrote this experience into a short poem, saying, "In the future I'll insist on expressing my opinions," that is, from now on I will use what I can of my writing as a weapon in the struggle; as Lermontov once said, "Let my song become a whip."

The War of Resistance came. For me, it came just at the right time, because I was no longer a pale-faced dreamer, or a coward; already, like an adult, I had a sense of responsibility: I believed that no matter where I went, there would always be something for me to do. I returned to Szechwan. I discovered that my native district was so backward that the work of teaching was absolutely essential. In the district school where I taught the teachers played mahjong almost all day long. When the news of the fall of Shanghai and Nanking appeared in the papers, they too seemed unhappy and sighed, but still they were more concerned about their jobs and their salaries than the war. The headmaster, who was half-deaf and in his fifties, and who had previously studied engineering in Japan, openly said in the staff-room that China would not be able to withstand Japan. However, he added, China was still indestructible. He said that in all its history, China had never been conquered. When everyone asked him whether or not the Yüan and Ch'ing dynasties counted as foreign rule, he pretended not to hear, putting an end to his political theorizing. Besides this, I did not like the way in which many of the students in my class were so quiet, so knowing. They had many opinions about the school, but seldom raised them in a positive way. Once I even went so far as to say to a class which was about to graduate, "I can see that you are more sophisticated than I." I hoped that they would become more concerned about things, starting with the school. Of course, it was not just their fault; I did not forget that the cultural backwardness, the military and bureaucratic rule, the low ebb of the revolution, and the intimidation of intellectuals in their professions and in their lives, all helped in the training carried out by certain groups of people, the training which crushed the ideals, enthusiasm and courage of the young. All I hoped to find was some vitality, some exuberance of manner. Later, a minor incident made me feel I had to leave these surroundings, for after all, I was no seasoned battler myself. I still needed companions, I needed encouragement and consolation. One fairly enthusiastic student wrote an article deploring the lack of concern shown in the district towards the War of Resistance. A person of responsibility in the school urged him not to publish it, saying, "You criticize others, but you should start with yourself." At this, he actually asked leave to return to the countryside to carry out propaganda work, and not long after came back to the school with money he had collected in donations. Then the person of responsibility spoke to me of him in one contemptuous phrase: "I think he is a bit neurotic."

I went to Chengtu, thinking that I could do more in a bigger town. I taught, wrote *tsa-wen*, and published a small magazine. Every week, I went to the printers' with a friend and corrected the proofs; I posted them to other districts in bundles of twenty or thirty copies, and took them around to various bookshops. At the end of the month I personally took the order book and collected all the bills. My articles attacked the heavy atmosphere of classical education, the cruelty of feudal thinking which despised women and mistreated children, the business of drugging young minds which was secretly being carried out, and the social ambitions of intellectuals; but when my pen chanced upon Chou Tso-jen for taking part in the "Committee for Cultural Renovation" in Peking, I aroused the ire of some people. There was one writer who had been on an archeological expedition to Greece. For some time he had been urging me to stop writing *tsa-wen* and to concentrate on "true creative work." Because I did not take his advice, he ridiculed me for turning into a young activist, or social activist; then, on the basis of that article alone, he decided that my time was certainly running out. Among the people I was associated with, including my own friends, almost no-one supported me; they either called me vindictive, or excessively hot-tempered. This made me feel extremely lonely, and I wrote, "Chengtu, Let Me Shake You Awake!" As if to encourage myself, I wrote,

Like a blind man whose eyes have been finally opened,
From the darkest recesses I saw the light,
That great light,
Coming towards me,
Coming towards my country ...

At the time, a friend living in another place, who used to enjoy the works of Chou Tso-jen, nevertheless repudiated his liking and respect for him in an article, saying that he wanted to get rid of the newspaper photograph of Chou Tso-jen sitting with Chinese traitors and Japanese; and then he mentioned me, saying that I should no longer call myself an individualist (up until then I still occasionally liked to call myself an individualist, of the type defended by Romain Rolland), because I had my companions, though they were in another place.

Yes, I should go to another place, I should go to the front. Even if I could not bear weapons and stand shoulder to shoulder with the soldiers on the firing lines, I should still go and live with them, and write down their stories; in this way I could to some extent lessen my own shame, and at the same time I could make those gentlemen leading comfortable lives in the interior reflect a little, and see whether they still want to ridicule these soldiers who are always ready to lay down their lives, as "confused" or "excessively hot-tempered."

From *Sparks*   171

I arrived in Yenan.

I wanted to pass through it to reach the north China battlefield. I still hadn't realised that I needed its education. At that time I was so stupid, when I was in the bus on the Szechwan-Shensi highway coming towards this holy city of the young, I had in mind a sentence by Bernard Shaw spoken just before leaving the Soviet Union: "You must allow me to reserve my freedom to criticize." But when I arrived here, I was so full of emotions and impressions. I reflected that I was the one who should be criticised, and not this place where a great and difficult revolution was in progress. I lifted my arms in acclamation. I wrote, "I Sing of Yenan."

I have been living here for ten months now, ever since I returned from the north China front. Here, because life is filled with light and joy, time flows past as easily and swiftly as a gentle song, and now I sing of it in my work, and defend it with my life, not just with words. Here, when I speak of mankind and the future with passion and dreams in my voice, no-one secretely mocks me. Here, despite my foolishness and sentimentality, I have learnt a great many things from the environment, from people and from work. I have made progress with a hitherto unequalled rapidity; I have taken a complete farewell of my former unhealthy and unhappy thinking; and like a small cog in a huge machine, with countless other cogs alongside me, I spin and whir in happy regulation. I am already lost among them.

8 April 1940
(*Sparks*, pp. 119-36.)

Poems from *Night Songs*

These poems were written between 1939 and 1942 in Yenan and collected for publication in 1945 under the title of *Night Songs*; I have also included here a long poem written in the same period but first published in the substantially revised and expanded version of the collection, which appeared in 1952 under the new title, *Night Songs and Songs of Day (Yeh ko ho pai-t'ien te ko)*. Apart from a few "occasional" poems produced at long intervals, Ho Ch'i-fang gave up writing poetry after the Yenan Forum on Literature and Art in 1942, at the age of thirty-one.

Chengtu, let me shake you awake! *(Ch'eng-tu, jang wo pa ni yao-hsing)*

> Certainly there is a great and
> noisy Peking, but my Peking is
> both small and quiet.
>
> Eroshenko*

I

Chengtu is both desolate and small,
And like someone who has spent countless nights in dissipation,
Is asleep,

Although there have been torches burning in procession,
Although there have been chilling alarms,

Although boatful after boatful of children
Have been transported to Chungking from every field of battle,
This remnant state is their only parent,
Although day and night the enemy bombs
Canton, our only remaining door to the sea,
Although our ten-thousand-*li*-long new Great Wall
Is the flesh and blood of our front-line soldiers.
Like Eroshenko, I cannot help but
Mournfully sigh:
Although Chengtu is asleep,
It is certainly not a place where men may sleep.

And this is not an age when men may sleep.
This age makes me want to laugh loudly,
And shout loudly,
But Chengtu makes me silent,
Makes me silently think of Mayakovsky's
Condemnation of Essenin's suicide:
"It is easy to die,
Living is more difficult."

---

*Eroshenko, a blind writer of children's stories and an associate of Lu Hsun in the
early nineteen-twenties and thirties.

II

Once in the north I sang:
"O north, with your wind-palsied ancient hands,
The robber's fists have struck at your joints,
Have you still not returned his blows?"

"O north, I want to leave you, and return to my native district,
Because on your plains as stiff as corpses,
Happiness is so rare,
And winter is so long."

Then came the sound of guns by Marco Polo Bridge,
Ancient and wind-palsied hands
Lifted high the banner of resistance,
Then the enemy seized our Peking, Shanghai, Nanking,
Countless towns groan under his brutal tread;
Then everyone forgot his individual sorrows and joy,
The people of the country united to form a steel chain.

In the long steel chain,
I am the tiniest link,
But I am as firm as the firmest.

Like a blind man whose eyes are finally opened,
From the dark recesses I saw the light,
That great light,
Coming towards me,
Coming towards my country . . .

III

But I am in Chengtu.
Where there is a pleasant, lazy atmosphere,
Like Rome in its decline and fall, it plays the epicure,
But because its all-accepting belly
Is stuffed with filth, putrefaction and iniquity,
On this glorious morning it is still asleep,

Although there have been torches burning in procession,
Although there have been chilling alarms,

Let me break open your windows, your doors,
Chengtu, let me shake you awake
On this glorious morning!

Chengtu, June 1938 *(Night Songs,* pp. 1–7.)

Night Song I *(Yeh ko)*

1.

Wake up from your dreams again,
And open your eyes to the morning light,
And think of days from the past.

Drop a few tears on the pillow,
Cry softly a little while,
It doesn't matter, it's not a sin,
Tears come for many different reasons.
Sometimes because of happiness,
Sometimes because of grief,
Sometimes because of tender feelings,
Sometimes because of sublime thoughts,
Sometimes they fly like songs
From the throats of people unable to sing,
Bearing away petty cares and sorrow.

2.

But you are still only a child,
You say you have grown up surrounded by love,
What unfathomable reasons
Keep you from sleeping at night?
You say you are a circle of fire,
Burn brightly then!
You say you know that wisdom invites suffering,
And that beauty is accompanied by grief.
No, the wise must not halt in suffering
The beautiful must not think only of their beauty.

3.

You should no longer feel lonely,
From the arctic circle to the tropics
Everywhere are the same gardeners
Rebuilding the garden of mankind.
We must change the seasons of nature
To make all living things more beautiful,
So that the very mud
Spreads warm and fragrant odours.
Oh, my companion, you've just entered our ranks,
Don't say your life is burdened with misfortune,
Our lives must grasp good fortune
Both for ourselves and for mankind.
If none exists among us,
Let us create it ourselves.

4.

Don't say there is a future for mankind
But not for you.
When all the world is laughing,
Surely you will share their happiness?
When children of the next generation
Play in the sunlight,
And in the proper season fall in love,
Surely you won't be jealous?
No, tomorrow we have our good fortune
Today we have our duty.

5.

So sleep a little longer,
The silence and the length of night
Are not designed for deep reflection
But so that we may rest
And build up reserves of joy and energy
To welcome a new dawn,
And bring to our arduous working life
A singing heart, a blessing.
So sleep a little longer!
Your eyelids softly close.

11 March 1940 (*Night Songs*, pp. 24–29.)

Night Song II *(Yeh ko)*

───

I sleep, but my heart waketh.
Song of Solomon

And my mind is an open window
And my thoughts, my multitudinous clouds,
Drift towards me in scattered disarray.

And in May,
The daytime sunshine is too brilliant,
The evening moonlight is too brilliant,

I cannot be like Maupassant's priest,
Who, unable to sleep,
Clasps his hands in prayer:
"O Lord, if you created night for sleep,
Why did you create this moon, these stars,
This wine-like air which hovers around my lips?"

I cannot rise from my bed and go into the forest.
To say each tree has a beautiful soul,
And weep along with them.

And I cannot be like you, Shelley!
I cannot say I am Ariel, an airborne sprite,
And fly across plains, over hill and dale,
I cannot sit upon the sand like you and sigh:
"Alas! I have nor hope, nor health,
Nor fame, nor power, nor love, nor leisure . . ."
I cannot sing of love simply, like you:
"I arise from dreams of thee . . ."
You seem to do nothing all day,
But prostrate on the grass of summer nights,
You sleep a tropical sleep.

"But, comrade Ho Ch'i-fang, if you don't like nature,
Why do you describe her
So beautifully in your books?"
Yes, I should talk about nature.
Nature to me is a background, an ornament.
Just as on my occasional strolls through the fields,
I occasionally stick a flower in my buttonhole,
Because I love mankind
More than nature.

We have already lost the simplicity of the nineteenth century.
We are men of the present.

But I should talk about war.
A civil war of man against man is now in frightful progress.
Along the borders of France
Two million troops engage in an orgy of mutual slaughter,
Tanks advance three thousand at a time.
The League of Nations, like a bankrupt shop,
Is gathering its documents, dismissing its people,
To each is given his severance pay.
And you Italy, hurry up for your share!

Hurry up all of you, come in for your share!
Who can hold you back,
Who can hold you back, like trains
Frenziedly racing towards your doom!

How many living men,
How many brilliant men,
How many good and simple men,
How many men who could have worked for this world and its future,
Have been forced to sacrifice themselves for you!
And I, if only I could clasp them in my arms!
Yet I do not weep.
I know they will awaken,
And change this war into another kind of war.
And in the midst of death and destruction,
A new Europe will arise, a new world!

And I should discuss Lenin.
And I see him,
I see him patting little children on the head:
"Their lives will be better,
Theirs won't be full of cruelty like ours."
I see him sitting by the dawn window:
"I am writing to a comrade working in the countryside.
He feels lonely. He is weary. I must comfort him.
Because one's state of mind is not a small matter."
And it seems the letter is for me.

And I seem to hear
His voice ring out in the Assembly:
"We must dream!"

Yes, I like doing some little work like this,
And I like to dream like this,

I cheerfully love myself like this,
And bitterly want to destroy myself like this,
To lift myself higher!

23 May [1940]   (*Night Songs*, pp. 30–37.)

Night Song III *(Yeh ko)*

My brother, why are you weeping?
You say you weep because life is so ugly?

You say you once saw,
When the moonlight had slipped behind the black clouds,
When the night wind made the thorny rose-bush tremble,
Lovers, not long parted,
Meeting at their first trysting-place;
Instead of vows and talk of dreams and passion,
They cross-examined one another, confessing their infidelities.

You say you once saw,
In a peasant family,
Among the spiders' webs and hemp-oil lamps,
After the wedding-feast,
The husband begin to curse and beat his bride
Because some petty detail bothered him?

You say you once saw
A four-year-old orphan,
Adopted by relatives,
Running along the sunlit road,
Run, then abruptly stop
And his lips began to quiver,
And abruptly he burst into tears?

Yes, life is very ugly, very ugly indeed.

You say you want to mention the short tale
That you have already told so many times,
How a swallow stole from a statue every night
Precious stones and carried them to the poor.

There were so many poor to help
That even when winter came it did not fly south,
But went on until it died of cold.

You say why cannot we live in fairy tales?
Why is it only easy to find in books
Pearl-like stories shining with a tender warmth?

You say you also want to mention your former way of thinking,
Which is now so old and stale.
You felt that we humans
Do not live as joyfully or justly as plants or animals,
Plants live out their lives so harmoniously,
Their lives whether short or long,
And reproduce their kind
Making the earth prosper.
And wild beasts,
Even at their hungriest
Do not savage and devour their own kind.
Even less in the moment before mutual slaughter
Do they put on smiling faces,
And murmur sweet-sounding words.

You say you know
That the things you have seen are still too few and trifling,
Is there more which is ugly, and much uglier?

Yes there is still more which is ugly, and much uglier,
This is why we finally arrived in the ranks of revolution.

You say
You have also spoken of revolution.
You say you know that revolution cannot be made with clean hands,
Washed sweet with soap and gloved in white,
Our hands are muddy,
Our muscles bulge,
Dirt and filth we cheerfully accept.
But have you the heart of a stripling,
To tremble so easily?

You say you know you should think of other stories,
Like the story of the fire-seizer,
The rebel against the gods, chained to a barren mountain peak,
His liver daily devoured by savage vultures,
Devoured and yet constantly renewed.
And in the history of mankind there is not just one fire-seizer,
And the fire-seizers of today are no longer alone,
They have countless companions,
And thus countless stories?

You say you have also seen
Light overcoming darkness,
Joy overcoming sorrow,
New life overcoming death,
Beauty overcoming ugliness,
And they are not far away,
They are not mere shadows,
Because not only do you see them,
You also breathe them in,
As if from the skies,
From the vast open plains,
From the fresh morning air?

Well, what else have you to say, my brother?

Well, what have you to weep about, you silly child?
You say you are weeping over your own weakness and folly?

Wipe away your tears,
Let us talk of bright shining stories,
Joyful stories!

12 June [1940] (*Night Songs*, pp. 38–46.)

Night Song IV *(Yeh ko)*

I must arise and go among the children,
I must go and live among them.
I must teach them to read,
And tell them simple but moving tales.
I must tell them of the importance of cleanliness,
And wash their hands constantly.

I must play with them.
"I'm coming, ready or not?"
"Ready."
From my loud replies,
They easily find me,
Hiding behind the door or in the curtains.
And because I am kneeling,
They can easily put their arms around my neck,
Laughing.

I must talk to them of many things.
And let them get right down to the roots
Of any problem they care to ask about.
I must tell them everything I know.
If I cannot answer,
I must tell them honestly, "I don't know either."

I must not get angry with them.
When they are too naughty,
When they misbehave in various ways,
Bullying their weaker playmates,
Or putting to death a sparrow,
I must explain things to them gently and patiently.

I must arise and go among the workers.
I must go and live among them.
I want them to tell me stories from their lives.

Should one have been a child-labourer,
He can tell me how he went into a factory as a boy,
How because a full day's work was too much for him,
He often fell asleep beside the machine.
Once he saw a boy younger than himself,
Caught in the conveyer-belt while dozing off,
The machine in its frenzied whirling,
Quickly devoured him,
Even his bones were ground to dust.

Should another be a female worker,
She can tell me how the first day she entered the factory,
She stood till her legs ached, her back hurt and her feet were on fire.
She had to go to the lavatory to steal a few minutes' rest.
But in the tiny, foul-smelling room, with its one tiny window,
Were many others of her work-mates, sitting and sleeping,
And some said, "We'd better hurry back,
The foreman will soon be coming round to look."

She can tell me how
A worker who was pregnant,
One evening suddenly stopped working,
And sitting on the wooden floor burst into tears.
They asked for leave to take her home.
Half-way there she could not go on. She collapsed.
The night was quiet. Only the sound of frogs.
She sat up. The baby was born.

Other workers can tell me other stories.
I must say: "Comrades, I haven't taken part in any struggle,
I am ashamed."

I must arise and go by myself to the river-bank.
I must sit on a rock,
And listen to the water-fowl chirping so brightly,
And think a while on myself.

I am already an adult.
I have many responsibilities.
But still like an eighteen-year-old adolescent,
I need tenderness.

What I have given is not much.
What I have received is even less.

I know it is shameful to speak like this,
To calculate like this,
But it is just as well,
That at last I have expressed my inner thoughts.
I must arise,
But I am not going anywhere.

I must arise and light my lamp,
And sit down at my desk,
To look at my comrades' examination scripts,
To answer my comrades' letters,
To read,
To plan tomorrow's work,
In short
To do the work I am supposed to do.

20 June [1940] *(Night Songs,* pp. 47–54.)

Our history is racing forward *(Wo-men te li-shih tsai pen-p'ao che)*

I

My dear sisters,
Young sisters,
Our history is racing forward,
See how quickly it runs!

You are studying economic theory,
You are studing revolutionary history,
Soon you will all be cadres,
And yet you are so much like little girls!
You say that each night before sleeping
You each take turns to tell stories,
Even going back to the ancient past.

You want me to tell something too.
Well, I shall tell a very ancient story,
The story of my aunt.

My aunt was an Ophelia.
My aunt was a madwoman.
Ophelia, the madwoman who was in love with Hamlet,
Reaching for the white aspen beside the river,
Reaching for the white aspen whose leaves were reflected in the water,
Fell suddenly into the water.
My aunt used to sit at the back entrance to our old home,
Singing mad songs,
Songs whose meaning only she could understand,
Swaying on the back gate until it squeaked.

Inside the back gate was the room where we ate,
Its walls crawling with mosquitoes.
At that time I used to enjoy
Killing them with my little hands.
Outside, a bamboo thicket, a shady ditch, a well.
The grape-vine bore tiny grapes,
The green plum-tree bore sour plums.

My aunt was really a still, quiet person,
With a still, quiet smile,
Such as people with good hearts often wear.
My grandfather gave her in marriage
To the son of a merchant in the district town,
Because their family had a great deal of property,
And owned a good many shops.
When her husband came to see us in the country,
Wearing shiny silk clothes,
Smoking a cigarette,
And humming the latest popular tune in town,
He and everything about him
Seemed utterly foreign in our old home.

Soon after she married she went mad,
And with her hands bound
Seated in a sedan-chair
She was sent back to us.
I do not know how it started,
But from the women's conversation,
I learned that her mother-in-law was his stepmother.

And so I had a mad aunt.

She recovered from her illness,
And was sent back to her husband's house.
When I went to town to see her
Even then she was a still, quiet person,
Wearing a still, quiet smile.

For many years she had no children.
Her husband then married a prostitute.

Finally she died still young,
From a strange illness.
When the women spoke of her illness,
They said it was a terrible ulcer,
Which made her whole body rot away,
And which no medicine could cure;
They would not speak its name,
But sadly, helplessly sighed.

It was not until I lived in the city,
And in the library uncovered all sorts of books,
That at last in an American book,
Sexual Knowledge by Dr. Robinson,
I found the name
Of the impure disease
Transmitted to my pure aunt.

II

My dear sisters,
Young sisters,
Our history is racing forward,
See how quickly it runs!

Perhaps I have told you an unpleasant tale.
I can imagine the future lives of men and women,
Happy and just,
But sometimes I also think of the past,
Of the people from the past,
As we sometimes want to stretch our hands
To fondle the heads of unhappy children.

My sister had a girlfriend,
Her father in the Ch'ing dynasty was a minor official at the capital,
In the Republic he was a conservative.
It was only when she was quite grown-up
And her father returned to his native village,
To hand her over to the man she had been betrothed to as a child,
That she finally had the opportunity to study in Peking.

My sister said that she was very clever,
Each time she came out of the cinema,
From a film she had seen just once,
She had learnt a new song.
Soon she became familiar with new ways,
And could make herself some fashionable clothes.

Soon she was introduced to a boy by a classmate,
Soon for him she fled from her fiance's home
And spent her honeymoon in Japan with this boy.

Soon my sister got a letter from overseas;
Written in a strange old-fashioned way;
She used an ancient saying,
"One false step brings a thousand miseries",
To sum up her life and fortunes after marrying.

Soon she returned to Peking and had a child,
But her husband then abandoned her.
A person always has a sense of self-respect.
So she raised her baby alone;
In a Szechwan boarding-house she lived in bitter poverty.

Peking is a desolate city.
Its broad streets reflect the pale cold light.
The wheels of large carriages raise clouds of dust.
Even the tramcars on their iron tracks move slowly, very slowly,
As if they were weary, stopping whenever they pleased.

The atmosphere was even more desolate in the boarding-house,
Formerly built by a Szechwan nobleman
For fellow-provincials to stay in while taking exams.
Now poor students lived there,
And the families of the unemployed.
On the locust-tree in the courtyard hung green silkworms,
On the cold-cloth over the windows crawled grey lizards.

She wrote many letters to her father,
But received not a single one in return,
Because he burnt them all unopened.
He gave her inheritance to a temple,
And afterwards he went blind.

Afterwards she married a junior official
And gave birth to another child.

Afterwards he also abandoned her,
And then we had no further news of her.

III

My dear sisters,
Young sisters,
Our history is racing forward,
See how quickly it runs!

But you see I shall soon burst into tears.
I do not even know myself
Whether I am happy that history is leading us away from the past,
That heavy, unhappy past,
Or grieving that in its course
So many nameless tragedies have taken place.

11 October [1940]
(*Night Songs*, pp. 55–69.)

I see a little donkey *(Wo k'an-chien le i-p'i hsiao-te lü-tzu)*

I see a little donkey
It is so lively, so cheerful,
The dry dusty road
Is like a grassy field under its hooves.
It does not know when it grows up
What sort of things will be loaded on its back.
It hasn't been in this world for long,
And can leap around so playfully,
And bray so cheerfully,
See how it shakes its ears,
Look at this little thing!

[1942] (*Night Songs*, pp. 152—53.)

I should like to talk of pure things *(Wo hsiang t'an-shuo chung-chung ch'un-chieh te shih-ch'ing)*

I should like to talk of pure things.
I think of my first friend, of my first love.

The earth has its flowers. Heaven, its stars.
Man — has a soul.
I know that nothing can endure forever.
In the cycle of nature everything passes away like morning dew.
But things which have gleamed with light are precious,
They have grasped eternity in their own radiance.
Once I sat on the grass with my first friend reading,
Or strolled under the stars, discussing our future,
To poor children the future is full of riches.
I was also silently in love with someone,
It made me happy to do things for her.
Unrequited, even undeclared,
My love was as full as a harvest moon.
Ah, the ashes of time have buried my soul,
Too much time has passed since I last thought of them.
My first friend has long been sleeping in his grave,
My first love has been a mother for many years.
And I too am no longer a young man.
But nature will not stop its cycle for me,
Youth is still in bloom throughout the world,
Everywhere young souls unfold,
Young comrades, let us go into the countryside,
I should like to talk to you of pure things
Under the soft blue sky.

13 March 1942 (*Night Songs,* pp. 162—64.)

Here is a short fairy tale *(Che-li yu i-ko tuan-tuan te t'ung-hua)*

Here is a short fairy tale:
A mermaid who wanted to become a mortal,
Lost her tail by a witch's magic spell,
And living amongst men
Soon learnt to speak.
She said, "Man, you are so beautiful,
You can play in the open air,
You can share thoughts and feelings through sound,
Please do not blame me for being so shy,
Or for the way I stammer,
Because I'm still not used to all these things."
Upon this someone ran up to embrace her,
And then released her,
Her whole body quivered lightly,
And for the first time flowed her tears.
Then she laughed her first laugh,
Since then have been both tears and laughter,
She has become a mortal, sister to man.

(*Night Songs*, pp. 165–66.)

How many times have I left my daily life *(To-shao tz'u ah tang wo
li-k'ai le jih-ch'ang te sheng-huo)*

How many times have I left my daily life,
That narrow life, that dusty life,
That busy life, filled with strident clamour,
To go to far-off places unknown to others,
To throw myself down on the grass,
As if returning to the ample bosom of my mother,
She doesn't say a word,
But lets me burst out sobbing on her bosom,
Or quietly rest a while,
And afterwards gently bathes me,
With the sound of running water, with the sky and clouds,
Until she has completely cleansed my heart of irritation, depression and
                    distress,   .
And I am like a man new-borne,
Or like someone who has left the world of men,
Eating wild herbs and drinking dew . . .
But soon I remember my daily life,
That narrow life, that dusty life,
That busy life, filled with strident clamour,
I love it so much,
I cannot leave it for a second,
I must run back hastily,
I must run along that grimy road,
Into that dense mass of people,
I must go and toil together with those sweaty people,
Earning my food with my own hands,
I must go and sleep under that low roof,
And dream alongside my brothers,
Or wake with them, singing their songs,
I must go into the ranks of the armed soldiers,
And go with them to war,
Together to seize freedom . . .

Ah, I want to live like this forever, with my brothers,
My fate is tightly intertwined with theirs,
Nothing can divide us, nothing can tear us apart,
Although individual peace may be easy to find,
I am so restless, so obstinate, so hot-tempered,
I cannot accept its enticement and embrace.

15 March [1942]
(*Night Songs*, pp. 167—70.)

North China is aflame! (Part I) *(Pei Chung-kuo tsai jan-shao — tuan-p'ien i)*

1. *Lanhsien*

Listen, our land is raging!
Our land is shaking, roaring with anger,
As if it has received a heavy blow,
A great drum sends out its summons,
Summoning us to welcome the battle.
Today, a week after coming here,
I hear for the first time the sound of war.

Today, when we were at breakfast with the commander,
Eating spinach,
The bugle sounded as if in alarm
And now, the commander stands on the town wall,
Ordering the guard to seek a hiding-place,

Getting the cameras ready to take the Japanese planes.
But in the sky there is no trace of them:
"Mother's, the Japanese planes are blind,
They have found Lanhsien by mistake!"

Silence is restored in the streets.
An empty silence in the streets.
This winter,
In this north-west plateau which produces oats and yams,
Days without wind or snow seem colder,
A drop of water freezes as it falls to the ground,
But I feel warm, comrades from the political group.
From your tales I can see
How before you came,
Ancient Shansi was weak and palsied
But when new blood flowed through her veins,
When the front-line Eighth Route soldiers recaptured many towns,
And you went into the villages
Subduing or chasing off the remnant troops everywhere,
Then she began to recover her health and youth.

And you, comrades of the mobilization committee,
I listen to you explaining the old customs here. You continue.
You say that the peasants believe in the White Dragon Father,
In June and July they offer incense and fulfil vows.
Offering incense, they lead in a sheep and kneel before the idol,
Pouring water from the mountain well into the sheep's ears:
If it shakes its head, the god has accepted it,
Otherwise, they must stay on their knees
And pray: "White Dragon Father, are you angry because my sheep is thin?"
They brand a mark with red-hot iron chopsticks,
On the horns of the sheep accepted by the god,
Then it is led away by the head of the temple who will exchange it for
                          banknotes . . .
I do not laugh.
I hear you go on to say you want to persuade the head of the temple
To use the money from selling the sheep to establish a p̃easant co-
                          operative.
It brings to mind the workers' representatives' meeting yesterday,
Where stonemasons, carpenters and bricklayers
Were discussing, demanding, enlightenment and knowledge.

2. The bombing

Stop! Don't run!

I had already stopped. I had already found a cave
In which to shelter from the storm overhead.
When the engines thundered like dense clouds covering the sky,
When confused footsteps pattered in the street like rain,
I closed the door, fastened the lock,
And edging along under the eaves,
Ran to the air-raid shelter at the foot of the town wall.

Don't push! Bombs rained on the ground.
After each one our cave trembled.
After each one our hearts took a dive and then floated up again.

Don't go out! How do we know the accursed Japanese planes
May not fly away and come back to bomb a second time.
The sound of bombing comes closer.
A black net drops over us,
We are frightened by its heavy shadow,
"They must have hit the chapel or the drum-tower!"
"Heavens, our commander is in the drum-tower!"

But after a long period of silence,
The bugle happy as a bird begins to sound.
I go outside the cave. I pick up a broken fragment.
I fondle it. I think even Socrates' brain
Could not withstand this iron fragment or a bullet.
I follow the crowd surging into the street,
And like getting off a steamer which has just moored against the bank,
Or from a train which has just pulled into the station,
Treading on solid ground,
Feel unaccountably giddy.
I go into my room.
The window-panes are broken, glass all over my desk,
And the plates and cups now filled with mud,
Recall to me a memory I had of time:
It was also one morning. Just as I was at breakfast.

I saw a corpse.
It was lying
Like a pile of torn clothing, cotton padding and blood.
But it was still moving,
Its elbows propped up on the ground
As if wanting to stand on the stumps of its severed legs.

A white-haired old man weeping over his mother,
She was too old. She was ill. She did not run away.
Now she was completely buried by the fallen wall;
Only a strip of cloth, a trace of blood, remained.

A young donkey from Supplies
Seemed to have been disembowelled.
In another street far away
One of its hooves lay turned upwards,
Its iron shoe gleamed with a dull blue light.

A crow dead under the eaves.

Halt! Halt our tour of inspection!
Ahead, our young commander approaches,
Let us go and honour him.
When a bomb fell on the church beside the drum-tower,
When he was so close to death,
It never occurred to him to desert his post.
And over there, the young orderly from the political group
Has just arrested a Chinese traitor,
Who had signalled from the wall with a white handkerchief,
Walking along beside him.
A child from one of the local families,
Also prevented another villain from escaping.
Even though during the chase,
An unexploded hand-grenade was thrown at him.

3. *The advance*

The yellow of the setting sun has faded,
Night shadows float in mountain gorges.
Along the dry and barren rocks,
A temporary military telephone wire is strung out, winding round
Our troops in long single file.
Step after step, horse after horse,
Like the belly of a crawling snake
We cannot see our head, we cannot see our tail.
We have been marching several days. Through plains and mountains,
Enduring cold, hunger and fatigue,
We have measured our motherland with our feet:
Even if it is a silent land, a barren land,
It is still our own land! We love it!
Here we will build a new Eden,
Transforming desert into grasslands, villages into cities,
In the daytime motors will turn and whir,
In the evening electric lights will twinkle under the starry sky . . .

Yes, you comrades who lived through the Long March,
Here you must live through a long, long struggle,
Longer than the twenty-five thousand *li* you marched before.
But we will continue marching, marching,
As we jokingly say,
"The worst roads in the world are ours to tread."
And you who have only just taken leave of your hoes,
New soldiers, you too understand
The foundation-stone for building a golden future
Is to drive out Japanese imperialism,
And today,
Every Chinese should share the burden of hardship . . .

Merging with my scattered thoughts, snow is whirling.
Snow is whirling, without a sound,
On our unbounded yet disputed land.
This is how I remember the first day of our advance.
When the order to start summoned me,
I breakfasted by lamplight, packed my bags,
And went to the assembly ground outside the town wall:
The drama group and the guards were welcoming each other with songs,
As if welcoming the morning;
Horses were stretching their necks, neighing long into the wind,
As if rejoicing that their hooves
Would soon be pounding over countless fields and forests.
When the long file of troops began to flow,
It inspired me
And pulled me happily and enthusiastically
Along with it, through boundless snows,
And vast plains,
And as I listen to men who have climbed Snow Mountain talk of Snow
                    Mountain,
And men from Suiyuan talk of Suiyuan,
I seem to see the lofty mountains untrod by man,
And the fierce winds and eternal snows
Beating against their faces.
Comrades, poor in health, climbing mountains,
Staggering, staggering, then suddenly falling dead;
And I seem to see the winter beyond the passes,
The earth deeply scoured, grapes frozen.
When the whirling snow dances, travellers cannot open their eyes . . .

The next day, we continue to advance.
The wind overnight has carried driven snow on to the plain,
Making it so pure and clean
That only bicycle wheels
And human feet have dented the ground,
Leaving white tracks, white footprints.
The sun shines with a dazzling brilliance
Like a swarm of golden bees in buzzing flight;
And opposite, lining far-off loess hills,
The sky is so blue . . .

But now there is no snow or sun,
The moon like a golden horn hangs in the sky.
We have passed the cliffs and come to level ground,
Running over moonlit plains,
To rest in the concealing shadows of marshy ground,
And then another burst of ten or twenty *li*.
We strictly observe night march regulations:
No talking, no coughing, no smoking,
And we keep watch for the small black or white flags
Planted on crossroads by our scouts ahead to stop us going wrong.
"Pass it back, don't drop behind!"
"Pass it back, don't drop behind!"
The order comes down from the front, each man turns his head
To pass it back in the same low voice,
The sound passes down in quick tremors,
As if through a metal megaphone.

A few *li* apart, parallel with us,
One of our brigades is on the left and a detachment on the right,
We in the centre "ladder-column" are mostly non-combatants,
The medical division donkeys carry drugs,
The drama group donkeys carry props,
The soldiers who are carrying rifles and hand-grenades,
Pass through the blockade line with us.*

---

* The march consisted of Ho Lung's 176 Brigade, plus a guerrilla detachment
and non-combatants. The "ladder-column" was originally a protected column
for officers, and was divided into sections or "steps" and guarded by special
troops. As a member of the political group, Ho Ch'i-fang would naturally be
travelling in the ladder-column.

By forced marches we cut across a broad
And sparsely tree-lined highway,
Then vault over the narrow track of the T'ung-P'u Railway,**
Like the night wind blowing through withered grass.
Like the dogs barking in distant villages,
The enemy uses its cannons to dispel
The fear that comes to them when night descends.
Our sentries crouch beside the railway track,
Waiting until the whole troop has passed.
It is past midnight. The horn-like moon has set.
The Dipper more brightly tilts its handle.

The cold pricks my nose, my face,
And one night spent sleepless out of bed,
Has left me now dozing, now awake.
But we continue forward,
Until the morning sun casts its yellow rays
Over the plains, lighting up
The white frost congealed on the upturned fur-trimmed collars of our
                    sheepskins.

** The railway from Tat'ung to P'uchou (Yung-chi) which bisects Shansi
   vertically, passing through the capital Taiyuan; it was at this time in the hands
   of the enemy.

4. *Hut'o River*

The Hut'o River sings loudly,
And flows to distant places.
It sings that the current flowing to freedom cannot be halted.
It sings that though keeping in company with time
It has flowed for countless years, it is still young and strong.
It sings of the sweat and groans of the peasants.
It sings that the darkness of feudalism is already shattered.
Hope grows up from it angrily
Like trees which grow along its banks,
Nourished by its moisture.

We have crossed so many, many mountains,
The "young devils" move forward by hanging on the horses' tails,
On the uphill climb it's like hanging on to an elastic band,
But downhill it's like shouting.
And we have gone through many, many villages.
Men and women happily crowd the streets,
Pointing at the big Japanese horses we have captured,
Laughing at the hempen camouflage on their backs.
Little children, who in the throng
Can't see at all, climb the roofs beforehand.
And we drink the water they place by the side of the road,
We see them, on a signal,
Raise their hands high in welcome.

Today we stopped to rest
Beside this river, in this burnt-out village
(Hut'o, you are a witness to that day).
The blackened, roofless walls
Tell how the fire
Consumed the peasants' homes and food that day,
And how a madman who did not run away
Was killed in the streets. Yes, we can imagine
When the enemy aimed their guns at his body,
He was still talking and laughing in his madman's way,
Thinking that they were playing with him.
I went into the Area Peasants' Association beside the ashes,
A former peasant is now the weapon-carrying secretary.
When he gave me a few figures,
How many district and village associations in the area,

How many members, how many guerrilla groups, how much reclaimed
                land,
It was like telling me how many children he had.
And he spoke like a statesman,
When the people in the room spoke all at once:
"Stop talking! I am discussing problems."
Finally he introduced their chairman:
"He is a proletarian."
Just listen to him talk. He talks with so much spirit.
Formerly he was a hired peasant.
Now, when the anti-Japanese forces need food,
He often does not sleep all night but goes out to mobilize supplies.
The organizing secretary who started life as a donkey-boy
Also broke in to tell of his enthusiasm for work.
When he leaves home he orders the children,
"You have to look after yourselves, and take what comes,
I am busy at my work. Work is important."
Saying goodbye to them, I go away.
I reflect on man's awakening, man's reform.
I reflect on how many peasants just like them
Have been tempered by the actual struggle and become aware
Of the importance of their own existence and the world.

Spring 1940
(*Night Songs and Songs of Day*, pp. 106–28.)

North China is aflame! (Part II)

---

1. *Before the dawn*

A vigorous chorus of roosters
Welcomes me as I wake from my dreams.
The sky is still dark.
In my dream I saw a lavish banquet,
In a dim corner where the lamplight could not reach,
A black-robed woman suddenly arose:
Her voice hoarse as if she had just been crying, she spoke:
"Where did we come from, where are we going?"

Why did I dream such a dream on such a night as this?
Why are my dreams much graver than my daytimes?
Is this a question I must answer?
Ah no, not any more!
In the ancient book it says, "dust thou art and into dust shalt thou
                        return."
Within this interval of time, the Indian prince saw nought but suffering,
And Tolstoy, the Russian aristocrat,
Said that man is suspended on a branch about to break,
There are poisonous serpents below, but he keeps on licking the honey
                        on the leaves.
What I am licking isn't even honey, it is bitter stuff,
And yet I am still so greedy and stubborn,
And cling so tightly to every single day.

My senses, my very body proves to me,
My whole environment proves to me,
That life is not empty.
We accept nature's limitations.
In striving within those limitations to perfect himself,
Man proves his value and wisdom.
But to be a man and yet deny the man he is,
To keep on living while repeating that life has no meaning,
This is the greatest sin and the greatest ignorance.

Once I was a lost soul
Like a survivor from a shipwreck clutching a plank,
I devoted myself to dreams and love.
But dreams shatter as easily as glass.
And even love cannot compensate for human failings.
My soul was a tiny flame burning in a vast plain,
It seemed so easy to extinguish.
Until I discovered and shouted out,
"It's unjust! The society man lives in is unjust!"
Then with sudden strength I opened my arms to the whole world.
I said, welcome me,
O ancient world!
I am your long-lost son,
I am the son you lost and now have found again,
Give me twice as much love! Twice as much education!
Let me rest my head on your bosom,
Let me clasp my arms tightly around your neck,
Then quickly wipe away my tears, my memories,
And raise my head to share the burden of your suffering!

But my voice was so weak,
It seemed as if no-one heard.
Before the whole world one man is very unimportant.
And louder than man's voice is the bugle and artillery.
Ah! It is war!
The greatest and also what should be the final war,
Is being waged! I must take part in it!
I know which side I am on.
I hear my companions call.
I must go quickly,
I have spent my last peaceful evening!

On the eve of a long journey, I always sleep badly,
And wake up too early. And wait for the dawn.
As if waiting for the whistle of the steamboat or the train.
Dawn, come quickly!
I will set out immediately,
And leave my home and family!

My mother,
Do you wonder why I am always roaming,
Never to build myself a cosy nest?
Last night when I took my leave,
You cried.
Am I a madman?
When I was faced with her grief-stricken state
I still said, "Why do you cry? –
You should laugh."
Do you think the burden is too great?
Am I still a child to you?

Tears, ah, tears that well up from the heart,
Tears of love, tears shed for others,
Are flowers suddenly blooming in a desert,
Bringing forth fruit!

Let me go then!
Let me shoulder all my heavy grief and trouble,
Let me shoulder another's warm and gentle tears,
And tread the road before me,
That long road, that difficult road,
That road where I do not know what awaits me!
That road I can travel only one step at a time!
I am destined never to rest,
I am destined to sing an elegy for the old world,
And sing paeans on the birth of the new.
I will bury myself with the old world,
And joyfully experience
My painful rebirth.

5 January 1942

2. *A Silent Land*

A strange silence. The silence of Chinese paintings.
The dawn, which looks like a new-born baby,
The sun, the wings of flying birds,
The smoke from breakfast fires that rises from the rooftops,
None of these disturbs its ancient sleep.
O temple, whose red walls appear among the trees,
Let the bells of your pavilion ring out!
I seem to have walked into time past.
I seem to be a little child again.
We played many silent games.
Nearby, with those peasant children,
Children of cowherds, shepherds, grasscutters,
We shifted the stones in the streams to catch crabs,
We crept into thorny bushes to pick red berries,
We pulled down mud-wasps' earthen nests from the earthen temple
                walls,
And broke the arms of the Earth God.
Nothing seems to have changed:
By the streams the blue flowers of the flat bamboo still bloom,
The water flowing beneath the bridge hasn't fallen dumb,
And forest, you haven't grown any higher or bigger.

But I have already lost my small companions.
They have become peasants. Following their parents,
They toil in the fields, every season of the year,
And on those mountain slopes, in silence
Reap the grain with bended backs and sweaty faces.
This is a miserly, mountainous land.
And the sky is always miserly with its rain.
But what has happened? Why are there so few harvesters?
Where is the former bustle of harvest-time?
Those lines of men in the field, reaping in rivalry;
The tall corn falls; the sickles swish;
The butterflies leap and fly, spreading
Their red, fan-shaped wings;
On the threshing floor the stone revolves; the occasional ox lows;
Around the square the grain is heaped up like hillocks;
In the evening the men sleep out in the open air;
Sometimes there is a silent shadow-play with borrowed ox-hide cut-
                outs . . .

What has happened now? Why is it all so quiet?
When did they lose their songs?

Ah, thatched hut by the roadside, what an unhappy story you hide!
The young shoemaker used to sit under your eaves,
We adored him when we were children
And often surrounded him and gazed in the sunshine
As he sewed shoes with two pig-bristle needles,
And told us about the Earthrunner, who could hide underground,
And Hairy Chiseller the Robber, who could fly up to the eaves and leap
                    over walls.*
His mother was very gentle and never scolded us.
For some reason someone later said he was in league with bandits;
The district head, who really did rob the people,
Arrested him, and eventually executed him.
And the mother who had lost her only son cried to everyone she saw:
"My son was not a robber or a killer."
One night she threw herself into the pond beside her house.
The event pierced my young heart so deeply;
When I walked by the pond alone, I never feared the drowned spirit.
I knew she would never grab me to gain re-entry into the world.**
Since then another family has occupied the thatched hut;
The peaceful countryside has swallowed up this unhappy tale,
Just as the pond became peaceful again, after swallowing the woman.

* Characters from local myth and legend.
** A suicide could only gain re-incarnation by taking another person's soul.

The road winds down from the mountain
And climbs up a high mountain again.
There are small shops on the top for the refreshment of travellers.
You are still here, small iron forge!
The bellows are still wheezing. Red flames dart from the hearth.
Hammering and sparks fill up the room.
Soot-streaked blacksmith, you have grown old,
Do you remember how curiously I used to stand outside the door,
To watch your powerful arms wield the tongs and iron hammer,
Turning the hard iron into hoes, sickles or shears?
How many days have you spent hammering, hammering!
There is the same small restaurant next-door with the same old ways.
Customers sit at the table. Choppers and pots still rattle and bang.
Our aproned host, who still remembers me, asks me in.
But today I cannot rest here, I must hurry along my road.
This is the land I grew up in.
These are the people among whom I drew breath.
Their latent strength is just sufficient to waste on an impoverished life.
The black misery in their souls is unknown to others.
In life, they are almost without hope,
In death, they have no imaginary heaven.

I emerged from their midst.
I am responsible to them.
My father did not till the soil yet I had food to eat,
My mother did not spin yet I had clothes to wear.
Although my grandfather's grandfather ploughed his own land,
And my grandfather's grandmother used to work in the fields,
They say that in the dog-days of June, because she didn't have a straw
                    hat,
She used to wear a tattered mat to do the hoeing.
But my father never had the slightest taste of peasant toil,
He only had a landlord's greed and miserliness.
Many silver ingots lay in his chests;
Every New Year's Eve he took them out and laid them on the table;
Gazing on them in the candle-light he smiled.
If my mother went into town without his consent
To buy the children some cloth or a pair of shoes,
He would rip them up and start a quarrel with her.
From this narrow world I emerged
Into the vast and boundless world.
Into the forest of human civilization.
I discovered many secrets.
I finally realized that there could be another life for man,
One which he could create for himself.

But when will such a day come?
Such a shining day? Such a sweet-song day?
Ah, my neighbours, my family, all my suffering brothers!

I walk forward. I go in welcome. I go in search.
Such a day will surely come,
When a gigantic storm, gigantic thunder
Forms from the mass of countless human hardships!

20 January

3. *A Story of Rebellion*

There are so many things which grieve my heart,
They press, they clamour to be turned into song.
I consider myself indifferent to my home district,
But now I have left it, many familiar faces,
Many griefs, many customs and many tales
Come to my mind and enwrap me.

You, the strongest force, emerge first out of the confusion!
I should like once more to relive that hardship with you!
Among those who have walked along the highway to the district town,
          as I have,
Some went to pay their taxes at the local offices,
Some were conscripted soldiers or roadmenders,
Some carried vegetables to market and brought back cloth,
But there was also a band of rebels.
The strongest force is the peoples' resistance.
Even if it is a resistance which failed, I will sing of it.

Before, men over sixty liked to talk about the White Lotus Sect,
It was the greatest disturbance within their peaceful memories,
Lan Ta-shun and Lan Erh-shun, the two rebel chiefs,
Led men and horses along the road to attack the town walls.

There were few Manchu soldiers in the district town then.
The college people met to discuss the crisis with the magistrate.
They proposed to hang a long row of lanterns
In a nearby wood and light them when the evening came,
Then send a detachment to make a surprise attack from the side.
Lan Ta-shun and Lan Erh-shun fell into the trap and dared not advance,
And when the battle drove them to the winter paddy-fields,
The deep soft mud caught the horses' hooves.
Thus they were captured. Their troops took refuge elsewhere.

For many years after there were no more major troubles.
Sometimes a passing army formed a press-gang
And chased the peasants like chickens or ducks
Scattering over the mountains or scrambling down the cliffs;
Sometimes small bands of robbers arose,
They called the mountains dragon-backs, and wealthy men fat pigs.
But one drought year when tigers came down from the mountains
Then deep in the mountains the "divine warriors" appeared again.
There it was a world to itself, cut off from the outside,
Only adventurous traders would go there to buy drugs,
When they returned they would sneer at those people for living on
    maize,
For townsmen that was only fit for feeding to the pigs.
It was here in the mountains that the Great Buddha and the Second
    Buddha appeared,
Dressed in yellow robes, holding goose-feather fans, they chanted spells
    and worked magic tricks,
They were called "divine warriors" by the peasants who believed in
    them,
They said that if you swallowed water they had blessed, you would gain
    strength divine,
And neither sword nor gun could harm you.
One day, this band picked up their choppers, hoes and fire-tongs,
And came down from the mountains to kill. They set out for town
    along the highway.
As they marched their numbers grew. Rich families, deathly scared,
Burnt incense before their gates and knelt in welcome.
Their fate lay in two pieces of bamboo root.
The rebels threw down roots in front of them:
If the roots turned uppermost they would live, turned downwards they
    would die.
The band of rebels continued to advance. They shouted "Kill the grey
    dogs!"
These "grey dogs", the local garrison,
Were beaten back into the town, behind the gates.
They really seemed invulnerable. When bullets pierced their flesh,
They still advanced, as if a drop of water had fallen on them.
They captured guns, the new-style weapons they despised,
And smashed them with stones, then threw them into the river.
The garrison was so hard-pressed that in the town
They killed black dogs and roosters and sought out pregnant women,
To use their blood to break the "divine warriors'" magic spell.

But then these invincible warriors scaled the walls
Only to die under machine-gun fire; the garrison soldiers regained their
                    confidence,
The news quickly spread: the "divine warriors" can be killed!
In the savage counter-attack which followed,
The rebels became a pile of corpses by the riverside.

Then order was restored and silence reigned.
Like coal in the grate, this story
Gradually turned into ashes and was gradually forgotten.
Afterwards when I went to the town to attend school,
In the window of the photographers' in the street
I saw the photographs of the rebels' corpses
(The photos were just old pictures now, which no-one noticed anymore).
There were adults and children,
Some had cloths around their head, some were barefoot,
Some had closed eyes, some had open mouths,
These stubborn fellows still seemed to wonder
Why all their strength did not avail
To smash the fate that bound them?

4. *The city*

O city, what a monstrous thing you are!
You great black spider,
Your net stretches everywhere like bloodsucking tentacles,
The hunger of countless people fills your belly!

Wartime prosperity. Abnormal prosperity.
Concrete bank buildings reach high into the clouds,
Cars from Shanghai and Nanking,
Speed as self-importantly as ever through this mountain city of
                    Chungking.

People. People pulling people. People carrying people.
And people hurrying down the street.
What thoughts revolve in their minds?
Who is laughing, flushed with personal victory?
Who is short of breath in his never-ending race for life?

Dreary inns on dreary nights.
Breaking thorough the reigning noise of mahjong, comes a sudden shout
"Waiter, waiter" and a pedlar crying "Melon-seeds, cigarettes".
The waiter goes to the rooms of the single guests to ask, "Sir,
Do you want a girl? Clean, for thirty dollars the night."
I seem to be standing, breathing in a garbage heap.
Even in a garbage heap people crawl looking for something to eat.

Evening paper! Evening paper! The evening papers report the capture of
          Wuhan.
The news makes me tremble: male and female, young and old,
Crowd the pavement, making it hard to walk.
Red flames ascend in the dark night, the sound of wooden houses
          burning,
The sound of stone houses exploding, can be heard clearly . . .
But this cannot break the daily routine here.
All proceeds as usual, from day to night, from night to dawn.
How I loathe it all!
All the cities I have lived in!
My memory is as round as a perfect circle,
And my present is equidistant from every point in the past.

Peking. I lived there many years out still disliked
Their use of the polite "you", the way they say goodbye,
And when you meet on the street you must bend your knee,
And when you ring someone up the formalities go on all day,
And the famous Three Lake Parks, Eight Lanes red-light district, and
          New Year market,
And the new dance-halls, billiard saloons and women attendants.
No-one thinks it strange that these exist.
But I felt that this city was sinking, sinking under the crust of the
          earth,
Its inhabitants will be buried alive, and I will be no exception.

Before the great professor went to Tinghsien to lecture, he didn't know
That the common people don't eat white buns but boiled millet.
How meaningless were the days I spent there!
Those days filled with dreams! The strangeness of those dreams!
I dreamt I was standing on a high platform. The whole city lay beneath
                    my feet.
A tram was running through the streets sending off sparks.
I said, "Something is bound to happen."
But I lost hope: "Nothing has happened."
Suddenly a fierce gust of wind blew up, blowing me awake.
Ah! Gunfire! Gunfire in Nanyuan and Peiyuan rings out like thunder.
Ring out! Ring out! Nothing but you can shake up this dead city.

Tientsin. The stinking Chiangtzu River. The notorious free market of
                    Sanpukuan.
Everyone tells me that if I go there by rickshaw, to hang on to my hat,
Otherwise the people in the street would reach out and grab it.
Black smoke from factory chimneys spreads across the sky.
Women workers flow through the dusk like flotsam from a shipwreck.
Japanese ruffians piss against the gates of the municipal council.
Heroin addicts on their last legs petition for an "East Hopei Government",
Like chasing a swarm of flies
I want to chase away these grey memories of mine:
Every evening I would sit under the electric light, in a rattan chair,
Listening to the sighs of a fellow-intellectual:
"To spend another five years as a junior member of staff —
It will only take five years to destroy us altogether!"
Or a bachelor colleague
Like asking me why I don't have a drink,
Asks me, "Why don't you have a love affair?"

How I loathe all of this!
All the cities I have lived in!
My fatherland, where lies your strength?
How can you resist the enemy and safeguard yourself?
Who are really your most loyal sons and daughters?
Speak!
Why don't you speak?
Who has got you by the throat?

I could not sleep for a very long time.
As if I were sleeping in a prison, I craved sunshine and air.
As if I were sleeping in a hospital, I wearied of moans and cries.
And as if I were on a heaving ship crossing distant oceans,
My belly was turning over and my eyes sought distant land.
Ah! Bring me soon to a safe harbour.
Let my feet soon tread on dry land!

But far in the distance
I hear a sound like an earthquake,
It is both discordant and harmonious,
It is both ancient and young.
It is my fatherland starting a new life,
It is our soldiers attacking the enemy.
It is countless people awakening, standing up,
Pushing history forward.

[1942]
(*Night Songs and Songs of Day*, pp. 175–204.)

CONCLUSION

Ho Ch'i-fang's literary achievement

Ho Ch'i-fang was always very conscious of the limitations of his literary talent, and continually apologized for it. But there was one firm belief to which he clung despite his own inadequacies: that art has its own laws of existence, which must be studied and mastered. Apart from this, he never bothered to work out a consistent theory of art or poetry; the philosophy he studied at university gave him little taste for systematic thinking, and he avoided any rigorous investigation of the assumptions which informed his creative activity. The chief characteristic of his early poetry and essays is their sensuous imagery and introspective sentimentality, though as he matured his work became more austere. Nevertheless, the basic principle which he held at least until the end of 1936 was that poetry is not simply the expression of personal feeling nor a form of communion with nature or with mankind, but the creation of beauty. In poetry, he believed, beauty is achieved primarily through the use of imagery or symbols, while various metrical devices are employed for extra effect. The metaphysical identity of beauty or the epistemological role of the symbol are questions which Ho Ch'i-fang may have encountered in his studies but which evidently failed to interest him.

The French symbolists of whom Ho Ch'i-fang was so fond justified the primacy of the symbol as a poetic device in terms of the "correspondences" between the natural and supernatural world of Swedenborgian mysticism; or, as Carlyle put it, "In the Symbol proper, what we can call a Symbol, there is ever, more or less distinctly and directly, some embodiment and revelation of the Infinite; the Infinite is made to blend itself with the Finite, to stand visible, and as it were, attainable there." Ho was familiar with the mystical function of the symbol through Arthur Symons' *The Symbolist Movement in Literature* (1911) (from which the quotation from Carlyle is taken) and he had certainly read this very influential work by the time he wrote his only two essays on poetry. His obsession with beauty is completely in accord with the symbolist approach as described by Symons, and yet, with the possible exception of his first published poem, "The Prophecy", there is no trace of any systematic mysticism or longing for union with the Infinite in his writing: Ho Ch'i-fang stopped short at the twilight world of dreams, fantasy and magic.

The nature of the relationship between a poet and his poetry is left equally vague. In one place, Ho Ch'i-fang likens himself to a lute: when the wind blows through, it gives forth beautiful sounds. Elsewhere, he describes the poet as a master craftsman, carving the obdurate material of everyday language to create a thing of beauty. Only the ultimate goal of poetry is made altogether clear: it is to release the imagination, to escape from reality into dreams and fantasy. These twin ideals of craftsmanship and imaginative release are described by the Spanish writer Azorin (1874-1967), who was an important source of inspiration to Ho Ch'i-fang in the mid-thirties. The metaphor of the wind-harp or Aeolian lyre for the poetic mind, however, goes back to early nineteenth-century romantics like Shelley.

Ho Ch'i-fang's rejection of expressionist and didactic views of poetry was also influenced by the new school of Imagism. He was very likely familiar with T.S. Eliot's "Tradition and the Individual Talent" (1919), for instance, in which Eliot wrote, "Poetry is not a turning loose of emotion, but an escape from emotion; it is not the expression of personality, but an escape from personality. But, of course, only those who have personality and emotions know what it means to want to escape from these things." Again, Ho Ch'i-fang seems not to have assimilated the whole range of ideas expressed in this and other essays, just as the more elaborate technical devices and the wider philosophical sweep of *The Waste Land* are missing from the most Eliot-like of Ho Ch'i-fang's 1934-36 poems.

According to his own account, Ho Ch'i-fang's earliest love was for tales of magic and fantasy. Traditional Chinese literature is full of stories and anecdotes of ghosts, demons and fox-witches, of beautiful young maidens and handsome scholars who succour them. Some are in the classical language, like the T'ang prose romances or the Ch'ing *Strange Stories from a Chinese Studio*, but many others are in the vernacular, a pleasant relief after the day's lessons in the Confucian classics. Ho Ch'i-fang remained fond of these stories all his life. He borrowed their plots for his early compositions, and as late as 1959 enjoyed the task of compiling (for political reasons) an anthology of *Stories About Not Being Afraid of Ghosts*.

If his imagination found release in these ancient tales, his emotions were first awakened by the fairy stories of Hans Christian Andersen. Andersen's stories can shock even adults with their cruelty and preaching, and smaller children can be frightened to tears by the pitilessness of "The Snow Queen", and the pain of "The Ugly Duckling". But to Ho Ch'i-fang, these exotic tales apparently brought comfort and consolation. "The Little Mermaid" affected him deeply with its tragic tale of unrequited love and self-sacrifice, and created a longing in him which took many years to fulfil. Another story he mentions is the slight and snobbish "The Princess and the Pea": Ho shared a little of Andersen's snobbery in his own writing but almost nothing of his moralizing.

A more important literary influence were the stories of Oscar Wilde. These were very popular in the early New Literary Movement, and were translated several times into both classical and vernacular Chinese. Ho Ch'i-fang probably read them in English, for he modelled his own early prose style on them. One of his autobiographical heroes had read "The Nightingale and the Rose" at middle school: there is no direct reference to any other story, but the general stylistic influence is obvious.*

At middle school Ho Ch'i-fang was introduced to the vernacular writing of the New Literary Movement, but he does not indicate what he actually read or preferred most within the rather broad range of the movement. In 1925-26, for instance, Wen I-to and Hsü Chih-mo were bringing out a poetry supplement for the Peking *Morning Post*, the *Short Story Monthly* was continuing with its realistic stories of contemporary Chinese life, the *Thread of Talk* was concentrating on essays and poetry of a more varied and personal type, and the Creation Society was launching its own strange combination of proletarian revolution and French neo-romanticism. By the thirties Ho Ch'i-fang was associated with the Crescent group of Wen and Hsü, and we could assume his early acceptance of their poetic programmes.

It may have been through the Crescent writers that Ho Ch'i-fang developed his fondness for English romantic poets, particularly for Victorians like Tennyson and Christina Rossetti. He was attracted by the melancholy of their poetry, which like his own, grew from an unhappy childhood. Some critics have ridiculed the expression of wretchedness and cynicism in the poems Tennyson wrote at the age of eighteen but as Ho Ch'i-fang shows in his essays, loss of faith in mankind can bring even greater despair to a child than to an adult simply because he lacks defences.

In the autumn of 1931, Ho Ch'i-fang went to Peking, where the keen bracing air moved him to celebrate in verse the traditional theme of the difference between north and south in China. The difference between northern Europe and the Mediterranean countries is

* Ho's poem "Night Song IiI" mentions the story of "The Happy Prince".

similarly a familiar theme in English and German poetry, from Goethe's "Mignon" on; one of its clearest presentations, Christina Rossetti's "Love from the North," may have been the source of Ho's first published poem, "The Prophecy".

"The Prophecy", apart from its regional contrast, is ambiguous in the best manner of the symbolists: the Young God could be a symbol for Love, impatient at being detained (cf. Christina Rossetti's "The Prince's Progress"), or for Inspiration, as in a prose-poem by Turgenev, "Stay!" Alternatively, he could stand for Beauty, as Ho himself suggested in another work the following year, Beauty which is only achieved at the sacrifice of friendship and comfort. The considerable technical skill exercised in the poem itself is derived more probably from French symbolism than from English romanticism; Ho Ch'i-fang had discovered Valéry's *La Jeune Parque* three years earlier, and his choice of a Young God for his chief symbol is presumably due to Valéry's example. "The Prophecy" remained for many years Ho Ch'i-fang's favourite poem; it is quoted several times in his later imaginative work and became the title piece of his first single collection of poems in 1945.

The summer of 1932 was unusually rainy for the north, where duststorms from the Gobi Desert make the summer months oppressively dry and gritty. The unseasonable weather reminded Ho of his home in the perpetual mists of Szechwan; it also witnessed his first experience of love. The autumn which followed was also unseasonable: the past few months had emptied the skies of the usual autumn clouds and rain, and the days were clear and brilliant. As the turbulent emotions of summer abated, in his reading and writing Ho turned towards different kinds of love poetry. The allusive eroticism of Late T'ang and Five Dynasty lyrics matched the sensuality of French symbolism, while the richer romanticism of Keats, Shelley, Poe and Swinburne replaced the plaintive songs of Rossetti.

In the autumn of 1932, the influence of classical Chinese poetry shows through very clearly in poems like "Gauze Robe Regrets", "Do Not Wash Away the Red" and "Moonlight on the Frontier Mountains". Two other poems from the same autumn are much more Westernized: "Autumn", atypically a purely descriptive poem, could have been modelled on Keats' ode of the same name, while "The Wreath" carries undeniable echoes of Thomas Gray's "Elegy in a Country Churchyard". Between the summers of 1932 and 1933, Ho Ch'i-fang ranged from the slightly morbid sensuality of Edgar Allan Poe in a poem like "Footsteps", to the Swinburnian theatricality of lines like

> Tell me, do you hear the throbbing in my breast
> Like tree-roots on hot summer nights stirring in the mud?

while from the French symbolists he learnt the technique of syn-
asthesia (the confusion of the senses), as in:

> The black night flows through the flower shadows like a lute,
> Its fragrance is the song it sets floating.

The same combination of classical Chinese and the romantic West
appears in the prose writings of 1932-33. The story "Wang Tzu-yu",
for instance, is based on a well-known incident in the life of Wang
Hui-chih (d.388; courtesy name, Tzu-yu), a third-century "retired
scholar", and depends heavily on reference to the earlier poets, Juan
Chi (210-263) and Tso Ssu (3rd century). The style in which it is written, however, its imagery, sentence structure and composition, is
remarkably close to Oscar Wilde, as the following excerpts show:

> The slight quavering sounds of the song scattered over the dark surface of
> the water, like pearls sinking, sinking deeply to the bottom of the river
> like a secret forgotten dream of the past. And lightly slipped upwards,
> like a flock of high-flying birds brushing against the sky, and dropping
> down because the sky was empty of clouds. Finally, they faded away, as
> the petals of fallen flowers are carried away by the flowing water to the
> land of no return, as the green silken stuff of dreams disperses in the
> awakening light of dawn.
>
> (from "Wang Tzu-yu")

> She sang first of the birth of love in the heart of a boy and girl. And on
> the topmost spray of the Rose-tree there blossomed a marvellous rose,
> petal following petal, as song followed song. Pale was it, at first, as the
> mist that hangs over the river—pale as the feet of the morning, and silver
> as the wings of the dawn. As the shadow of a rose in a mirror of silver, as
> the shadow of a rose in a water pool, so was the rose that blossomed on
> the topmost spray of the Tree.
>
> (from "The Nightingale and the Rose")

Ho Ch'i-fang's only attempt at drama, the one-act *Summer Night*
is self-admittedly modelled after Maeterlinck and Hauptmann: its
love-problem is close to Hauptmann's *Einsame Menschen* (1896) but
the "poetic" vagueness of the dialogue, or "the words of the mind",
as Ho puts it, is in direct imitation of Maeterlinck.

The influence of French symbolism is particularly evident in a
series of prose-poems written in late 1932 and early 1933. Ho Ch'i-
fang's initial inspiration was from Villiers de l'Isle-Adam, though the

form of derivation is not altogether clear. The stories of Villiers de l'Isle-Adam are written in a lucid, precise prose, and their sophisticated themes are radically different from the pastoral sentimentality of Ho's first attempt, "The Grave". Ho's little Ling-ling, whose maiden grave is tended by a lover she never knew in life, is scarcely of the same order of beings as the heroine of "Véra" (one of the *Contes cruels*, 1883), whose fascinating presence is preserved after her death by her besotted husband. Ling-ling, the friend of the mountain grasses and the tiny ants, is more like a domesticated version of Rima, the jungle girl of W.H. Hudson's *Green Mansions* (Hudson was a favourite author of Ho's close friend, Li Kuang-t'ien). The remaining prose-poems are mainly derived from Baudelaire and Mallarmé (though Ho Ch'i-fang does not mention Mallarmé, he was undoubtedly acquainted with his work), and seem to owe little, for instance, to Turgenev, another writer he much admired.

The political crisis which forced Ho Ch'i-fang home in the summer of 1933 brought an abrupt change in his work. The luxuriant imagery of his verse was toned down, and under the tutelage of his more sophisticated friend, Pien Chih-lin, his prose style also became more refined. Ho Ch'i-fang says that he was influenced here by contemporary English and American poetry, T.S. Eliot and the Imagists, but there were other very strong influences in his work at this time. The poems written between the autumn of 1933 and the following summer typically consist of three major elements: an atmosphere of melodrama, the scenery of an ancient city, and the emotional "wasteland" of despair, variously culled from Edgar Allan Poe, T.S. Eliot, Dostoevsky and Baudelaire. The two surviving prose-poems from the same period (March & June, 1934), are similarly laden with the intense despair of Werther, Hamlet, Juan Chi and the young Gautama. It can be noted in passing that the "ancient city" of Ho Ch'i-fang's poem of that name is literally and poetically the same as Coleridge's Xanadu.

Ho Ch'i-fang emerged from these black depths—presumably the aftermath of his failure in love—to create a new, spare prose in the autumn of 1934. The models for the semi-narrative essays he first tried are possibly Turgenev's prose-poems or "Sportsman's Sketches", or Lermontov's *A Hero of Our Time*, but by 1935 he had found his own authentic voice. The three short anecdotes or stories under the title of "Sketches of Painted Dreams" are to my mind his most skilful technical achievement. Like "Wang Tzu-yu", each story is based on an incident from Chinese fiction or legend. The first, "Ting Ling-wei", is about a Han dynasty Taoist who becomes a crane. The second story is about Ch'un-yü Fen, a soldier of fortune who dreams in a drunken stupor that he has entered a kingdom in the base of an old locust tree. This story first became popular as a prose romance of the T'ang dynasty; in the original version, the matter-of-fact tone, the regard for realistic detail and the straight-forward narrative style contrast pleasantly with the fantastic nature of its subject. In retelling it, Ho Ch'i-fang discards most of the detail, the straight chronological sequence of events and the strong, unadorned prose: the unreality of Ch'un-yü's dream is extended to his awakening, and by implication, the reader's certainty about the reality of his own existence. The final story, "The White Lotus Monk", has the same air of dream-like unreality, and the same faint touch of humour.

Poems from the same period, like "The Fan", "The Wall", and "Day of the Duststorm", also have the theme of confusion between illusion and reality, and a similarly ambiguous structure. Only in "The Fan" does the poet stay completely within the dream or fantasy; in the others, he is forced abruptly awake, suddenly aware of the dangers of unrestrained fantasy. There may be an echo of Valéry's early poetry here, either directly or indirectly through a similar kind of poetry then being written by Pien Chih-lin. Of the individual poems, "The Wall" is mainly Western in feeling, "The Fan" is wholly Chinese, and "Day of the Duststorm" is an odd pastiche of Shakespearian and other quotations, perhaps in imitation of Eliot or Pound.

The final work of Ho Ch'i-fang's Peking days is a series of essays based on his childhood memories of Wanhsien. Here he writes simply and warmly about his family and friends, including the lonely, enigmatic figures of his pretty young aunts, the pedlar and the fortune-teller, and a remote ancestor who studied magic and practised divination from the *I Ching* (Book of Changes). Ho Ch'i-fang may have been impelled towards a simpler, more lucid style by the example of Azorin's delicate sketches of sixteenth-century Spain or other short pieces translated by Pien Chih-lin in the early thirties. Like Azorin, his simplicity covers a considerable technical achievement: the essay "Lute-strings", for example, is written in the putative mood, creating a vaguely pathetic, dreamlike effect.

The unfinished novel of 1936, *Sketches of the Passing Scene*, unmistakably owes its characterization to Turgenev, but its impressionistic composition is more akin to Virginia Woolf or some later author. In total contrast to the Wanhsien essays of the previous year,

Ho Ch'i-fang here allows himself unrestricted name-dropping, from Greek philosophy and myth (Archimedes and Narcissus), through English and German romanticism (Goethe, Byron, Elizabeth Barrett Browing, Oscar Wilde), to Russian literature (Lermontov, Turgenev, Dostoevsky, Tolstoy) and French (Maeterlinck, Maupassant). In the preface to *Painted Dreams*, written about the same time, Hamlet makes a reappearance, accompanied by Adam and Eve, William Blake, and Turgenev's last novel, *Smoke*.

The travel essays written the following autumn are considerably more subdued. Apart from the impassioned evocation of the Biblical curse on Adam and Eve, the only literary references are to Russian writers; Turgenev and Dostoevsky are accompanied by Ivanov, Tretiakov and Zoshchenko, who provide Ho Ch'i-fang's first acknowledgement of Soviet Russian literature.

The Laiyang poems of that winter are, in fact, Ho Ch'i-fang's farewell to the world of Western culture which he had treasured since childhood but which ultimately failed to sustain him. It is the funeral of Byron, Essenin and Gerard de Nerval, the repudiation of Baudelaire and "wine and books and honey-dripping lips". Yet Ho Ch'i-fang could not cut himself off from the past with one swift blow: the intensity of his emotion does not hide the careful contrivance of his verse, which can be shown to be a simplified imitation of Eliot's Prufrock and Waste Land poems. The poetry of the socialist world in 1936 was not like this at all, either in China or in the West; Ho Ch'i-fang was as far away as ever from proletarian poetry or literature for the masses. He still lingered in the wasteland of his imagination.

Ho's writing over the next six years showed clearly that he was reaching new levels of political and social maturity. It also shows evidence of increasing technical skill, particularly in the shorter poems and essays, and yet at the same time there is a new kind of clumsiness, as he directs his work to a new audience. In *Night Songs*, the liberal use of references to Western poetry and history, the direct quotations from Western poets and the use of free verse patterns are joined by new borrowings from Soviet literature, or a new kind of foreignism. Despite the simplified language and positive attitudes he wants to adopt, therefore, the poems and much of the prose still stand as a weakened postscript to his old life rather than a signpost to the new.

"Love, thoughtfulness and self-sacrifice"

Ho Ch'i-fang spent his childhood in the traditional Chinese extended family, with three generations under one roof and a horde of boisterous young uncles and cousins as well as his own young brothers and sisters. Why then does he continually harp on the loneliness of his childhood, the lack of love and understanding, and the distrust he soon extended towards the adult world? Love, thoughtfulness and self-sacrifice, he wrote, came to him as concepts from books, and his rare mentions of his own parents are unusually bitter for a Chinese writer. When Ho Ch'i-fang grew up and fell in love, he did so timidly, almost against his will. In his autobiographical writings, he describes at length the anguish of his love-affair and the effect it had on his thinking, but he fails to give a clear picture of his beloved or the reason why they parted. Even in the love poems of 1932, the image of the beloved is presented so shallowly that it seems initially at least only a vague poetic fancy. A more flesh and blood heroine appears in his prose writings, against a fairly consistent story of reluctant betrayal on her part and timid acceptance on his, but except in *Passing Scene*, she remains a shadowy figure. Perhaps there is a reason for Ho Ch'i-fang's reticence, and it may be impertinent to doubt the sincerity of his involvement; I can only quote these lines from "After Dreaming":

> *"Man delights not me, no, nor woman either,"* Prince Hamlet, do you laugh? I am in the process of learning to love my own self. We frequently feel hatred towards ourselves. To love others is even more a kind of learning, a difficult kind of learning in which it is easy to fail.

Thoughtfulness was his second ideal. Escaping from his unhappy solitude in books, he devoted himself to literature with patient diligence. Despite his fondness for poetry and fiction, he elected to study philosophy in order to understand better the basis of thought and culture. But he lacked the will towards objectivity, or to systematic, logical speculation. Turning back to art, he refused to regard it simply as a vehicle for his own emotional release, but conscientiously strove to create an "object" that was its own justification. When he realized the frailty of his own ability, he still respected the objective existence of beauty and art; he referred sadly to the "tragedies of art", where the sincerity of the poet is not a sufficient condition for producing good poetry. In his own case, Ho seemed to think that the solitude of his childhood had somehow crippled his powers of feeling and thinking. He looked around for someone else to believe in: if he were not strong enough to find his own way, he could still follow a friend or teacher towards some worthwhile goal. But as he knew his own weakness, he perceived the weakness of those around him: their voices were as thin, as lost as his own.

Ho Ch'i-fang had been able to ignore his country's misery when he still believed in love and poetry; when these seemed to have failed him, he found at last another way to self-sacrifice. His fellow-students and young intellectuals had already been fighting and dying for many years for the abstract ideals of social justice, national integrity and individual rights. Up until 1936, however, Ho had stubbornly closed his ears to the clamour around him, in order to safeguard his independence. Had he possessed a larger gift or a more generous nature, he might have realised earlier the social injustice of his own position. It was evidently not sufficient for Ho to take part in the coming battle still flying his own flag. While he was able to achieve a certain amount of objectivity in his poems and essays of 1937-39, on his return to Yenan he found it difficult to adjust to the demands of the new life, and turned to poetry this time as a means to relieve the tension between his individual feelings and his duties towards society: even as late as 1942, he was still fighting his personal demons and not the enemy.

BIBLIOGRAPHY

Bibliography

The poems and prose translated in this volume are from the following:

The Han Garden (Han-yüan chi), a selection of poems by Ho Ch'i-fang, Li Kuang-t'ien and Pien Chih-lin, compiled by the latter, in the series Wen-hsüeh yen-chiu hui ch'uang-tso ts'ung-shu, March 1936, Commercial Press, Shanghai. Photocopy by Ta-hsüeh sheng-huo she, Hong Kong (n.d.).

Record of Painted Dreams (Hua meng lu), stories and essays in the series Wen-hsüeh ts'ung-k'an, July 1936, 9th edition 1947; both editions Wen-hua sheng-huo Press, Shanghai. Photocopy of 1st edition Mee Ming Book Centre, Hong Kong (n.d.).

Painstaking Work (K'o-i chi), poetry and miscellaneous prose, in the series Wen-hsüeh ts'ung-k'an, October 1938, 2nd edition 1939, 3rd edition substantially revised, 1941, 4th edition 1946, 5th edition 1948; all editions Wen-hua sheng-huo Press, Shanghai. Photocopy of 2nd edition reprinted by Mee Ming Book Centre, Hong Kong (n.d.).

Diary of a Visit Home (Huan-hsiang jih-chi), travel essays, in the series Hsien-tai san-wen hsin chi, August 1939, Liang-yu fu-hsing Press, Shanghai. Photocopy reprinted by Mee Ming Book Centre, Hong Kong (n.d.).

Notes on a Visit Home (Huan-hsiang chi), 2nd & revised edition of *Diary of a Visit Home*, c.1943, Kung-tso she, Kweilin.

Random Notes on a Visit Home (Huan-hsiang tsa-chi), in the series Wen-hsüeh ts'ung-k'an, 3rd & further revised edition of *Diary of a Visit Home*, 1949, Wen-hua sheng-huo Press, Shanghai.

Prophecy (Yü-yen), poems from *Han Garden* and *Painstaking Work*, plus five others written in Laiyang 1936-37, in the series Wen-chi ts'ung-shu, February 1945, 2nd ed. 1946, reprints to 1951; all editions Wen-hua sheng-huo Press, Shanghai, new revised edition 1957, Hsin wen-i Press, Shanghai.

Sparks (Hsing-huo chi), miscellaneous prose, September 1945, Ch'un-i Press, Chungking; 2nd edition 1946, Ch'un-i Press, Shanghai; 3rd edition substantially revised 1949, in the series Ch'un-i wen-i ts'ung shu, Ch'un-i Press, Shanghai; 4th edition, further revised, 1951; new ed. [5th?], 1955, Hsin wen-i Press, Shanghai; new ed. (6th?), 1959, Wen-i Press, Shanghai.

Night Songs (Yeh ko), poems, in the series Shih wen hsüeh ts'ung-shu, May 1945, Shih wen hsüeh she, Chungking; 2nd edition 1950, Wen-hua sheng-huo Press, Shanghai.

More Sparks (Hsing-huo chi hsü pien), November 1949, Shanghai; new edition January 1955, Hsin wen-i Press, Shanghai.

Night Songs and Songs of Day (Yeh ko ho pai-t'ien te ko), substantially revised edition of *Night Songs*, 1952, 3rd impression 1953, 5th impression 1954, all from Jen-min wen-hsüeh Press, Peking. Photocopy of 3rd impression by Ch'uang-tso shu-tien, Hong Kong (n.d.).

Selected Essays (*San-wen hsüan-chi*), reprinted essays, 1933-46; 1957, Jen-min wen-hsüeh Press, Peking.

Dusk (*Huang-hun*), reprinted essays by Ho Ch'i-fang, 1932-37, & Li Kuang-t'ien, in the series Hsin wen-hsüeh hsüan-chi, 1970, Wen-hsüeh Press, Hong Kong.

Late Evening Flowers (*Ch'ih-mu te hua*), reprinted essays, 1961, Tung-ya shu-chu, Hong Kong.

Other books by Ho Ch'i-fang include:

The Revolutionary Story of Comrade Wu Yü-chang (*Wu Yü-chang t'ung-chih ko-ming ku-shih*), a biography, in the series Pei-fang wen-ts'ung, Hsin Chung-kuo Press, Hong Kong, 1949.

On Realism (*Kuan-yü hsien-shih chu-i*), critical essays, March 1950, Hai-yen Press, Shanghai; new (4th) edition, 1951, Hsin wen-i Press, Shanghai; new (5th) edition, 1954, Hsin wen-i Press, Shanghai; new edition 1959, second impression 1962, Wen-i Press, Shanghai.

West Park Collection (*Hsi yüan chi*), critical essays, Jen-min wen-hsüeh Press, Peking, 1952. Photocopy Mee Ming Book Centre, Hong Kong (n.d.).

On Writing and Reading Poetry (*Kuan-yü hsieh shih ho tu shih*), essays on poetry, Tso-chia Press, Peking, 1956; 2nd impression, 1957.

On 'Dream of the Red Chamber' (*Lun Hung lou meng*), September 1958, Jen-min wen-hsüeh Press, Peking.

Without Criticism There is No Progress (*Mei-yu p'i-p'ing chiu mei-yu ch'ien-chin*), 1958, Jen-min wen-hsüeh Press, Peking.

The Appreciation of Poetry (*Shih-ko hsin-shang*), essays on poetry, Tso-chia Press, Peking, 1962; 4th impression, 1964.

The Springtime of Literature and Art (*Wen-hsüeh i-shu te ch'un-t'ien*) critical essays, Tso-chia Press, Peking, 1964.

Ho was also the editor, with Chang Sung-ju, of *Folksongs of North Shensi* (*Shen-pei min-ko hsüan*), Hai-yen Press, Shanghai, 1951; new edition Hsin wen-i Press, Shanghai, 1955; and as the Director of the Institute of Literature of the Chinese Academy of Sciences he wrote the Preface to *Stories About Not Being Afraid of Ghosts* (*Pu p'a kuei te ku-shih*), a collection of Chinese folk tales compiled by the Institute and published by the Jen-min wen-hsüeh Press in Peking in 1961. An English translation of selections from *Stories About Not Being Afraid of Ghosts* by Yang Hsien-yi and Yang, Gladys was published by the Foreign Languages Press in Peking in 1961, and includes Ho's preface.

Translations of poems by Ho are contained in Acton, Harold & Ch'en Shih-hsiang (editors), *Modern Chinese Poetry* (Duckworth, London, 1936); Hsu Kai-yu (editor), *Twentieth Century Chinese Poetry* (Doubleday, New York, 1963); Payne, Robert (editor), *Contemporary Chinese Poetry* (Routledge, London, 1947).

The most comprehensive account of modern Chinese literature is Hsia, C.T., *A History of Modern Chinese Fiction, 1917-1957* (Yale University Press, 1961). Personal accounts of Peking literary circles in the thirties are Acton, Harold, *Memoirs of an Aesthete* (Methuen, London, 1948) and Hsiao Ch'ien, *The Dragon Beards versus the Blueprints* (Pilot Press, London, 1944) and *Etchings of a Tormented Age* (Allen & Unwin, London, 1942).

For background notes on Szechwan during the period described by Ho see Kapp, Robert A., *Szechwan and the Chinese Republic: Provincial Militarism and Central Power 1911-1938* (Yale University Press, 1973) and a report compiled in June 1948 by Barnett, A. Doak, "The Status Quo in the Countryside", in his *China on the Eve of Communist Takeover* (Thames & Hudson, London, 1963).

Traditional life in the *hu-t'ungs* or lanes in Peking is described in Bouchot, Jean, *Scènes de la vie des hutungs: Croquis des moeurs pekinoises* (Albert Nachbaur, Peking, 1926); for other places in north China lived in or mentioned by Ho Ch'i-fang, see Gamble, Sidney D., *Ting Hsien: A North China Rural Community* (Institute of Pacific Relations, New York, 1954), Smedley, Agnes, *Battle Hymn of China* (Gollancz, London, 1944), Yang, Martin C., *A Chinese Village: Taitou, Shantung Province* (Kegan Paul, London, 1948) and Gillin, Donald G., *Warlord: Yen Hsi-shan in Shansi Province, 1911-1949* (Princeton University Press, 1967).

For background to the lives of young intellectuals during the twenties and thirties see Israel, John, *Student Nationalism in China: 1927-1937* (Stanford University Press, 1966) and Eastman, Lloyd E., *The Abortive Revolution: China under Nationalist Rule, 1927-1937* (Harvard University Press, 1974); Nym Wales gives personal recollections of the December 9th movement in her "Notes on the Chinese Student Movement, 1935-1936" (mimeographed manuscript, Stanford University, 1959). For political and military developments leading up to the early stages of the Sino-Japanese War there are a number of eye-witness reports, such as Bisson, T.A., *Japan in China* (Macmillan, London, 1939), Oliver, Frank, *Special Undeclared War* (Cape, London, 1939), Strong, Anna Louise, *China Fights for Freedom* (Lindsay Drummond, London, 1939) and Utley, Freda, *China at War* (Faber & Faber, London, 1939). Two other "reporters" were Auden, W.H., and Isherwood, Christopher in their *Journey to a War* (Faber & Faber, London, 1939). A more formal account of the opening of hostilities is the Royal Institute of International Affairs' report, *China and Japan* (Information Department Papers, No. 21, London, 1938).

The classic account of the Red Army on its arrival in Yenan is Snow, Edgar, *Red Star over China* (Gollancz, London, 1937). In a later book, *Scorched Earth* (Gollancz, London, 1941), Snow describes the route also travelled by Ho Ch'i-fang from Szechwan to Shensi, one year later but apparently much the same. A few observers were able to see the Eighth Route Army (the former Red Army) in action; two reports which include descriptions of Ho Lung's divisions are Bertram, James M., *North China Front* (Macmillan, London, 1939) and Smedley, Agnes, *China Fights Back* (Gollancz, London, 1938); Belden, Jack, *China Shakes the World* (Gollancz, London, 1951) and Carlson, Evans F., *Twin Stars of China* (Dodd, Mead, New York, 1941) describe respectively peasant and military life behind the lines in the areas which Ho Ch'i-fang also passed through in 1938. For an overall assessment of the progress of the war and the growth of communist power, see White, Theodore H., *Thunder Out of China* (Sloane, New York, 1946) and Johnson, Chalmers A., *Peasant Nationalism and Communist Power: The Emergence of Communist China, 1937-1945* (Stanford University Press, 1963).

On the literary scene in Yenan during the war and the role played by Ho, see Hsia, T.A., "Twenty Years after the Yenan Forum" in *China Quarterly*, No. 13 (January-March, 1963) and Goldman, Merle, "Writers' Criticism of the Party in 1942" in *China Quarterly*, No. 17 (January-March, 1964). Ho's subsequent career is described in Goldman, Merle, *Literary Dissent in Communist China* (Harvard University Press, 1967), and his official appointments are listed in Boorman, Howard L., *Biographical Dictionary of Republican China* (Columbia University Press, New York, 1967-1970), *Who's Who in Communist China* (Union Research Institute, Hong Kong, revised edition, 1969) and Perleberg, Max, *Who's Who in Modern China* (Ye Olde Printerie, Hong Kong, 1954). In January 1966 a poem by Ho on the war in Vietnam was published in *China Reconstructs*; two months later, when the Cultural Revolution began, Ho came under attack for his association with reactionary elements in the literary world. He is now thought to have been re-instated in his academic position, and appeared at Chou En-lai's funeral as a representative of educational circles.

INDEX

Index

"After dreaming", 85, 231
"Afterword to *The Swallow's Nest*",
    51–53
"Ancient city, The", 41–42, 228
Andersen, Hans Christian, 151
    (quoted), 165, 195, 224–25
Archimedes, 230
Azorin, 75, 82, 224, 229

Baudelaire, 126, 228, 230
Biblical references, 208; Adam and
    Eve, 54, 63, 117, 230; Eden,
    201; King David, 74; *Song of
    Solomon*, 179
Bisson, T. A., 8
Blake, 52, 63, 230
Book of Changes, 77–78, 229
Browning, Elizabeth Barrett, 230
Byron, 122, 230

Carlson, Evans F., 25–26, 27
Carlyle, 223
Chang Hsüeh-liang, 10
Chaplin, 148
Chengtu, 16–17, 20, 23–24, 55,
    91–92, 94, 127, 130, 133, 134,
    138, 140, 142, 144, 170, 174–
    76
"Chengtu, let me shake you awake!",
    171, 174–77
Ch'eng Fang-wu, 150
Ch'i Hsieh, 63
Chiang Kai-shek, 3, 4, 10, 17, 25
Chou En-lai, 10
Chou Li-po, 25
Chou Tso-jen, 19–23, 171
Ch'u (state), 46, 58
Chu Kuang-ch'ien, 20–21, 171
"Chun-yü Fen", 68–69, 229
Chungking, 15–16, 90, 91–92, 134,
    165, 174, 216–17
"Cliffs", 85
"Clouds", 126, 169 (quoted)
Coleridge, 228
"Common people and the army,
    The", 59–60

Crescent Society, 13, 225
Croce, 21
"Cypress grove, The", 40, 54

"Day of the duststorm II", 49–50,
    229
Diary of a Visit Home, 8, 81–120
"Do not wash away the red", 37
Don Quixote, 86, 167
Dostoevsky, 50, 96, 168, 228, 230
"Dusk", 61, 65, 133

"Early summer", 43–44
Einstein, 28
Eliot, T. S., 18, 57, 168, 224, 228,
    229, 230
Eroshenko, 174
"Essay and I, The ", 81, 82–88, 168
    (quoted)
Essenin, 122, 174, 230

"Fan, The", 47, 62, 229
"Footsteps", 34
"Funerals", 122, 230

Gautama Buddha, 54, 167, 207, 228
Gide, 50, 82
Goethe, 226, 228 (Werther), 230
Gorki, 19
"Grave, The", 85, 228
Gray, Thomas, 226

Hamlet, *see* Shakespearean references
Han Garden, The, 7, 31–44, 50, 51
Hankow, 15–16, 23–24, 89–90,
    92–93
Hauptmann, 168, 227
"Here is a short fairy tale", 195
Ho Chien, 139
Ho Lung, 26, 27, 204
Ho Ying-ch'in, 133
Hochien, 27, 161
Honan, 26, 89, 91
Hopei, 5, 6, 15, 26, 27, 127, 218
"How many times have I left my
    daily life", 196

Hsiao Chün, 25
Hsü Chih-mo, 13, 225
Hu Shih, 12, 17
Huang T'ing-chien, 105
Hudson, W. H., 228

I Ching, see *Book of Changes*
"I see a little donkey", 193
"I should like to talk of pure things", 194
"I sing of Yenan", 25, 147–52, 172
"In the countryside", 111–18
Ivanov, 145, 230

Juan Chi, 227, 228

Kant, 82
Keats, 226
Kou Mo-jo, 12, 16

Laiyang, 8–9, 13, 15, 86, 87, 88, 96, 121–26, 169, 230
"Lament" (*Ai-ko*), 72–75
"Lament" (*K'ai-t'an*), 35
Lanhsien, 26–27, 158, 198–201
Lenin, Leninism, 4, 23, 181
Lenin in October, 148
Lermontov, 87 (quoted), 169, 228, 230
"Let's get drunk!", 126, 230
Li Kuang-t'ien, 7, 20, 82–83, 228
L'Impartial (Ta kung pao), 7, 51, 59, 61
Li Po, 105
Liang Tsung-tai, 132
Lin Yü-t'ang, 12
"Love", 36
Lu Hsün, 14, 20, 21, 137, 174; Lu Hsün Academy of Arts, 25, 147, 150
"Lute-strings", 79–80, 229

Maeterlinck, 227, 230
"Magic plants", 76–77
Mallarmé, 228
Manchuria, 5, 9, 10, 26
Mao Tse-tung, 23, 25, 28, 147, 148, 151
Mao Tun, *see* Shen Yen-ping
Marx, Marxism, Marxist literary theory, 12, 19, 23
Maupassant, 179, 230

Mayakovsky, 174
"Mists and clouds on a fan", 57 (quoted), 62–64, 86
"Mr Yü Yu-lieh", 123, 183 (quoted)

Nankai Middle School and University, 6–7, 8, 83–84, 91, 168–69
Nanking, 3–5, 15–16, 27, 91–92, 94, 130, 170, 175, 216
Napoleon, 52
Narcissus, 230
Nerval, Gérard de, 122, 230
"Night of the full moon", 39
"Night song I", 177–78
"Night song II", 179–81
"Night song III", 182–84
"Night song IV", 185–87
Night Songs, 173–219, 230
Night Songs and Songs of Day, 173, 198–219
"North China is aflame!" (Part I), 198–206
"North China is aflame!"(Part II), 207–219
Northern Expedition, 3–5, 12, 25, 164
Notes Ancient and Modern, 50
"Notes on the Szechwan-Shensi road", 142–46

"On basic culture", 16–19, 27
"On saving the children", 137–41
"On work", 19, 128–33
"Ordinary story, An", 127, 163–72
"Our fortress", 118–19
"Our history is racing forward", 188–92

Pa Chin, 61
Painstaking Work, 31–67
Painted Dreams, see *Record of Painted Dreams*
pao-kao (reports), 14, 24, 127
"Paths in dreams", 54, 85 (quoted)
Peking, 3–10, 12–13, 15, 20–22, 27, 56–57, 87, 89, 94–95, 133, 144, 165–68, 171, 174, 175, 190–91, 217–18, 225, 229
Peking University, 5–7, 20, 82
P'eng Teh-huai, 26
Pien Chih-lin, 6, 51, 82–83, 146,

228, 229
"Pillow and its key, The", 47, 57
Po Chü-i, 11
Poe, Edgar Allan, 226, 228
Pound, Ezra, 229
Prometheus, 184

"Record of painted dreams, A", 61,
    66–71, 228–29
Record of Painted Dreams, A, 7, 61–
    80, 84–85, 86, 87, 133, 163, 230
Richards, I. A., 21
Rolland, Romain, 18–19, 22, 23, 28,
    132, 135, 171
Rossetti, C. G., 56, 225, 226
Russia, Russian Revolution, 4, 12,
    18, 19, 89, *see also* Soviet Russia

"Scenery of the district town",
    104–10
Shakespearean references, 49–50,
    229; Hamlet, 62, 228, 230, 231;
    Ophelia, 188
Shanghai, 3, 5, 12, 15–16, 55, 90,
    109, 130, 134, 165, 170, 175,
    216
Shansi, 7, 15, 23, 25–27, 153, 198–
    206
Shantung, 4–5, 7–8, 15, 87, 169
Shaw, G. B., 22, 172
Shelley, 179, 224, 226
Shen Ts'ung-wen, 21
Shen Yen-ping (Mao Tun), 12
Shensi, 10, 16, 23–24, 26, 131, 140,
    142–46, 172
Sketches of the Passing Scene (un-
    tinished novel), 7, 84, 87, 229,
    231
Smedley, Agnes, 6–7, 25
Snow, Edgar, 24
"Sobbing Yangtze, The", 89–96
Socrates, 200
"Soliloquy", 85
"Sound", 124
Soviet Russia, 4, 12, 19, 21, 92, 172,
    230, *see also* Russia
Sparks, 127–72
Spinoza, 72
Stalin, 19
"Step insects", 46
Stories About Not Being Afraid of

Ghosts, 224
Strange Tales from a Chinese Studio,
    50, 224
"Streets", 97–103
Su Wu, 22
"Summer night", 38, 39, 52
Sun Yat-sen, 4, 156
Swallow's Nest, The, 31, 51, 54, 57
Swinburne, 226
Symons, Arthur, 223
Szechwan, 3, 5, 15–16, 24, 28,
    89–96, 97–103, 113–15, 119,
    129, 137, 142–45, 170, 172,
    191, 226

Ta kung pao, see *L'Impartial*
Tagore, 131
Taiyuan, 15, 26, 130, 153–58, 204
"Taiyuan primary school boy, A",
    153–58
T'ang poetry, 56, 58, 104, 226; prose
    romances, 224, 229
Tangku Agreement, 6, 133
Tat'ung-P'uchou Railway, 26, 153,
    204
Tennyson, 56, 225
Tientsin, 3, 6–7, 8, 10, 15, 61, 86,
    168, 218
"Ting Ling-wei", 66–67, 229
Tinghsien, 218
Tolstoy, 207, 230
"Tragedy of the Japanese, The", 26–
    27
Tretiakov, 110, 230
tsa-wen (satirical essays), 14, 17, 18,
    19, 20, 127, 170, 171
Tsinan, 5, 15
Tsingtao, 9, 15, 126, 169
Tso, Ssu, 227
Tu Fu, 11, 104
Turgenev, 63, 91, 226, 228, 229, 230

"Wall, The", 45, 229
"Wang Tzu-yu" (Wang Hui-chih),
    227
Wanshien, 3, 6, 8, 16–17, 61, 87
    96, 97–103, 104–10, 115, 170,
    210–13, 214–16, 229
Wen I-to, 13, 225
Wen T'ing-yün, 59
"White Lotus monk, The", 70–71,

229
White Lotus sect, 43, 78, 214–16
Wilde, Oscar, 50, 182 (quoted),
    225, 227, 230
Woolf, Virginia, 229
Work, 16, 140, 170

Valéry, 5, 18, 132, 226, 229
Villiers de l'Isle-Adam, 85, 227–28

Yang Sen, 3, 5, 107–9
Yangtze River, 3, 15, 34, 89–96,
    104, 106, 108–9
Yellow River, 26, 42, 43
Yenan, 16, 24–25, 28, 127, 131,
    147–52, 163–72, 173, 232

Zoshchenko, 89, 230